NIGHTSTALKERS: THE RIFT

NEW YORK TIMES BESTSELLING AUTHOR
BOB MAYER

AREA 51

THE NIGHTSTALKERS BOOK 3

NIGHTSTALKERS: THE RIFT

47NORTH

Published by 47North, Seattle

www.apub.com

ISBN-13: 9781477818114
ISBN-10: 1477818111

Cover design by Brian Zimmerman

Library of Congress Control Number: 2013953508

Printed in the United States of America

NIGHTSTALKERS: THE RIFT

PROLOGUE

On August 21, 1945, Harry K. Daghlian was stacking blocks just fifteen days after the bomb they'd put together at Los Alamos blew the dragon's breath onto Hiroshima and twelve days after Nagasaki received the same fate.

Enrico Fermi called what Daghlian was doing "tickling the dragon's tail."

He had no idea how right he was.

On this day, Daghlian dropped a block.

Everyone has dropped something. Sometimes one hits the big toe and hops about and curses. Sometimes the thing dropped breaks. Unfortunately, the blocks Daghlian was stacking and what he was stacking them around were both rather unusual.

Rarely does the thing dropped kill, but when connected to the dragon, nothing good can happen. Daghlian was part of the Critical Assembly Group and was attempting to build a neutron reflector by arranging bricks of tungsten carbide around a plutonium core, trying to achieve criticality.

He was moving the last brick into place—sort of like how one should never do the last run on the ski slope, except a lot more dangerous—when the neutron counters in the room went off, alerting him that the last brick would be a mistake. What physicists call going supercritical and laymen call a "big oops."

As Daghlian withdrew his hand, he dropped the brick.

This caused the core to go into what's technically called "prompt critical region of supercritical behavior resulting in a power excursion" and what laymen would call "oh shit."

Give him credit. Daghlian didn't run away. He didn't spin in circles and scream and shout. He attempted to knock the dropped brick off the pile.

Without success.

He then stuck to the job and began disassembling the pile to halt the reaction. He managed to do so and in the process received an estimated dosage of 510 rem.

He was dead twenty-five days later.

Exactly nine months later to the day, as if Daghlian's death had conceived and was giving birth, another scientist working on the exact same core, in the exact same room, poked the dragon's tail with a screwdriver.

Scientists.

He'd been warned. After they buried Daghlian, everyone muttering proud words at the funeral service and remembering the good times building the atomic bombs, Fermi looked Louis Slotin in the eye and told him, "Keep doing that experiment, tickling the dragon's tail that way, and you'll be dead within a year."

For a betting person, anyone who took the under of three months from the year made a lot.

In front of seven of his fellow scientists, Slotin was maneuvering two half-spheres of beryllium around the same plutonium core. He had his left hand on one of the half-spheres, with his thumb in a hole drilled into the top and a screwdriver in his right, which he was using to keep the two half-spheres apart.

He'd removed the safety shims that usually did that.

They're called *safety shims* for a reason.

He didn't drop the half-sphere in his left hand. He missed with the screwdriver in his right, the blade slipping and allowing the two halves to touch, ever so briefly. Slotin flung the half in his left hand to the ground, but the damage had been done.

Everyone in the room saw a blue glow, an indication of the air in the room being ionized. They were all washed by the dragon's breath, a blast of warm air, also known as *radioactivity*. Slotin's hand was burned and he had a strange taste in his mouth, as if he'd swallowed something sour. In fact, his entire body had absorbed something deadly. As his colleagues hustled him from the lab, he began vomiting.

That was just the beginning of the bad. While Daghlian had died in a coma, Slotin wasn't so fortunate. Over the next nine days, his body disintegrated until death brought a merciful end.

———

Two days after Slotin died, a convoy of heavily armed army vehicles pulled up to the front gate of Los Alamos. The base had the highest security clearance possible, given it headquartered the Manhattan Project, so it was rather amazing that the leader of the convoy could produce paperwork that cleared that high hurdle and the vehicles were allowed access.

The men inside the convoy were dressed in army fatigues but had no rank, no names stenciled above their breast pockets, no unit insignias. They just carried weapons in a way that indicated everyone was a hardened combat veteran looking for an excuse to use those weapons. They seemed to have a particular dislike for scientists.

The convoy drove straight to the lab.

Fermi was waiting outside, having been alerted by the gate guards.

"Might I help you?" he inquired of the hard-looking, gray-haired man who led the phalanx of soldiers to the door of the lab. A scar crossed the man's face from above his left eye to the right of his chin. It made his smile look terrible, but since he didn't smile, it didn't matter. He wore aviator sunglasses, hiding his eyes from not only the sun but also everyone else. A set of pilot's wings adorned his chest.

"My name is Thorn. Colonel Thorn."

"And what can I do for you, Colonel Thorn?" Fermi asked. "The guards said you had authorization directly from the White House to access the base. I called Washington and that order was verified."

"I want the plutonium core that killed Daghlian and Slotin."

Fermi didn't budge. "Why?"

"Because you idiots play with things you don't understand."

Fermi raised an eyebrow. "And you do?"

Thorn removed his sunglasses, revealing dead eyes. "We like to keep people alive."

"We understand what we're doing here," Fermi said. "We developed the bombs that ended the war. You do remember that they worked." It was not a question. The entire world knew that Little Boy and Fat Man worked.

"And two of your people killed themselves playing around with that core." Thorn reached into his breast pocket and pulled out the same sheet of paper he'd shown the gate guards. "I have the authorization to take the core."

Fermi reached out to take the paper, and for a moment Thorn didn't let go. Then he released and Fermi put on a pair of reading glasses and scanned the document.

"What is this Majestic-12 organization?" Fermi asked.

"You don't need to know."

"Where is Area 51?"

"You don't need to know."

"Who exactly are you and your men?"

"You don't need to know."

Fermi took off the reading glasses and handed the paper back. "Do you have the proper facilities to store the core?"

"We do."

"Do you have scientists who understand what they're dealing with?"

A grimace flickered for the slightest of moments on Thorn's rough visage. "We do."

Fermi frowned. "We have the best physicists in the country here. Who do *you* have?"

"You ask too many questions," Thorn said. "I'm taking that core. We can do it easy or we can do it hard, Professor. My men would prefer hard. Personally, I like it easy." That was such a blatant lie that even Fermi—a scientist, not someone skilled in the subject of psychology—could read it. Thorn was itching for the hard way.

Fermi stepped aside. "It is all yours, then, Colonel."

Thorn waved and his men went into the lab, rolling a large lead box they'd taken off a specially built truck. A cluster of guards, weapons at the ready, surrounded them.

"A bit overly dramatic, don't you think?" Fermi observed.

"No."

"The guards, not the box," Fermi said.

"Protocol is important," Thorn said. "Didn't Slotin violate protocol by removing the shims?"

Fermi had no response to that.

After several minutes the men reappeared, rolling the box down the short ramp to the truck, muscles straining to control the weight.

"By the way, Colonel Thorn. Do you know what we call what you've just taken?" He indicated the large lead box the men were now maneuvering onto the truck.

Thorn had put his sunglasses back on, hiding his eyes. "I figure you're going to tell me, so go ahead."

"The demon core. Beware of tickling it."

CHAPTER 1

Roland stood on the open back ramp of the Snake, fifteen thousand feet above St. Louis, as calm as if he were waiting in line at Pottery Barn. Of course, Roland had no clue what a Pottery Barn was, but if one mentioned the term to him, he would deduce that it had something to do with a recurring fantasy about fine china and a bull, which was pretty much the definition of Roland—the bull part. Roland was six-four and two hundred forty pounds of muscle, bone, and pure killer. He had a scar running along the right side of his head, starting from his temple and curling behind his ear. On his last trip to Vegas, he'd had it tattooed with barbed wire, which earned him a big-time ass-chewing from Moms, because Nightstalkers weren't supposed to have tattoos (the body could be identified), but in this case Ms. Jones intervened because the tattoo actually sort of hid the scar, which had been more noticeable than the black ink covering it and raised more questions.

And Roland was noticeable no matter what was on his skin.

The Snake was at fifteen thousand above ground level (AGL), because any higher and everyone inside would have to be on oxygen. As it was, the breathing was hard for normal people, but the people inside were anything but normal.

They were the Nightstalkers.

The best of the best, the cream of the crop, the tip of the spear, et cetera, et cetera, so secret they even wondered if they existed, in their more existential moments, of which there weren't many, except when Eagle, the pilot, got to thinking.

"There's a lot of lights," Roland observed, looking down.

"It's a city," Mac said, as if talking to a three-year-old, which is the way Mac talked to Roland pretty much all the time, except in combat, when Roland was everyone's best friend. "A big city."

"I know it's a city," Roland muttered. "But it's three in the fraking morning."

The team had recently done a *Battlestar Galactica* marathon in the Den, buried underneath the Ranch outside of Area 51, and *frak* was now the buzzword, as Moms frowned on cussing. They had adopted it as adjective, adverb, verb, noun, and simple exclamation. It had caught on with some, but not all.

"Two minutes," Eagle announced from the cockpit.

Roland took a short step closer to the ramp. Moms came up and ran her hands lightly over his rig, doing a last-minute jumpmaster parachute inspection (JMPI), redundant, not needed and not Protocol, but Moms always checked Roland before a jump. Tradition trumped Protocol sometimes. She slapped him lightly on the shoulder and gave him a thumbs-up.

Roland blushed, because he always blushed when Moms paid him special attention. It wasn't a sexual thing but a deep and abiding affection, much like a Doberman for its owner, because Moms had once saved his life in combat and for Roland there was no deeper love than that of combat.

Roland had concocted a unique rig for this jump and he was overly excited about trying it out, even though there was a good chance he was jumping into a real-world equivalent of the Hellmouth. (They'd tried a *Buffy* marathon, but only Roland had wanted to see it through; that was 'cause he had immediately identified Buffy with Moms. The Nightstalkers dealt with things that made vampires look tame, so the rest of them felt the show was kind of lame.) Roland had done thousands of jumps in many different configurations and situations, but this one was unique even for him. The prospect of a combination of an aircraft free-fall jump directly to a landing, where he would then do a BASE jump tickled his tiny, tiny imagination—or so Mac had said as Roland had prepped.

Roland, as usual, had ignored his poking.

"It is a city," Nada said, his voice, more a growl, coming into each team member's earpiece. "Even at three in the morning there's likely to be civilians. We've got Support en route, but as always, we're on our own for a bit. Remember—containment, concealment, and control. And the local law is as dangerous as anyone else because they give those people guns, even though most of them shouldn't have one."

A couple of the Nightstalkers exchanged glances, because those three C words were their mantra and deeply imprinted in each of their brains. For Nada to feel he needed to repeat them reminded them not only of the mantra, but also that things had been a bit frayed in the past year on various missions.

"One minute," Eagle said.

"Doc?" Moms asked.

Doc was staring at his laptop screen, his forehead furrowed above his thick glasses. "A Rift is indeed forming. But different."

"Not much help," Nada said. "Different how?"

"Bigger." Doc looked up. "Someone's using the Gateway Arch to make a Rift."

"Frak," Mac said, vocalizing what every Nightstalker thought at the moment.

"You know," Eagle said over the net, "the guy who designed the Arch said it symbolized, and I quote, 'the gateway to the west, the national expansion, and whatnot.'"

"Looks like we're heading for the whatnot," Kirk, the team's commo man, observed.

Moms began chanting Warren Zevon's "Roland The Headless Thompson Gunner," and the team picked it up.

"Go!" Eagle ordered from the cockpit.

Roland stepped off into the glowing darkness above St. Louis. In his earpiece he could hear the team finish the second line of the song.

He wished he had a Thompson gun, with its big .45-caliber slugs. He spread his arms and legs, got stable, then pulled the rip cord. The opening shock jerked him upright, and he looked up to make sure he had good canopy while he grabbed the control toggles for the chute.

Then he looked down.

"Oh, yes, yes, yes!" It could have been the soundtrack for a porn movie, except the young woman exclaiming the words was fully clothed, sitting cross-legged in the grass, had a laptop on her knees, and was watching six different data boxes on it.

We all get our kicks different ways.

She was so focused on the data that she was missing the real show. The Gateway Arch towered 50 feet in front of her, 630 feet high and 630 feet wide, making it the tallest memorial in the United States and the tallest stainless steel structure in the world. It had been dedicated in '65 and opened to the public in '67, not the greatest decade to celebrate the westward expansion of the United States, as the country was embroiled in an unpopular war abroad and unrest at home.

At three in the morning, the woman had the park to herself, which is why she'd picked three in the morning to run her test. The numbers and indicators on her laptop screen showed that the program she'd started two hours ago was reaching culmination. She was completely unaware that the initiation had also set off flashing lights and a loud clicking alert deep underneath Area 51 in the Can, and that was why the Nightstalkers were descending from above like avenging angels or, as Mac said in his grumpier moments, flying turds, especially with regard to Roland, the largest turd of them all according to Mac.

He never said it within earshot of Roland, though, because Mac had an innate survival instinct.

A single thin cable ran from the USB port of her laptop across the grass and was attached to the left leg of the Arch with a magnet.

As with most of the scientists the Nightstalkers ended up dealing with, she thought she knew what she was doing.

As with most of the scientists the Nightstalkers ended up putting in body bags or more likely listing as MIA, she really didn't.

A crackling noise caused her to finally look up. Her mouth dropped open and she couldn't even moan her excitement anymore. The entire interior of the Arch was flickering, a slightly golden sheen illuminating the space framed by what Eagle could have told her was a weighted catenary form of stainless steel. Eagle could have even gone into the math involved, something to do with x and y and cosines and fractions and whatnot, but that wasn't what Melissa Eden was interested in, even though she was very good at math, having earned a PhD in physics from Stanford, which required more than a few math courses along the way.

Just as quickly as she'd seen it, the gold coalesced inward from the metal arch to a single tiny, golden, glowing arch, about ten feet wide and high, in the exact center on the ground.

It wasn't a sign for McDonald's.

Eden felt the hairs on her arms tingle and there was another crackling sound. She had a sour taste in her mouth. She squinted, because through that small arch, there was something, like there was another side, which was the whole point of this experiment, except even in her most excited dream, she'd never really imagined it would work. Because no one had ever published on it, saying they had succeeded.

That should have been a hint.

She didn't realize she'd gotten to her feet, the laptop forgotten on the grass. Through the golden arch, she saw rows of . . . something. Even though she couldn't make out what the somethings were, she had the distinct sense the somethings were facing this arch and if it stayed open much longer, they were going to come through.

In the way ancient man used to stare out the mouth of the cave into the darkness, knowing danger lurked out there, Eden felt a primeval fear of those somethings.

Here there be monsters used to be written on ancient maps to fill in the blank spaces. In this case, it should be written in capital letters. With one or two exclamation points.

As quickly as she thought that, though, instead of a bunch of somethings, a single someone stepped through and the golden arch snapped out of existence.

Roland was focused on the Arch and the area around it. There was a golden glow underneath the stainless steel structure, which was never a good sign.

As he passed through eight thousand feet, he checked in, because it was Protocol that he check in at eight thousand feet.

"Eagle, thermals?" Roland asked as he adjusted his descent.

"I've got one hot spot near the Arch. On the landward side. Probably our genius scientist."

"That's the side on the other side from the river," Mac added, in this case probably a smart add, because Roland had been a bit puzzled by the landward part, although Mac's explanation didn't help much with its redundancy.

Roland was using a clockwise spiral to descend, checking all directions.

"Beyond that, looks like a couple of homeless on the riverfront," Eagle continued. "And then there's the city. You've got I-70 cutting the park off from it."

Doc's voice cut in. "The Rift is closed. I'm getting nothing. That was different. Like it snapped shut."

"Roland, see any Fireflies?" Moms asked.

"Too high up," Roland replied.

Roland started to dump air, increasing his downward speed.

The someone was a man. He was walking straight toward Eden. He wore a long tan bush coat, inappropriate for the warm night, and a fedora, pulled low over his eyes.

"What—" Eden began, but then she saw his face under the fedora and the next words were clenched in her throat. His skin looked like he'd been through a shredder. He paused about five feet from her and cocked his head, revealing more of his disfigurement.

"Does my face disturb you?" he asked. As he spoke, his skin rippled and smoothed out. "Better?"

Eden still couldn't find words.

"I guess not." He looked down at the laptop and tsked. "One should not interfere with things beyond one's comprehension. My associates on the other side are getting rather irritated with the whole thing and believe it's getting near to time that this be brought to a conclusion."

He leaned over to pick up the laptop, and that move finally stirred Eden to action. "That's mine!" She stepped toward him and grabbed his arm, her other hand going for the computer.

Her second mistake of the evening.

And her last.

With his free hand, the man grabbed the top of her hand, seizing it in a grip that froze her muscles, and he lifted her off the ground. She dangled from his hand as he peered into her eyes. They remained like that for several seconds; then the man dropped her.

Eden lay stunned for a second; then her spirit came back and she jumped to her feet. "That's—"

She never finished as the man drew a silenced pistol from inside his coat, pressed it against the side of her head, and pulled the trigger. The round went into her skull with a soft chugging sound, then fragmented, shredding her brain. She was dead before she hit the ground, but the man fired again, this round into her forehead.

"Nada Yada," the man said with a grin, the scars returning to his face. "Always double-tap and make sure they're dead." He stared down at her. "I saved you considerable pain."

He holstered the pistol, snatched up the laptop, and tucked it under his arm. He began walking toward the nearest road.

As he was about to pass through four thousand feet, Roland took a moment to get oriented. It was easy, given the size of the Arch. The M240 machine gun was rigged tight against his body on one side, a flamer on the other, the fuel for it underneath the parachute case on his back. Protocol said he was to reverse directions after passing through four thousand feet, so Roland regained the toggles and reversed. Roland was a big believer in Protocol.

"Wind?" Roland asked.

"Negligible," Eagle reported. "You're still clear. We're holding at three thousand to the west." There was a pause. "We've got a second person with the first."

"Where did that one come from?" Roland asked, peering down.

"I think out of the Arch," Doc said. "No indication of Fireflies, though."

Roland couldn't make out the people on the grass, but he did see a church across the road from the Arch. It stirred memories of a wedding, a buddy in the army, and holding a sword forming an arc, but not much more of the wedding itself since he'd been drunk and there'd been a bunch of singing and girls crying and crap. The reception, on the other hand, he could remember clearly. He'd gotten into a fight with the best man, and the bride had been pissed, but his army buddy, the groom, had laughed, because what was an army wedding without some blood being spilled?

It had been a great reception, but as Roland went through three thousand feet, he had a feeling this reception wasn't going to be as good.

Keith was drunk, it was 3:00 a.m., and he could have sworn the Arch had been shimmering just a minute ago. Maybe some special promo, like when they'd shone pink lights on it in support of breast cancer research. He was stopped at a red light, left turn signal on, nervously drumming his fingers on the steering wheel, constantly glancing in his rearview mirror, dreading that a cop car would pull up behind him.

He couldn't afford another DUI. He'd lose not only his job, but also his license. And how could he get another job if—

Just as the light turned green, the engine stalled out, which was almost impossible to tell since he was driving a Prius and the battery had been powering the car, but a warning light flashed on the dash and nothing happened when he pressed the accelerator. Keith cursed and punched the start button to no avail.

The rap on his window startled him. A man wearing a raincoat and a fedora stood there. The man signaled for Keith to roll down his window. Keith panicked, thinking the man was a cop and knowing he couldn't roll the power window down without power and that the cop would think—

The man placed his hand on the window and slid it down, the glass going with the hand. Which was weird.

"What? Who the—" Keith began, but the man reached in and grabbed him by the throat. With a distant part of his mind, Keith heard and felt his seat belt unbuckle, but that was impossible because the man was holding him by the throat. As he was lifted out of the open window, gasping for breath, Keith saw the terrible scars on the man's face. The man held him in the air, peering into his eyes as if evaluating him like a side of beef he was deciding whether to devour.

"Don't drink and drive," the man said, and then Keith was flying through the air, landing in a drunken tumble.

Being drunk actually saved him from serious injury as his body simply absorbed the contact without the resistance sobriety brings to impacts. He lifted his head, watching the man get in his Prius. The turn signal changed from left to right and then the car drove off, heading for the bridge over the Mississippi.

Roland landed on the very top of the Gateway Arch. Eagle had told him on the flight from the Ranch to St. Louis that someone had tried doing a double jump in 1980: landing on the Arch using a main and then jumping again and deploying his reserve. That person had died, because he'd gotten no purchase on the slick stainless steel. Instead of being able to launch again off the top, he'd slid along the north leg to his death, the reserve never deploying.

Roland had solved that problem by duct taping large magnets to the outside of both his boots. When he clanged down on the top and his main deflated, his feet were locked in place. Roland cut away the main, letting the wind blow it toward the Mississippi.

The riverward side, Roland thought, but that hurt his head so he focused on his mission.

He leaned over and looked below. There was a body on the grass.

Roland sighed, a true believer in Heinlein's principle that the only capital crime is stupidity, a Nada Yada before Nada even thought of his Yadas. M240 now readied in one hand, he reached for his knife to cut the magnets loose from his boots.

"Sitrep?" Moms's voice echoed out of the earpiece.

"We've got a body," Roland said.

"Eagle?" Moms asked.

"The body is going cold. Someone walked out of the Arch to the body, grabbed the laptop, went to a car, tossed the driver, and is now driving away. The driver is still alive."

"Roland, secure the Arch. I'm sending Nada and Mac down to assist. We're going after the car."

Moms finished giving orders as Nada and Mac jumped off the ramp in tandem. The second they were clear, Eagle banked the Snake and took chase after the car. The Snake was a prototype of cutting-edge flight technology: similar in design to the tilt-wing Osprey, except instead of rotors, the Snake had powerful jet engines, whose noise was muted by running them through baffles. The outside of the aircraft was also coated with radar-reducing material. It was all angles and flat surfaces, everything designed to lower the radar signature of the entire craft to that of a duck in flight, a comparison that Mac constantly goaded Eagle about.

Not a Snake but a flying duck.

Moms moved forward in the cargo bay until she could lean into the cockpit, looking over Eagle's shoulder. Moms was a tall woman, almost six feet. She had broad shoulders with narrow hips, making her appear a bit awkward, although she was anything but. Her hair was growing grayer by the year and by the mission. She had a vague Midwestern accent that indicated a childhood anywhere from eastern Kansas to western Kansas, which is actually a long spread, but for a kid, not much different.

"Where's the target?"

Eagle nodded to the right front. "Going onto the bridge. Red Prius. Someone's driving it."

"We've got to get containment," Moms said.

Eagle flipped a switch. "Chain gun deployed." Underneath the nose of the Snake, a door slid open and a thirty-millimeter chain gun poked its ugly snout out. It was a gun designed to destroy tanks, so the Prius shouldn't be a problem. Whoever, and whatever, was in it might be more of an issue.

"If it's not a Firefly, who's the person?" Moms wondered. "Kirk, get me Ms. Jones."

"You're live with the Ranch," Kirk announced.

"Ms. Jones, we're losing containment," Moms said. "At least one human in a car, escaping on the I-70 bridge over the Mississippi. I need to go wet."

"Authorized," a voice with a Russian accent replied. "I am mobilizing more support for containment and concealment."

Eagle hit the throttle and they raced over the dark Mississippi to the Illinois side, beating the Prius across the river. Eagle spun the Snake to face west and descended until they were less than twenty feet above the roadway, the thirty-millimeter pointing directly ahead.

"Pretty desolate here for about two klicks," Eagle said. "If we want to fire, this is the place."

There were several sets of headlights on the bridge, but containment took priority. The Nightstalkers and their support had binders full of cover stories for civilians who might get caught up in the action.

"Acquiring target," Eagle said as he centered the chain gun's sights right between the headlights of the oncoming car.

Moms was just about to order him to fire when there was a flash of gold. It leapt from the car and hit the Snake at light speed, faster than they could dream to react.

Everything electric on the aircraft shut down.

Eagle jerked the controls with all his strength, using what little altitude he had to manually force the hydraulics to move the Snake to the side of the freeway where it crashed, then rolled.

■■■■■■■■■

Nada and Mac hit hard, their bodies instinctively doing what had been drilled into them years ago at Fort Benning in jump school, using the five points of contact: balls of feet, calf, thigh, buttocks, and the pull-up muscle along the side. Then they were on their feet, cutting away their chutes, readying their weapons.

Nada was the longest serving member of the Nightstalkers, which meant he was both good and lucky. His parents were Colombian and his face was pockmarked and scarred. During the *Battlestar Galactica* marathon, Mac had started calling him Adama, but he'd only done it twice before Nada cut that crap off at the mouth. He had short gray hair, racing Moms to see who could go totally gray first.

"Status, Roland," Nada demanded over the net.

"One KIA, one wounded," Roland reported.

They could see Roland standing near a body, his machine gun tight to his shoulder, scanning the area through the scope on top. They could also hear sirens approaching. Sometimes the locals were almost as dangerous as the threats the Nightstalkers had to contain.

Almost.

"Fireflies?" Nada asked, leading Mac over to Roland.

"I didn't see any," Roland said. "But someone shot this woman. Double-tap."

Nada stared down at the body. One round on the side of the head (some blood, so the first shot), one in the forehead (no blood, so she'd already been dead from the first bullet). His skin went cold, because that meant a well-trained professional. The first bullet had done the job, but the second was insurance.

Nada shook the premonition off. "If she's the scientist who opened the Rift, where's her computer?"

"Shooter must have taken it," Roland said. He pointed. "Got a wire running to the Arch."

"Moms will get 'em," Nada said with more confidence than he felt. "Let's—" he began, but an urgent transmission cut him off.

"Snake down, Snake down." Eagle's voice was faint, but the words were clear.

"Moms?" Nada asked.

"I'm trapped in the cockpit," Eagle said. "I can't see the cargo bay. Transponder is on. We're on the other side of the river. We've lost containment."

The first police car roared up, cops leaping out, screaming for the three Nightstalkers to drop their weapons.

"Fuck me to tears," Nada muttered as he lowered his automatic rifle.

CHAPTER 2

"I'd like some French toast," Scout said, and her mother shot her a look as if she'd asked for a shot of pure heroin.

Scout's mother was terrified of calories. She was making an egg-white omelet and some asparagus. And not much of either.

Mother also didn't like that her daughter insisted that her name was now Scout. This change had occurred the previous summer when all sorts of strange things had happened in the gated community in North Carolina they'd lived in while Scout's dad worked in the Research Triangle. Gas explosions, mysterious fires, strange people out and about; it had all been quite unnerving for Mother and she'd been happy to see North Carolina in the rearview mirror. Unfortunately, Tennessee in the windshield didn't seem much different, with just the Smoky Mountains in front or behind.

At first she'd ignored Scout's name request, an irresistible force against an immovable object.

The object won, because Scout simply refused to acknowledge her given name, Greer.

It only took her twenty-six days and forcing her mother to watch *To Kill a Mockingbird* and then leaving it on, playing off the DVR on a constant loop. Every time her mother turned it off, Scout turned it back on. It also didn't hurt her cause that she had an aunt, a cousin, and a grandmother who were also named Greer and the whole mess got quite confusing at times.

Scout was easier all around was the way her mother finally rationalized it. A phase the seventeen-year-old would grow out of.

But Scout was who she was.

Of course, Scout also knew giving up Greer meant she was the outsider, not of the clan, but she'd never really been inside, so it shouldn't have bothered her that her mother now called her Scout. She'd wanted it and her mother had given in. Victory.

But the still-child part of Scout kind of wished her mother hadn't given in. She was wise enough to realize that sometimes people gave in when the fight wasn't worth it because they simply didn't care that much.

Awareness was a bitch.

Scout's hair was now red with blue streaks, since Scout believed change was good. Short and spiked. A lot of kids laughed at it in the new school that first day in January, but Scout had noted the ones who didn't laugh. Who watched. She knew Nada would have approved. Eggs and ham, or ham and eggs. There was a lot of difference.

She missed Nada. She missed the team. She didn't even resent that they'd knocked her out to go do whatever they'd gone to go do, although the online newspaper had reported a lab explosion on campus at UNC. *Yeah, right*, Scout had thought upon reading that. Had Nightstalkers written all over it. The team really needed better cover stories. They'd left without a good-bye or fare-thee-well. Still, she'd understood on a base level that Nightstalkers never said good-bye.

It was too permanent a thing in a business where there were more serious permanent things.

"I'm going riding today," Scout said, settling in on the bar stool at the perfectly clean granite kitchen bar. "I need the carbs."

The sun had come up over the Smokies to the southeast an hour and a half ago and Scout was raring to go, way too early for most seventeen-year-old girls, but Scout was anything but normal.

The house was new, but unlike cars, it didn't have a new house smell. Actually, it smelled pretty much of nothing. No character, no essence. It sat alone at the end of a cul-de-sac in a new, isolated subdivision outside of Knoxville, Tennessee, on the wrong side of the river but the right side of the railroad tracks. Scout often said the latter to irritate her parents, who'd sacrificed distance from Dad's work for price per square footage. She had no idea which side of the railroad tracks they were on, although she could hear the train coming through, hooting and tooting every so often.

The nearest house was still under construction and it depressed Scout to count the five electrical boxes lined up along the street between their house and that one, because that meant while the houses were large, the lots were small and if this place got fully developed, she'd be able to jump from rooftop to rooftop. Big houses, tiny lots.

And the closest tree was a quarter mile away, as the developer had bought out a dairy farmer's field and was trying to squeeze every possible nickel out of the real estate. Beyond that tree, huge power lines crossed the river, metal towers on each shoreline holding them up. This was TVA country, Tennessee Valley Authority, and the whole place thrived on power. The Smoky Mountains were to the southeast, but not visible from the front of the house, because rolling hills blocked the view. They could be seen from the roof if one stood on one's toes; Scout knew this because she'd gone up on the roof one day when no one was home and stood up on her toes.

On the plus side, unlike Senator's Club in North Carolina, there was no gate. Of course, as far out in the middle of nowhere as they were, it didn't seem like there was going to be much traffic. No one came to this neighborhood by accident; it was on a bend of the Tennessee River, a thumb of land four miles long by two wide. To get to the other side of the river, where Knoxville was, one had to wind through miles of mostly single-lane roads to a larger road, to Interstate 140 (which ran all of twenty miles from I-40 to Maryville) and cross on the I-140 bridge, or take Alcoa Highway into downtown Knoxville. Traffic on that road (locals called it "I'll Kill You") was so bad, one literally took their lives into their hands just trying to merge into the speeding flow of people anxious to get to wherever was so important they were willing to risk their lives for it.

On the upside, the sloping backyard ended at the Tennessee River. And even better, beyond the cul-de-sac, on the other side of the wooden fence, was a huge spread with an old house and a barn and a bunch of cows, and most importantly a stable where Scout's horse Comanche was housed.

Scout could tell her mother was wavering, glancing at the pantry.

"Please? Comanche gets carbs. I won't get any lunch and I'm starving." Scout wasn't sure if oats were carbs, but Comanche definitely ate better than she did.

"A moment on the lips—" her mother began, but Scout cut that one off at the fridge.

"If you say a lifetime on the hips, I'm gonna scream." Scout opened the door to the fridge and pulled out the real eggs. Then she opened the bread bin. "Face it, Mother. The food thing is your deal and I don't float my boat by keeping my lips sealed to real food. That's yours."

"It's everyone's deal," her mother said. "This country is in bad shape."

"Yeah," Scout muttered, putting the eggs on the bar. "Everyone's worried a size two is twice as fat as a size zero."

"What was that, dear?"

"Nothing," Scout said as she headed for the stairs.

She glanced over her shoulder before she turned the corner on the landing and saw her mother staring into the bread bin as if it contained a snarling possum. Scout sighed and continued the trek to the upper level, thinking of her grandmother, Nana, who couldn't feed her enough and her mother who wanted her to subsist on air and egg whites. Why the disconnect in subsequent generations? As if a parent had to do opposite their own, and everything skipped one generation, causing never-ending turmoil and misunderstanding.

Scout paused as she wondered what kind of mother she'd be, and decided that Nana-mode wasn't so bad, but it had produced her mother.

So.

Seemed like a lose-lose all around. Was there a third option? She bet the Nightstalkers could figure out a third option.

Scout flipped the sign on her door to DO NOT, and walked into her new room. Sometimes she missed her old room in North Carolina with its nice window to the roof where she could climb out and sit in the dark and smoke and watch Nightstalkers parachute out of the sky.

Once at least for the latter.

But this room had its upsides. There was a lovely window seat looking out onto the river and all her books were on built-in shelves. She liked snuggling up on the cushions on the window seat and reading and watching the action on the river. The locals called it Fort Loudoun Lake because there was a dam about twenty miles to the west. But Scout called it the Tennessee River, because the river was here before the dam and it had river barges, and barges didn't go in circles on a lake. They ended up somewhere on a river. Point A to Point B. On one tug she'd seen *Chattanooga, TN* painted on the stern, and she knew that was a long way past the dam, downriver, traveling through a lock in that dam and the others. A bunch of dams on the river, each one dropping the level seventy feet. She'd researched it, and on some base, explorer level, it excited her to think one could get on the river in her own backyard and travel over six hundred miles, meandering southwest through Tennessee into Alabama, turning back north, crossing back into Tennessee, past the Shiloh battlefield, and then into Kentucky where the river links up with the Ohio at Paducah. And from there, of course, the Ohio went to the Mississippi and the Mississippi went all the way down to New Orleans and beyond there to the Gulf of Mexico, and from the Gulf, the Atlantic, and from there the world.

Sometimes Scout wondered if she ought to consider a career in the merchant marine. Or if the lure of the Mississippi was from all the Twain she'd read.

She'd read all the Twain there was to read.

On the far side of the river, the original rocky side (her house was on the drowned farmland side created when the dam was put up during the early 1940s by the TVA), a barge was anchored, putting in a dock for a house on the cliff. The barge was old and battered and every piece of metal on it was covered with rust, but it had a crane and a pile driver to pound the long wooden poles down into the river bottom, and lately she liked to just sit on her window seat and watch that power in action, listening to the rhythmic thud during the day.

Her mother complained every time it was working and had already called the TVA to complain about the noise.

As if.

Scout likened that to people who bought a house in the flight path of an airport and then complained about the noise of the planes taking off and landing. Speaking of which, while they weren't on the civilian flight path to Knoxville Airport, only a few miles away as the crow flies, for some reason big military planes flew overhead every day, taking off and landing. She figured the air force just had to take a different runway from the civilians, just like the Nightstalkers hadn't been able to fit in her old gated community. The military was just different.

Scout liked the river and overall she rated this place better than Senator's Club, although she missed her window egress and the ability to sit on the roof and smoke. For that, she now climbed under the wood fence and then went down to the riverbank and hid behind a wooden seawall the owner of the barn had put in. It was okay, but she had a feeling once summer really hit, the mosquitoes were going to be a bitch to deal with.

She could smell the French toast, but it was a thin smell because her mother had held back on the sugar and cinnamon, which her nana would have piled on to make the heady aroma of a real, vibrant dish. One that would draw you downstairs, just to be in the presence of its creation.

Scout also liked the new bathroom because a bunch of the plugs were built into the cabinets and drawers so her mother didn't complain about tangled wires or scummy electric toothbrushes out in the open. If it was hidden in a drawer, her mother was of the "out of sight, out of mind" persuasion, at least when it came to her daughter.

Scout hit the face of her iPad and music came out of the speakers built into the ceilings, which was also a cool feature. The whole house could be controlled by iPad, and not just the music: lights, locks, garage doors . . . pretty much everything. It was a smart house, according to the real estate brochure. Scout thought it was probably getting smarter than her three-person family and would one day turn on them.

She'd seen a house do that back in North Carolina.

The Nightstalkers had blown it up and then burned it down to ashes.

She didn't think her mother would be happy if that happened.

Sometimes, though, when she saw her dad at his computer and the Quicken program was open, she had a feeling he wouldn't be too upset to collect on the insurance.

Scout turned on her toothbrush and stuck it in her mouth, keeping her lips shut so the drool didn't run down her face. She wanted to be out of here as soon as she wolfed down the skimpy breakfast her mother was preparing. She wandered back to the big window and watched the barge across the river. The crew had just arrived and tied off their skiff and were getting ready for a day's work. A speedboat roared by, some guy water-skiing behind it in a wet suit, because May was too early, even in Tennessee, plus it was slightly chilly at 7:15 in the a.m. There was a cluster of ducks near their dock and Scout tried to remember what that was called—a gaggle? Or was that geese?—which got her trying to remember the difference between ducks and geese.

Her family had two Sea-Doos on lifts on one side of their dock, but the boatlift was empty. Her dad sat every evening after work with his catalogues and laptop and looked at boats the way her mother went through her yoga attire catalogues and *Southern Living* magazines. Weird the way everyone wanted different stuff and spent so much time looking—

Scout yelped because her mouth suddenly got hot and her back molar was tingling like she'd lost the filling and hit a nerve.

She jerked the toothbrush out of her mouth so quick, she forgot to shut it off, spraying herself and the blue window seat and the window with spittle and toothpaste. Before she hit the off button, it stopped. As did the music and the lights overhead.

Her first thought was she'd have to clean the window and wash the seat cover.

Great. Her mother couldn't even make French toast without flipping a circuit breaker.

She looked over and the iPad screen was dark, which was weird, because even if the power went out, its battery should keep it on. And then she realized the battery-powered toothbrush wasn't wired in to a circuit breaker either.

Scout tossed the toothbrush in the sink and went downstairs. Her mother was standing in front of the stove, the French toast sizzling, the lights on.

"What's up with my room?" Scout asked.

"What do you mean, honey?" Then the range exhaust fan stopped, as did her mother. "Well, that's weird."

"Must be the breaker box," Scout said, even though she doubted her mother knew what one was, never mind where it was.

And she knew it wasn't the breaker box. One could hope.

Sometimes hope isn't a good thing.

Then all the lights went off and the two just stood there for a moment staring at each other.

Scout was about to tell her mom she'd check the box in the garage when the fan started with a low whir and the lights flickered, coming back on. Scout realized she still had a dull pain in her molar and went into the downstairs half-bath and turned the light on. She looked in the mirror, opening her mouth wide. There was the faintest golden glow in the tooth, which slowly faded out.

The skin on the back of her neck tingled. Scout ran back upstairs, ignoring her mother. The iPad was on, music was coming out of the speakers, and the lights were bright.

The toothbrush was rattling in the sink, vibrating the water, which was also glowing golden. Scout hit the sink stopper and the water drained out, taking the golden glow with it.

With a trembling hand, Scout picked the brush up and hit the off button.

It shut down.

Scout waited, not sure what to expect but having a feeling it wasn't going to be good.

Tentatively, she tried the toothbrush. It rattled to life, no golden glow, and shut off when she hit the button.

So far, so nothing.

Which was good. Perhaps.

Scout went to the window and sat on the window seat. She squinched her eyes shut and thought hard: Was the toothbrush new or had it been recovered from her destroyed bathroom in North Carolina, where her curler had been possessed?

She realized there was no way of knowing without asking Cleaner, who'd supervised the reconstruction of the room after the Nightstalkers had taken out the Firefly that had possessed the curler.

Or had they?

She'd been on the porch with Nada. But Moms, she'd been in there and she'd said they done it, and although Scout had only known Moms for a couple of days, Scout knew Moms wasn't a woman who imagined things or guessed.

If Moms said they got it, they got it.

So what didn't they get?

And where was it now?

She looked toward the bathroom and mentally traced the flow: gold in toothbrush, into water, down the drain. Drain went to septic tank to drainage field, which was in the backyard.

Her mother called for her and Scout reluctantly went downstairs to get her meager breakfast. It looked like her mother had cut the slices of bread into even thinner slices, which required the skill of a surgeon, but her mother was quite good at paring food down. There was, of course, no maple syrup to drench the French toast in. Scout took the plate and went to the nook table, where her mother was always trying to get the family to eat meals together.

This took Mother by surprise, since Scout always wolfed her food down at the bar or trudged upstairs to her room to eat alone.

"Are you all right, dear?" Her mother had taken to calling her dear, not Scout. A compromise.

"I'm fine," Scout said. The nook gave a nice view of the yard and the river.

Her mother shouldered the heavy bag of workout gear and whatever else she hauled around to make it through her day. "Enjoy your ride, dear."

"You, too, Mother."

Her mother stood in the doorway to the garage, staring at Scout as if she'd grown two heads. "You know, Greer—" she began, and Scout perked up.

"Yes?"

"Nothing, dear." Her mother shrugged and the door shut behind her.

And then Scout was alone. She took the plate to the sink and washed it.

Then she went to the back door. She wanted to just gear up and go ride Comanche. But then she thought, *What would Nada do?*

He'd wait and watch. Something strange had happened and it was easy to ignore an anomaly.

Easy was bad.

So Scout waited and watched and then she saw it, thirty minutes after the water had gone down her sink, a golden shimmer in the grass in the backyard. Scout was tempted to walk out there, but that was tempting fate.

So she waited a bit longer and then she saw a translucent snake of golden water surface in the river, and then disappear underneath the muddy surface.

"This isn't good," Scout muttered. She went back into the house to her room.

Scout grabbed the Leatherman multitool out of her backpack and went to the air intake grill on the wall. She carefully unscrewed it, making sure not to mark the perfect white paint. A lockbox was set inside. She dialed up the combination and opened it. Inside there were the usual items a normal seventeen-year-old girl would hide, but even more items an abnormal seventeen-year old girl would hide.

Such as some spent shell casings of various sizes she'd scavenged from the fence line of Senator's Club where the Nightstalkers had destroyed the backhoe—Cleaner's team was good but not perfect. An empty eggs and ham MRE packet, a tribute to Nada's willingness to take one for the team. And a postcard from the Little A'Le'Inn, located in Rachel, Nevada, along Highway 375, aka Extraterrestrial Highway. She'd received it just a week after the events in Senator's Club, her name and address printed on a label.

And the only thing where one would send endearments or "wish you were here" was a phone number. And the words *Text in case of emergency*. Then someone—she assumed Nada—had scrawled, *But it will take a while.*

Scout took the card to the window seat and placed it in her lap as she sat down. Something was different. She closed her eyes and focused, and then realized it was the lack of something that had caught her attention. She opened her eyes and saw that the guys on the barge across the river were staring at their pile driver, one scratching his head.

The driver was silent, frozen in mid-movement.

With trembling fingers, she typed in the number on her iPhone, knowing she was initiating something that could have tremendous repercussions.

Then she typed in a message: *Nada. Scout. In TN. We have a golden problem.*

Scout pressed send and the message shot to the top of her page.

She waited, then realized the odds were low there would be an immediate reply based on Nada's addendum. She put the phone in her pocket.

Looking up at the sound of a thud, she saw that the pile driver was working again, doing its job.

Then she stared at the river, the water flowing by so slowly, held up by Loudoun Dam downstream, so much so that they called this a lake. And she felt it again, that feeling of trouble having arrived and more trouble coming.

Looking out the window again, she could see a boat was stalled out, about a quarter mile downstream, the driver fussing over the engine.

Yeah. There was a problem.

CHAPTER 3

"Welcome to Area 51," the old man in desert camouflage fatigues said to Ivar. The small plane that had dropped him off just moments ago raced down the runway and was airborne within seconds, as if the pilots were anxious to get out of here. Its running lights twinkled in the dark sky; the only hint of dawn was a slight red tinge on the eastern horizon.

Ivar looked around. "This isn't Area 51."

Nothing but desert in all directions. The runway was a pitted concrete strip, half covered with drifting sand, with just a tattered windsock hanging limply on a rusting pole.

"Sure it is," the old man said with as much spirit at the windsock. "I'm Colonel Orlando. You're"—he paused and looked at a clipboard—"Ivar. For now," he added.

"Area 51 has the longest airstrip in the word," Ivar pointed out.

"Well, third longest," Orlando said, "and that's the main strip. Which is a long ways thataways." He pointed vaguely to the southwest. "This is an auxiliary strip. We're having some, uh, well, security issues, so we thought it safer to bring you here."

"What kind of security issues?" Ivar was tall, thin, but no longer stooped as if afraid of the world. Seeing the Rift open at the University of North Carolina, the Russians die, and a year of

Special Operations training had changed him. Into what, even he wasn't sure yet.

But he liked the changes.

His face was still thin, his hair brown and thinning. His eyes were dark and there were lines around them that hadn't been there a year ago; before the Nightstalkers blasted their way into the lab he was working in at the University of North Carolina in Chapel Hill.

Colonel Orlando might have stood tall once upon a time, but the years of working in the covert world had accumulated on his shoulders, much like the way the gray crept into Moms's and Nada's hair.

Instead of answering, Orlando turned toward an old battered jeep, indicating for Ivar to follow.

"I wasn't done with my training," Ivar said.

"Ms. Jones believes you are and when she says you're done, you're done."

"Who is Ms. Jones?" Ivar read more into Orlando's statement than the obvious, which he had a feeling was intended.

"I'm taking you to her." Orlando got behind the wheel. "Coming? It's a long walk to anywhere from here."

Despite being the subject of numerous documentaries, blogs, newspaper reports, movies, and so on, very little of the truth of Area 51 is known to the outside world. It's in the Middle of Nowhere, Nevada, and you have to want to get to it to even take any road close to it. And you couldn't get to it, unless you were invited, which few people were.

Ivar was now one of those.

To the west of Area 51 is the Nevada Test Site where 739 nuclear weapons had been exploded by the U.S. Department of Energy.

And another one, just last year, by the Nightstalkers. That one wasn't listed on Wikipedia.

Nobody wanted to get to the Test Site. And even if someone got to it, they wouldn't last long, given the lingering radiation.

Going back to its origins, the location received its name when a large chunk of Nevada was bought (appropriated) by the government during World War II because the military at Nellis Air Force Base needed some place for its pilots to practice dropping bombs and strafing targets before shipping them overseas to do the same against the Japanese and Germans.

Traditionally, the military took training posts and divided them into training areas. It was easier to do numbers, and sometimes, surprisingly, even the military took the easy way. So the portion on the map surrounding Groom Lake had received the number 51. It might have easily been 50 or 52, but 51 it was.

The conspiracy theorists do have one thing right. Majestic-12 did begin at Area 51 and from there on out the place became the hub for a lot of super-secret activity, including mundane things such as testing beyond-state-of-the-art aircraft.

As far as the aliens from Roswell being brought there?

No such luck.

There were no aliens from Roswell.

It really was a weather balloon.

But the best cover-up is a cover-up of something that never happened to cover up something that happened. Anyone in covert ops knows that, and if one can wrap their brain around that concept, they might have a chance of surviving in the Black World. Roswell was leaked to the press and appeared to be a cover-up for recovery of an alien artifact and bodies, because one state away, at super-secret Area 51, they were dealing with another problem altogether: a Rift.

Over the following decades, enough weird stuff happened around Area 51 that couldn't be completely covered up, and UFO enthusiasts began to focus on it. Every day a flight from McCarren Airport in Las Vegas took off and landed at Groom Lake, on the aforementioned third-longest runway in the world, depositing workers. It returned to Vegas each evening, taking them back home.

While the stuff they worked on was classified, the real work happened farther underground, at levels none of those on the plane would ever get access to. Nor did any of them particularly want access to those levels. Sort of like you might find the Mines of Moria interesting to traverse if you absolutely had to, but you don't want to know what's way down there in the darkness.

Speaking of which, Ivar asked Orlando as he got in the passenger seat, "I thought I'd be taking Janet in?"

Orlando laughed. "Been checking Wikipedia?" He threw the jeep into gear. "Nightstalkers don't take Janet. Hell, son, they aren't even stationed in Area 51 proper. You'll see." The jeep moved forward with a lurch.

"The government actually got some stuff right there at Groom Lake," Orlando said as he spun the wheel and they rolled onto a paved road, heading south. "They been flying worker bees in and out of Area 51 since '72. The planes and pilots were under several front companies for the National Security Agency, until someone got smart and said fuck it, let's just let the air force do the flying for the government, since that is what the fucking air force is supposed to do, right? But they still paint the fuckers weird, red stripe down the side. Like they was trying to draw attention to the fact that the flights weren't fucking normal."

Orlando had not taken part in the *Battlestar Galactica* marathon.

Orlando glanced over at Ivar, who could swear he smelled

alcohol wafting across the jeep from the colonel, but who also picked up the challenge. "So they're a diversion too?"

"Don't say it with a question mark," Orlando said. "The Nightstalkers like statements, not questions. And the big jets, the 737s, they got the red stripe. The little ones, like the one you just flew in—"

"Had a blue stripe."

"So you were paying attention," Orlando said as he shifted gear, the jeep's transmission protesting loudly. "That's how folks like you get in and why you land out here, rather than at Groom Lake."

"How do I get out?"

Orlando laughed. "You might be smarter than you look. You aren't even there yet and you're asking about leaving." He had one hand on the wheel, the other on the gear shifter, and he slammed it into the best the old jeep could do. "It's easy. You just say no."

"No?"

"Did I stutter?" Orlando said. "When Ms. Jones asks you, you just say no and you get to leave, go home, go back to whatever fucking rock you crawled out from under."

"That's it?"

"That's it." Orlando then reached into his pocket and pulled out a flask. He expertly unscrewed the top with the same hand holding it and took a deep drink. He held it out to Ivar.

"No thanks."

"Suit yourself." Orlando screwed the top back on and slid it into his pocket. "Funny thing is, no one has ever said no to Ms. Jones. That I know of. Now, of course, I do think some should have. But she's got a way of putting things."

"So she's going to ask me what?"

"To be a Nightstalker, son," Orlando muttered, then in a low voice, "*Maybe.*"

Ivar leaned closer. "What was that?"

"You met some of the Nightstalkers in North Carolina," Orlando said. "That's what they're called now, but they've had a lot of names over the years."

"It's a cover name," Ivar said.

"So you listened in some of your classes," Orlando said.

"The army's elite Special Operations helicopter unit is called the Nightstalkers," Ivar said. "Task Force 160 is its official designation. They flew us on some of the training missions. I assume these Nightstalkers aren't helicopter pilots."

"Yeah," Orlando said, clearly not impressed. "The team has had some dumb-ass names over the years, but we all kinda like the current one: Nightstalkers. Go after things that go bump in the night. Catch 'em and destroy 'em."

"What about study them?" Ivar asked.

"Spoken like a true fucking dumb-ass scientist," Orlando said. "Anyway, the team was first based at Area 51, because some dumb-ass scientists opened the first Rift there, way back when. Most of those idiots ended up getting snarked through, never seen again. The ones that weren't sucked through the Rift ended up dead." He glanced across at Ivar. "Ms. Jones must have seen something in you, boy, because if she just wanted you to be a scientist, she'd have made you an Acme, one of the Support people. Maybe even an on-call Acme. But she sent you to Spec-Ops training so that you'll know which end of the rifle the bullet comes out of. So she wants you to be a Nightstalker. There's a big difference."

"A scientist can't be a Nightstalker?" Ivar asked.

"Not many." Orlando snorted. "It's real simple. When it comes down to it, do you want to study the fucking problem or solve the fucking problem? Nightstalkers solve problems, usually caused by scientists, so that the human race can go on, ignorant and blissfully unaware of the shit they just avoided. Little things, like the end of the world."

Orlando twitched the steering wheel to avoid some road kill. "The team moved out of Area 51 proper when it got too popular. TV shows, news reports, all that bullshit, even the CIA releasing data on it via the Freedom of Information Act. The Nightstalkers hate media almost as much as they hate scientists. We call our new home the Ranch. Because it actually was a ranch, which we bought. It's technically private land, which is good because we can use deadly force to protect the grounds while the guards at Area 51 just escort dumb-asses off the perimeter and wag a stern finger at them. Ought to stick that finger up their ass."

They came to a stop sign where the road T'ed. Orlando actually stopped, even though they could see to the horizon in either direction and there wasn't a vehicle in sight. Orlando put on his turn signal.

But he left the jeep in neutral, staring straight ahead out the windshield. Ivar waited patiently, for at least thirty seconds, which doesn't sound long, but most people can't sit behind someone at a green light for two seconds without blaring their horn.

"Something wrong?" Ivar finally asked.

"Yes."

Ivar looked where Orlando was staring. "What?"

"There's an intruder out there."

Ivar peered ahead. In nautical terms, it was BMNT—begin morning nautical twilight—where the horizon to the east was clear but the sun had not yet broken the plane.

"Where?"

"You can't see it. But I can."

"What *it*?"

"But you can see the M4 in the bracket in front of you, right?"

It wasn't hard to miss the automatic rifle clamped to the dashboard in front of the passenger seat. "Yes."

"Slowly, very slowly, take it."

Ivar looked out into the desert. There was nothing moving, nothing out of the ordinary. Not even a rabbit.

Ivar removed the M4 from the bracket.

"Careful, son, there's a round in the chamber."

"I know how to use a weapon. Now," he added, and nodded. "The bullet comes out of that end."

"Big difference between the firing range and real life," Orlando said. He still hadn't moved.

"What's out there?"

"The enemy."

Ivar stuck the M4 out toward Orlando. "Here. You see it, you shoot it."

"I can't," Orlando said. "I'm being targeted. Don't you see? On my chest?"

Ivar look at Orlando's chest, but all he saw was the name tag and the Combat Infantry Badge Velcroed to the uniform.

"I don't see anything."

"Good," Orlando said. "If you can't see it, maybe it can't see you. Ready your weapon, soldier."

Ivar had the rifle in his hands. He stared at Colonel Orlando hard, then put the stock to his shoulder, his eye to the sight. "What am I aiming at?"

"One o'clock. One hundred and fifty meters. See that pile of rocks?"

"Yes."

"Eight inches to the left of the last rock. It's about four feet tall."

Ivar saw nothing. He curled his finger around the trigger.

"Fire."

Ivar pulled the trigger. He saw a puff of sand about forty meters past the "target."

"Damn, son," Orlando said. "Close. About six inches to the right."

Ivar adjusted.

"Give it three rounds."

Ivar quickly pulled the trigger thrice, riding out the recoil. Three puffs of sand.

"Hot damn!" Orlando exclaimed, slapping Ivar on the shoulder. "Stand down, son, stand down. You got 'im."

"What did I get?"

Orlando threw the jeep into gear and turned left.

"Aren't we going to get whatever it is I shot?" Ivar asked, still grasping the M4.

"Why?" Orlando asked, as if truly puzzled by such a strange request. "You got it."

Blake was sitting by the pool in the Myrtle Beach complex, wondering if his grandkids had enough sunscreen on. He was also trying to remember if they even had sunscreen when he was a child. But he couldn't conjure up an image of ever being at a pool as a kid. Growing up in Detroit, the summer season was short and pools were in even shorter supply.

His daughter always griped that he forgot things, but he wondered how she'd have turned out if she'd grown up in Detroit. She'd dropped the kids off on her way to work, expecting him to babysit them all day 'cause her nanny was out sick.

Right. Out sick. Sick of the damn kids, more like it.

He'd done it right. Slathered it on both the little beasts and then made them stand around, fidgeting for the requisite time indicated on the side of the bottle. They complained, naturally, being his daughter's children, that none of the other kids had to wait to get in the water. Of course, there weren't that many kids here at the pool this early in the morning, but he was damned if he was going to let them run around his apartment.

"That's 'cause their parents are stupid," he'd informed them, and regretted it right away, because they'd tell and then his daughter would lecture him about saying negative things about people, but the fact is, most people are kind of deserving of negative, in his experience.

He'd seen that working for the government—well, sort of the government—for thirty-four years.

"All right," he said, and the two monsters dashed for the pool and cannonballed in. Blake's focus was now on a young mother across the water, rubbing sunscreen on incredibly long legs. He was wishing he could do it for her. He started analyzing the problem, the mother being the objective. One of the first things he'd learned working for the government was never, ever, take the frontal assault.

At least not yet, he thought with a grin.

He scanned the kids and located the one that was obviously hers. Too small, too near the water, no vest, no floatie things on the arms and the mother was too focused on getting every square inch, probably worried about skin cancer, to notice for the moment. The narcissism of the young never failed to surprise him.

Perfect flank maneuver and Blake grinned once more as he made his move, considering the double entendre of the thought.

He caught the kid just as he was about to fall into the water and smiled at the startled mother. He had his line ready, but then the phone in his bag across the pool rang. Not his phone exactly, but *the* phone, the distinctive ringtone of the chorus of Warren Zevon's "I'll Sleep When I'm Dead." He dropped the kid—*kerplunk*—and strode back to his bag, the angry exclamations from the young mother falling upon his back like splashes from the pool.

Irritating but ineffective.

Damn job, Blake thought as he looked at the text message.

He sighed. He'd have to go pull the cache to get the *other other* phone and encryptor in order to relay the message. And, of course, encrypt it. But first, he had to figure out the source, then the path and additional messages that went with this particular number.

Damn, damn job.

━━━━━━━━━

"We did not contain," Moms summed up the "Clusterfrak at the Gateway," as the team had designated the mission. Moms had a couple of broken ribs, making any deep breath difficult. According to Doc, it would be especially painful if she laughed, but she hadn't laughed since the Snake went down and didn't see much laughter on the horizon. It was early morning at the Ranch, but underground, time often meant little. They'd been flown back from St. Louis, landing at Groom Lake instead of the Barn, since the Snake was out of commission, and driven back here, a rather unhappy group.

No singing, no Roland in the gun turret of the Humvee.

Ms. Jones was actually seated at her desk, making the journey from her hospital bed in the suite behind her office with the assistance of Pitr, her right-hand man. She looked like a wreck of an old woman, hunched over, emaciated, an IV in each arm, because she was a wreck of an old woman. When she spoke, her voice held the Russian accent of her childhood and early adulthood.

"It is worse than that," Ms. Jones said. She gestured with a bony finger at a display for Moms and Nada to watch. They were in Ms. Jones's office, the rest of the Nightstalkers in the team room beyond the flimsy door separating them. The team could hear everything that was said, a deliberate ploy on Ms. Jones's part to make them feel there were no secrets, which, Eagle often reminded them, was the very definition of irony since they were so far in the dark, they might have been at the heart of a black hole.

The screen flickered and then showed the highway coming out of St. Louis. "From the nose camera of the Snake," Ms. Jones said.

Headlights flared as the Prius came down the road.

"Pitr," Ms. Jones said, and her assistant paused the display. "Observe," she said to Moms and Nada as Pitr magnified the view. The windshield of the Prius expanded and then they could see the face of the driver.

"We also received positive identification of the carjacker from the owner of the Prius," Ms. Jones said.

"Fuck me to tears," Nada said, giving up on the *Battlestar Galactica* verbiage. He even threw protocol out the window as he announced loud enough for the team in the other room to hear: "It's Burns. He's back."

"That was a test," Ivar said, a statement, not a question. The sun had cleared the horizon and was sending long fingers of light across the desert floor.

It was almost pretty.

For such a desolate place.

"Good." Orlando nodded. "Scientists always want to know why. Why this? Why that? And that's great, brought us indoor plumbing, because some scientists way back when figured out shit flows downhill. Fucking geniuses, they were. But they still don't know exactly how gravity works, do they?"

That stirred the scientist in Ivar. "Well. Sort of. There are theories and all great science starts from a theory. Nobody has directly observed them, but we believe gravitons exist and they act like photons, except instead of carrying light, they carry gravity."

"Right. A theory. Theories get you killed."

Ivar was not deterred. He might shoot at nothing, but science wasn't nothing. "Einstein defined the space-time continuum, which is a theory, and it's worked pretty well so far. And gravity is a product of that theory."

"But you're not sure."

"We don't know everything. When we finally break out the unified theory, we'll understand gravity like we understand electromagnetism. Let me ask you something. Do you know how your cell phone works?"

"I know how my weapon works," Orlando said. "And you know how yours works. On an op, the big thing is you get an order to do something, you do it. You don't ask why. You don't bring up whether it makes sense. I coulda had you shooting Harvey out there. You know who Harvey is?"

"No."

Orlando sighed. "Jimmy Stewart? Big rabbit no one else can see?"

Ivar shook his head.

"You might be a scientist, but you don't know a lot of important shit. I miss Eagle."

"We can—" Nada began, but a flutter of Ms. Jones's hand silenced him.

"We have a potential team member coming in. If he accepts, we will name him. It's the tradition."

Nada wasn't sidetracked. "Burns is—"

Once more, this time just a lift of a finger, and Nada's mouth snapped shut. He glanced at Moms and she shook her head ever so slightly. Everything was off, out of step. They'd lost containment. They'd lost the Snake. Burns was back, from wherever it was that was the other side of a Rift. If that thing in the Prius was even Burns.

"The scientist was named Melissa Eden," Ms. Jones said. "The initial check on her body indicates she received a fatal dose of radiation prior to expiring. So she was dead regardless. The bullets saved her some misery."

"I'll be glad to save Burns some misery," Nada said. "We can—"

"Please let me in-brief the new team member," Ms. Jones said, and the weariness in her voice was palpable. "And, before that, I must make a call to determine our next step. Go upstairs and welcome our arrival. Colonel Orlando is almost here."

She took a deep rattling breath. "You should also know that we pulled video surveillance from cameras in the area. As best the Acmes can determine, the only thing that came out of the Rift was

Burns. No sign of Fireflies, so this is a very different situation. Thus it must be handled differently."

Nada blinked in surprise and glanced at Moms as he got to his feet. They all knew Ms. Jones reported to someone, but she'd never been so open about it. She'd never outright said she had to defer a decision to someone else.

Moms and Nada quickly left the office, Nada carefully shutting the flimsy door behind them, Moms with a finger on her lips to keep the team from exploding in fury over Burns's return.

CHAPTER 4

Somewhere near Knoxville, Tennessee. That was all Blake had as far as an indication of who had sent the text. The code that went with this particular number indicated a path for the message to be passed. A path that consisted of five cutouts.

Blake stared at the screen of his laptop. He'd never heard of using five cutouts. One was usually sufficient since the very definition of a cutout was someone who knew both sides, but the two sides didn't know each other. Thus the cutout was expendable and once expended, both sides were safe. Five meant whoever had set up this commo line was being extra, extra, extra, extra careful. Some paranoid son of a bitch, which defined a lot of people Blake had worked with over the years.

In this case, Blake didn't know either side other than the message received and the mode by which he was to forward the message.

Which meant there was more to this than simply keeping it secure. It had to be a heads-up for each cutout along the way.

Regardless, he had a duty to perform and he knew the immediate task wasn't going to be pleasant.

He missed the pool, he missed the young mother, and he even missed his grandchildren as he headed out to his truck.

"Fancy digs," Ivar said as they passed a plywood sign with NO TRES-PASS: WE WILL SHOOT YOUR ASS spray-painted on it along with a skull and crossbones. "I assume someone would indeed shoot my ass if I wasn't supposed to be here."

Again not a question, so Orlando didn't respond. They'd left the tar road a minute ago and were rattling down a dirt road toward what appeared to be a deserted filling station, which Ivar assumed was anything but deserted.

Orlando braked a football field short of the station. He looked bored as two men appeared out of holes, camouflaged with ghillie suits and weapons at the ready. A third man appeared from behind and scanned Orlando's eyes. Then the man did the same to Ivar. He seemed disappointed that the scanner beeped, his finger twitchy on the trigger. He waved Orlando on and the three disappeared back into their holes.

"They seem anxious," Ivar observed.

"Told you," Orlando said. "Security issues."

Orlando shoved the stick into gear and they rattled up to the service station just as an old soda machine slid aside and a group of people climbed out of stairs that had been hidden behind it, arguing. All seven had the look that Ivar was now used to: Spec Ops. Competent, quiet (though not at the moment), professional. Well, except for the short, Indian-looking guy with thick glasses, but even he exuded something.

Scratch the professional, too, though, as one of them, movie-star good-looking, drew an MK23 from under his shirt and fired, punching holes in an old gas can and sending it tumbling.

"At ease, Mac!" the only woman among the
in a voice that clearly indicated she was in charg

Mac holstered his weapon and they all tu
stopped the jeep with a screech of brakes.

They didn't seem happy to see Ivar. He recognized several from
the hectic events at the University of North Carolina last year, but
his memory of that event wasn't the greatest, since he'd been under
the influence of forces he still couldn't comprehend.

"Fresh meat," Roland said.

"Just what we fucking need," Mac said with a Texas drawl,
and Ivar sensed he would have preferred to shoot him. "Another
rookie to break in."

"Kirk did okay," Roland said, indicating another member of
their group. Kirk was of average height, lean. His face was almost
skull-like, all angles, and he sported deep blue eyes that fixed Ivar
with their gaze.

"Hey, Eagle," Orlando called out. "My man here doesn't know
who Harvey is, even after I had him shoot the bugger back yonder."

Eagle, a tall black man without a hint of hair on his head,
laughed. "The Harvey test is so old school, Colonel." The left side
of Eagle's head was covered with a burn scar, a gift from an Iraqi
IED years ago.

"It's not old if you haven't done it before," Orlando said.

"Who's Harvey?" Roland asked.

"Big rabbit," Eagle said. "But only one person can see him."

"Nada killed a rabbit in the *Fun Outside Tucson*," Roland
said.

"Yeah," Mac said bitterly, "where Burns got wounded."

"And most likely infected," Doc threw in.

"We're not sure of that," Moms said.

What are we sure of?" Nada muttered, and Ivar threw a look at Orlando as if to say, *See?*

"So who the fuck—excuse me, the frak—are you?" Mac asked.

"My name is Ivar."

"No one gives a shit what your name is," Mac said.

"Roger that," Eagle said. "Because if you say yes to Ms. Jones, you get a new name. And that will be that."

Nada peered at Ivar. "I remember you. You're from the lab in North Carolina." He sighed. "A fraking scientist."

They all turned and looked at Doc as if he were already Harvey.

"You going somewhere?" Nada asked.

"Not that I am aware of," Doc said. "But we all know our lives here are full of uncertainty and—"

"Give it a break, Doc," Mac said.

"So why do we need another scientist?" Nada asked, knowing there was no answer forthcoming from this group. Ms. Jones had her own ways, and trying to figure them out was a waste of brain energy.

Orlando got back in the jeep. "You gentlemen, and lady, have a fine rest of the day. Until next time."

"Stay safe," Nada said, and Orlando paused for a moment, as if that admonition was more a premonition.

"You too." In a cloud of dust, Orlando drove away.

Ivar shifted from one foot to another, uncomfortable under the gaze of the other seven. Finally Nada jerked his thumb at the rusting soda machine. "Punch grape soda."

Ivar went over to the machine. He had four choices: Dr. Pepper, Pepsi, orange, and grape. The faded writing said .25 CENTS. He paused, thinking this through even as Mac called out, "Don't hit the orange or we'll all become part of the desert."

Ivar didn't have twenty-five cents. He also had a feeling it didn't matter. He hit the button for grape. Driven by pneumatic arms, the soda machine slid to the side and a stairway beckoned.

"Got eight seconds," Nada said, startling Ivar, since he hadn't heard him come up right behind him. Along with the rest of the team. Ivar scuttled down the stairs, the others following. Before he reached the last stair, the steel door at the bottom slid open.

"Welcome to the Den," Moms said as they came out of the hallway into a large circular room with dull gray walls and old battered furniture. It all looked like stuff the government should have auctioned off decades ago. Apparently the Nightstalkers weren't working on the $10,000-per-toilet-seat federal budget. Ivar saw an assortment of tables; flip charts; whiteboards, some with incomprehensible writing on them; and a row of lockers. There was also a six-foot-high log impaled with throwing weapons: knives, axes, even a spear.

"You don't get to throw," Mac said to him, grabbing the handle of a hatchet and jerking it free of the log.

"Not yet," Roland added, pulling the spear loose. "Not until after your first op."

The woman stood in front of Ivar, having a two-inch height advantage. "I'm Moms. Team leader. We met once, but it wasn't under the best of circumstances." She pointed as she introduced him. "Nada, team sergeant. That's Eagle, pilot and walking font of useful and useless information. Kirk, our communications man and contrarian. Roland, the one with the spear, naturally is weapons. Mac, the hatchet man, our engineer or as he prefers, demo man." As she pointed him out, Mac threw the hatchet and it whirled, hitting the log with a solid thud, blade sinking in.

"What's a contrarian?" Mac asked.

55

"I don't think I am one," Kirk protested.

"See?" Eagle said.

Moms pointed at the last person. "And Doc is Doc. He's our scientist and doctor. I don't know what you're going to be, but you're meeting Ms. Jones now and she'll let you know. Then we'll pick your name."

"*If* you say yes," Nada added. "Listen to what she has to say very carefully."

"You might want to consider saying no," Mac yelled from across the Den as he retrieved the hatchet. "Given recent events, that is." He didn't flinch as Roland threw the spear and it passed eighteen inches from him, burying its point into the log, the shaft quivering for a moment.

"There's no shame in saying no," Nada said. "You leave here and go on with your life."

"He don't look like he got much of a life," Mac added, pulling the spear free along with his hatchet.

They all seemed to ignore Mac, except when he was shooting gas cans, so Ivar tried to ignore him also.

"We need more shooters," Roland said. "Not scientists."

"We need more brains," Mac said. "Not sure this guy qualifies, though."

"We need a bigger boat," Eagle said, but no one got it, as usual. It was a sign of his frustration that he explained, "*Jaws?* Big shark? Need a bigger boat?"

"I got it," Kirk said, "but I'm not a fan of the allusion."

"The illusion," Mac threw in.

"Yeah," Roland added. "A shark I can handle. I don't need a bigger boat. I need a bigger gun."

"And since you crashed the Snake," Mac added, "we ain't got no ride."

A muscle twitched on the side of Eagle's face. "I lost all power. I had no choice."

"We know," Moms said, shooting Mac a shut-the-frak-up look. "We all did the best we could."

Nada tapped on the door, then swung it open. "Sit in front of the desk. Don't get out of the chair until dismissed. Then you come back out here. Violate these instructions and I'll kill you."

Ivar nodded. After shooting at Harvey, nothing much was surprising him and he had no doubt Nada meant it. Everyone in the Den looked like they had a lot of experience killing, except for Doc.

Ivar walked in and sat in a hard plastic seat facing a large desk. There were several papers scattered on the surface. On the far side was a large, wing-backed chair, set in the shadows cast by large lights pointing directly at Ivar. He squinted, trying to see who was in the chair.

As far as he could tell, no one.

He heard a door squeak and then a man appeared, carrying someone in his arms. He was a tall, well-built man with silver hair. He ignored Ivar as he deposited an old woman in the chair, where she disappeared into the dark shadow. He went back to the door, then returned, rolling two IV drips. He reached into the darkness with the lines from the drips and did something.

Then he straightened. He turned to Ivar, shooting him a withering look, as if blaming him for this trouble.

"Do you want me to stay, Ms. Jones?" he asked. He had a slight accent, which Ivar guessed was Russian or Eastern European. When Ms. Jones replied, there was no doubt hers was Russian.

"You may, Pitr."

He nodded and folded his arms across his chest, glaring at Ivar, who had no idea what he'd done to earn the man's enmity.

"And," Ms. Jones said, "I'd like the rest of the team in here."

Pitr was obviously startled. "It is the tradition that—"

"Please," Ms. Jones cut him off.

Pitr spoke in a louder voice, through the door, to the team room. "Moms. Nada. Please bring the team in."

The door swung open and the Nightstalkers trooped in, spreading out along the rear wall, Moms and Nada in the center. They all looked like they'd rather be facing a firing squad.

Ms. Jones said, "Pitr, please turn off the spotlights."

Pitr's mouth flopped open, ready to protest, but he'd known Ms. Jones too long. He reached behind him and hit a switch. The lights behind the chair went off, leaving only dim recessed lighting around the edge of the room. It took a few moments for everyone's eyes to adjust.

Ms. Jones looked somewhere between eighty and a hundred, give a decade or take a day. A withered old woman, skin lashed with red sores and old scars. She wore a thick gray smock, almost a sackcloth. Shunts went into her chest and one arm, the IVs feeding in whatever was keeping her alive. She had no hair, her skull crisscrossed with scars from surgeries.

"Yes, I am real," Ms. Jones told them. "Although, Mister Doc has been right. There are occasions I was projected into here as a hologram, during some of my more difficult times."

If this was a "good" time, no one wanted to see what she looked like during a "difficult" time.

"Since you all hear everything anyway, you might as well be present. I'm not sure how much longer I will be occupying this chair, and I think it's time to stop some of the"—she paused, searching for the correct words, finally settling on—"pretense and mystery. We have"—she gestured with the claw of a hand at Ivar—"to give our latest member the option of joining our merry band

and, if he decides yes, a name. Then there are some things I have to tell you, some of which will not please you."

She shifted her gaze to Ivar, ignoring the others for the moment. Ms. Jones spoke so low, Ivar had to lean forward to hear her. "You do know, of course, that someone has to guard the walls around our civilization in the middle of the night? The walls between all those innocents out there who go to bed every evening, troubled by thoughts of such things as mortgages or the garbage that needs to be taken out tomorrow, or the car that is going to need new tires? The normal things most people worry about. There are even those who have grave, serious worries, such as divorce or illness or a loss of faith. But the things we in the Nightstalkers worry about, they are far graver than any of those worries.

"You know some of this because you were part of the event in North Carolina," Ms. Jones continued. "You were there when these Nightstalkers behind you closed the Rift you helped make in the lab there."

There was no accusation in the tone, but Ivar stiffened anyway and shifted uncomfortably on the hard plastic chair.

"Tell me," Ms. Jones said, "what do you think Rifts are?"

"Ms. Jones, I've been in training—" Ivar began, but Ms. Jones cut him off.

"Do not try to obfuscate the truth," Ms. Jones said. "I have neither the time nor inclination for it. Any spare moment you had from training, you were on the Internet, researching Rifts. And you are the only person we know of who actually opened a Rift and is still with us. Everyone else either is dead or disappeared, where we know not. I don't know if that is a good thing or a bad thing, but it is a reality and the reason why I've had you pulled out of training early."

"Why now?" Ivar asked, and Nada half stepped forward to smack him on the back of his head for his impertinence to dare interrupt Ms. Jones. Ivar pressed on. "Colonel Orlando said there were security issues. Is that why?"

Ms. Jones shook her head. "Things have occurred, but we are not under threat here. There is a situation, but it does not appear urgent."

Moms and Nada exchanged a what-the-frak? glance.

Ms. Jones paused and they could hear her struggle for oxygen for a moment. Then she spoke again: "What do you think a Rift is?"

"A gate," Ivar said.

"To where?"

"Three possibilities," Ivar said without hesitation. "Either distinct or combined. First, it could be a shift in space. So, that would mean to another place or even planet. If whatever is on the other side is even on a planet. It could be some other"—Ivar paused, then gestured a circle with his hands—"space. Second, a shift in time. The Rift could be punching through to the future. And, if time travel is invented in the future, that means they're here now. Perhaps the past, but not likely. Third, the Rift could be to a parallel universe. When you start considering it might be a combination of two or all three, it becomes a bit overwhelming."

Doc made some sort of noise but not enough to earn a rebuke from Ms. Jones, who was still focused on Ivar.

"What do they want?" Ms. Jones asked.

"They?"

Ms. Jones sighed and Ivar quickly spoke. "I don't know. There were times in the lab when other Ivars materialized. I couldn't quite figure out if I was real or one of them." He rubbed his forehead. "I definitely sensed intelligence behind it all."

"Did you sense a threat?" Ms. Jones asked, which caused Pitr to glance down at her in surprise and the Nightstalkers to fidget.

Ivar grimaced, obviously reluctant to answer. "There was so much going on—the Russians, the Nightstalkers coming, the other Ivars."

Ms. Jones made a noise; what it meant, Ivar had little clue, but he was picking up the hints.

"Not particularly," Ivar said. "Not in the lab. But there were no Fireflies there, like the team faced in Senator's Club." He gestured at the people behind him. "On the other side, whatever was there and trying to come through, I didn't have a good feeling about."

"'Good feeling,'" Mac muttered with a snort.

"At ease," Nada said in a low voice.

"Do you know what a criticality accident is?" Ms. Jones asked Ivar.

He nodded. "Of course. An uncontrolled nuclear chain reaction."

Unnoticed by everyone, except Ms. Jones and Pitr, a frown crossed Doc's face at this shift in questioning.

"How many have occurred?" Ms. Jones asked.

"Twenty-two outside of reactors," Ivar said.

"And sixty, known, including reactors and assembly facilities," Ms. Jones said. She lifted a hand toward her scar-covered head. "I experienced one directly at Chernobyl. It was the largest of the sixty. Known. Explain to the team what a criticality accident is exactly."

"Well, uh, it's the unintentional bringing together of a mass of fissionable material outside of a shielded environment. The critical mass releases radiation and neutron flux. The radiation can be very dangerous to any humans nearby."

"The woman who opened the Gateway Rift," Ms. Jones said, "had received what would have been a fatal dose of radiation—fatal, that is, if she'd lived long enough to have died from it."

"Lucky her," Mac muttered.

"That's new," Doc said. "Usually they're sucked through the Rift."

Ms. Jones ignored him, focusing on Ivar. "What if the critical mass is done intentionally?"

"Then it isn't an accident," Ivar said. "Did this woman have fissionable material?"

"No."

Doc tried to keep his hand in. "Then it had to come from the other side."

"Duh," Mac said. "Even Roland could have figured that out."

"Yes," Ms. Jones said, ignoring the team interplay as she usually did. "I fear we are approaching our own form of criticality."

"How so?" Moms asked.

Ms. Jones shook her head. "I don't know. But for many years the Rifts and the Fireflies were relatively the same. But the last few have been different, evolving. That concerns me. Almost as if there were a plan being played out."

"And Burns?" Moms asked. "How does he play into this?"

"That is a good question," Ms. Jones said. "I fear we might not ever know the answer."

"I'll get the answer out of him," Nada vowed.

Ms. Jones waved that comment off and focused back on Ivar. "Will you destroy Fireflies, and whatever they're in, if ordered?"

Ivar didn't hesitate. "Yes."

"Will you be a Nightstalker?"

"Yes."

Ms. Jones gestured and Pitr picked up a thick folder from among the papers on her desk. He disappeared behind Ms. Jones's high-backed chair. A shredder went to work.

"You no longer exist," Ms. Jones said. "All tangible proof of your existence is gone. Teams in the field have also erased your existence in the outside world. You might be a memory for people you've met in your life, but that is all. And memories fade, faster than most people realize."

Ivar swallowed hard, trying to search his own memory for those who might have a memory of him.

Apparently he wasn't giving up much, he decided.

Ms. Jones finally shifted her gaze past him. "Names?"

"Fred," Nada said right away, as Nada was wont to say. He felt every team needed a Fred and they hadn't had one in a long time. This was met with a few eye rolls but was so expected it was pretty much ignored.

"Mini-Me," Mac said. "We already got a Doc, so he can't be called that, but he is a scientist. Kind of looks like a mad scientist to me."

This nomination didn't seem to light anyone's fire.

"Roland?" Ms. Jones asked.

The big man didn't like being singled out, especially by a woman. He had a thing about women in leadership roles—not a bad thing, but they made him kind of nervous. He'd rather be shot at.

"Buddy?" Roland suggested, at a loss for anything else and not having paid much attention to the candidate anyway.

"He ain't a dog," Mac drawled.

"A nice name," Ms. Jones said, and Roland blushed, the barbed wire standing out in stark relief against the scar. "Eagle?"

"Chowder," Eagle said.

"Clarify?" Ms. Jones said.

"The only Ivar I know of is a chain of seafood restaurants around Seattle," Eagle said. "Ate at one while waiting for a ferry. Had chowder." Eagle shrugged. "Best I could do. Under the circumstances."

Ms. Jones moved on. "Mac?"

"Rat."

Everyone in the room turned to look at Mac, including Ivar.

Mac clarified. "Not 'cause I think he's a rat or nothing, just that when we rescued him in that lab, there were rats there, and he was kind of weird about them." Mac shrugged also. "It's all I know about the man."

"Moms?" Ms. Jones asked the last member of the team.

"Ivar."

Ms. Jones blinked.

"Heck, Moms," Mac said, "we know that's—" Then he trailed into silence.

Ms. Jones cracked a smile, which actually appeared like her face was crumbling. "Yes. I like it. He is an original. He is the only one to open a Rift and still be among us. Therefore he should still retain his name. Ivar it is."

"Welcome to the team," Mac said, taking a step forward and slapping him, a bit too hard, on the shoulder. "Usually we celebrate with beer, but this ain't a beer day."

The rest of the team shuffled by, uncomfortable under Ms. Jones's gaze, and shook Ivar's hand.

Then everyone regained their positions and waited for the bad news.

"I will not bore you with more 'why we are here' talk," Ms. Jones said. "You all have heard it many times and Ivar will have time here at the Ranch for me to discuss it with him one on one."

Moms and Nada exchanged a glance. They'd both expected to be gearing up and moving out to go after Burns ASAP after this. Perhaps they were leaving Ivar behind and—

"The issue of Burns has been appropriated by a higher authority," Ms. Jones said.

"Frak," Mac muttered.

"Fuck me to—" Nada couldn't finish it.

"Excuse me, Ms. Jones." Moms was the only one who would dare to stand up to the old woman. "Burns was one of us. We clean up our own messes. He killed the scientist at the Arch and he killed one of our Support in Utah along with an innocent girl. He's ours."

"He was ours," Ms. Jones clarified. "But we lost him, didn't we? We discarded him and then he turned on us. It is my fault," she added, because she always took responsibility for everything that went wrong. "I chose him for the team. It was a mistake. One I hoped we could rectify in-house. I also made the mistake of letting him go. Believe me, Miss Moms. I want us to go after Burns very badly."

Nada stepped up next to Moms. "Whose responsibility is it now?"

"The Cellar," Ms. Jones said, and they all glanced over at Roland, because he'd spent some time with a Cellar operative after their joint mission during the previous holidays, saving the world from nuclear Armageddon.

Roland put both his big paws up, as if to ward off the stares. "I ain't heard nothing from Neeley since we dropped those two CIA dickheads." When Roland said *dropped*, he meant it literally, cutting the two men's climbing rope and letting them fall to their deaths on a mountaineering expedition in South America. Such was the price of betrayal in the world of covert operations.

"It does fall under the province of the Cellar's mandate to deal with rogue agents," Ms. Jones said.

"Yes," Moms agreed, "but whoever the Cellar sends, will they understand if a Firefly is involved?"

"There's no indication a Firefly came through," Ms. Jones said. "I told you: We have video from six different cameras of the gate. The only thing that came out was Burns."

"What looked like Burns," Nada corrected. "And who knows what's in him. He took down the Snake pretty effectively. The Burns we knew couldn't have done that."

Ms. Jones inclined her head in agreement. "True. Burns was on the other side. We have no clue what's over there. We have no clue if he's even Burns anymore. But policing the ranks of the covert world is the Cellar's province."

Moms wasn't ready to give up. "Does the Cellar know how to close a Rift? Because it's highly possible Burns is here to open one. He took the computer from the Gateway Rift."

"You raise valid points," Ms. Jones agreed. "Points I made to my superior. That is why you will be heading to Fort Meade to consult with the Cellar personally."

"At your request or their request?" Moms asked.

Ms. Jones nodded at the import of the question. "Hannah wants to meet you. And I want you to be my personal liaison to the Cellar, as it appears we're going to be working together more often in the future."

Moms didn't move. "And the team?"

"Is in stand-down," Ms. Jones said. She held up a hand as Moms prepared to protest once more. "Again, I made all the points you are prepared to make, but again, I was listened to but not agreed with. The Snake was badly damaged and is in depot maintenance. The team was damaged. It is time for various members to rest, refit, retrain." She shifted her gaze. "Nada, I believe you have personal business to attend to in Los Angeles. A birth?"

Nada blinked, not surprised that Ms. Jones knew about his family, but that she thought he would ever consider it a priority, especially with someone like Burns loose. But the way she'd shot down Moms told him there was no argument he could use. He was going to Los Angeles.

"I do," he said.

"Good. Take the time to visit your family. After you give Ivar the Protocols to study, of course."

"Yes, Ms. Jones," Nada said, resigned to having to visit his family and taking time off. A condemned man would have looked happier. The last time he'd been in California with family, he'd had to bail out on his niece Zoey under less-than-optimal circumstances, and he wasn't expecting to be welcomed with open arms.

"Doc." Ms. Jones had already moved on. "You will be in charge of Mr. Ivar after Moms and Nada give him the Protocols. Show him the Can. Take him into the Archives. He is to know everything you know about Rifts and Fireflies."

Mac snorted, as if to indicate he didn't think that was much.

"Yes, Ms. Jones," Doc said, bowing to the inevitable and ignoring Mac. He cleared his throat, something on his mind.

"Yes?" Ms. Jones asked.

"What role on the team does Ivar take?" Doc asked. "I'm the team scientist."

"He is your assistant," Ms. Jones said.

"No one else has an assistant," Doc pointed out.

"No one else needs one," Ms. Jones snapped. She held up a frail hand as if to stop the impact of the words. "I do not say that to disparage you. I say that because it's the other way: We need more help understanding the problems we deal with, particularly Rifts and Fireflies. Ivar is the only person who has opened one and is still with us. That brings a unique perspective to the table. We need one because Burns walked through a Rift and is with us now. The Nightstalkers and all the iterations of our predecessors have been dealing with this problem since its inception in 1947. We've been on the defensive. It is time to change that. To be preemptive. I want the two of you to work on that."

Doc took a step forward. "Does that mean you want us to consider opening a controlled Rift?"

Nada shook his head. "No one has ever opened a controlled Rift."

"Not yet," Doc said.

"I did," Ivar said.

Mac snorted and Doc began shaking his head. Ivar held up his hand. "When you can open it and close it, you control it. I admit I have little clue how I did either, and I wasn't in charge of my own faculties, but still."

"Exactly," Ms. Jones said. "And that is why you are here and that is why you and Doc will work together. Any more questions, Mr. Doc?"

"No." Doc took a step back.

"Mac, Kirk, Eagle, and Roland." Ms. Jones said the names ominously. "You need to relearn some basic lessons about following rules, after your stunt in Arkansas, which we never had time to address. You need some training. A flight is awaiting you at the auxiliary field. Colonel Orlando will escort you to Fort Bragg."

"Oh *shiit*," Mac muttered. "Not Bragg."

"You all have your instructions. Please follow through. Of course, as always, you are on immediate recall."

The Nightstalkers exited Ms. Jones's office, a defeated group if ever there was one.

That was still living.

When the door shut behind them, Pitr reached down and unhooked the two lines. Then he gently scooped Ms. Jones up and carried her to her room. He laid her in the bed, reattaching the lines and then the monitoring gear.

They'd known each other since Chernobyl and it was obvious she'd gotten the worse of that event. She'd saved his life, warning him against flying over the reactor to dump a load of concrete. At the same time, she'd risked her own life, going into a control room to rescue another engineer—one of the engineers who'd helped make the disaster.

That was a basic contradiction in nature that Pitr still couldn't reconcile in his old friend. Of course, others couldn't understand why a Russian was running one of the United States' most highly classified units.

It is as it is.

Ms. Jones sighed and collected her energy. Meeting the entire team face-to-face, a first, had drained her. But she'd been worn out prior to the meeting from her discussion/argument with Hannah, the person she reported to in the covert world. She'd thrown every argument that Moms had tried to start, and more, at Hannah and had been denied at every turn. It was more than just the issue of Burns, the failure of the Gateway mission, and the loss of the Snake. Tension between the Ranch and the Cellar had been building for over a year. Having to run the Nuke Op last December together had been both beneficial and disturbing.

Hannah's insistence that Moms come to Maryland and meet with her brought its own set of questions, with most of the answers being bad ones.

"Please put me through to Hannah," Ms. Jones ordered Pitr.

——————————

"What do you think?" Hannah Masterson asked Dr. Golden.

In another time and another place and another universe, they might have been two housewives chatting about their children. Or, given their business attire, two professionals discussing a client.

But they were three hundred feet below the main building of the National Security Agency at Fort Meade, Maryland. In an office where lives were evaluated, judged, and decided upon with regularity.

There was no chitchat. Hannah had once done chitchat. When she was Mrs. Masterson, appendage to her husband and doing all she could to help him climb the corporate ladder in the aerospace industry in St. Louis.

The fact he'd failed to mention his involvement in illicit covert activities in his past was something that had cost him his life and brought Hannah, by a very hard road, to her current position as head of the Cellar. It had also come close to killing her. And Neeley.

Hannah was half Ms. Jones's age, in her late forties, with thick blond hair. She was fit, something she did for the job not for vanity, and her skin was pale, which was to be expected of someone whose quarters and office were deep underground. Her most striking feature was her chocolate-colored eyes.

She never thought of them as striking and only noticed the deepening lines around them when she looked in the mirror, which wasn't often.

Dr. Golden was of roughly the same age, also blond, also fit. She wore glasses, which both she and Hannah knew was an affectation, something to give her more cache when she met with others. Even now, in the second decade of the twenty-first century, women still had to fight to be taken seriously, especially in worlds dominated by men. Hannah let her position and, when needed, operatives like Neeley implement her seriousness.

Often it was the last thing some people saw.

Hannah rarely ventured forth out of the Cellar, wielding her power in the darkness through her agents. Golden, on the other hand, as a psychiatrist, had to meet people to do her job. Many of those people were covert ops, toughened veterans, who conjured up initial impressions quickly and had little time or tolerance for those who tried to probe into their minds, especially a woman.

Even when that probing could determine whether they lived or died at Hannah's command.

"Childhood trauma," Golden said. She had no notes to refer to. Hannah didn't believe in a paper or electronic trail. If one came into her office and couldn't remember what they had to say, perhaps what they had to say wasn't that important. The only papers Hannah kept were in the desk behind which she sat. There were no copies.

Hannah gave a wry smile. "Don't we all have childhood trauma?"

Golden nodded. "Pretty much. But it's the manner of the trauma and which parent figure it comes from that is the key. And then the environment in which one grows up." This was Golden's specialty: profiling backward, looking not at crime scenes but at lives, seeing the patterns to them, particularly in the formative years.

Golden did it first as a student, writing her PhD on it. She'd wanted to determine who had the predilection to be a killer long before they killed. Serial killers were born and also made in her opinion, and she wanted to study the combination that made the cauldron of evil. She then expanded her field and was drawn to further study in the military because they kept such good records of their members. Hannah's predecessor, Nero, had done it instinctively, keeping files on numerous candidates, sensing the traumas and, most importantly, how the betrayals in their lives would cause them to blossom into adults of a certain nature.

Hannah had been one of those candidates. Nero had been looking for a person who could withstand the most base betrayal yet still be able to function, to perform their duty.

For Nero it had been an instinctive art; for Golden it was a science.

Hannah's husband's betrayal had been like the smash of a blacksmith's mighty hammer on a misshapen lump of metal, splintering it, revealing a finely honed edge of steel hidden inside.

Sometimes, alone in the dark, and she was often alone in the dark, Hannah mulled over the issue of free will. Were we all a product of our genes and then our environment shaping those genes, as Dr. Golden postulated? Was it all just fate? Was her presence here, behind this very desk, a predetermined event, in which she was just playing her part? If she got up and walked away, quit her post as head of the Cellar, was that also preordained? A person could go crazy trying to understand the ramifications and possibilities.

However, this didn't bother Hannah much. She only thought about them as a means of exercising her mind when she was bored.

Which wasn't often. There was almost always something in the world of covert operations that demanded her attention.

Golden folded her hands in her lap as she waited on Hannah. The office was spartan, essentially little different from when Nero had occupied it, minus the medical equipment near the end of his tenure. And a bit more lighting, since, unlike her predecessor, she could see. Nero had lost his eyes at the hands of the Nazis after being captured on a covert operation during World War II.

After being betrayed. Making him the perfect candidate to head the Cellar.

"Bottom line?" Hannah said, because she always dealt in bottom lines.

"Moms appears to be a loner but she isn't," Golden said. "She took care of her brothers, all younger than her, while they were growing up, nurturing them, giving them what her mother wasn't capable of. She works best on a team."

"Neeley liked her," Hannah said. "Thought she was effective," she amended, surprising herself a bit at the term *like*. *Like* had nothing to do with what she had to do here at the Cellar.

"That was more a product of the observation than the observed," Golden said.

Hannah graced her with a smile, revealing perfect teeth. "I enjoy how you phrase things. I imagine therapy with you would be most interesting."

"Therapy for you would be counterproductive," Golden said.

"True. I am who I am and who I am is what this job needs. So Neeley is"—Hannah searched for what she wanted to say— "needy?"

Golden swallowed and shifted uncomfortably. She didn't have the full story, but she did know that Neeley and Hannah had come to the Cellar together after a trial under fire. When the toughest jobs came up, it was Neeley whom Hannah dispatched to deal with them. Perhaps for too long now? That was the question that had caused Hannah to summon Dr. Golden.

"You will admit," Golden said, "that it is rather amazing Neeley is still alive after all the missions she's been on. While her body is intact, I have concerns about her mind."

"And," Hannah concluded, "you don't think Moms would be a good replacement."

It was a statement, so Golden didn't reply.

Hannah leaned back in her chair and gazed off, lost in thought. She was like that for almost a minute before returning her gaze to Golden. "Can you help Neeley?"

Golden was startled. This was not what she had expected. "I can try. When can I meet with her?"

"As soon as she finishes her current mission," Hannah said. "Also consider the possibility that Moms might replace Ms. Jones, not Neeley. Our Russian friend is getting on in years."

Dr. Golden wouldn't be sitting in this office if she hadn't already considered multiple possibilities, playing the game out several moves ahead. She knew she would never be a move ahead of Hannah, but she tried her best to keep up. "That is a much better fit. But her emotional connection with the team could cloud her judgment."

Hannah shrugged. "Teams can be rebuilt. It is the head that is most important." She nodded. "Thank you, Doctor. Please listen in later today when I meet Moms."

Golden nodded. She got up and left the office, the heavy security door swinging shut behind her, sealing the room.

Alone, Hannah lifted her hand in front of her eyes. She stared at it, noting there was a slight tremor.

This all would be so much easier if she were a psychopath. Or even a sociopath.

She wasn't that lucky.

The phone rang and Hannah's secretary, Ms. Louise Smith, announced a call from Ms. Jones. Hannah picked up the receiver.

"Yes?"

"Moms will be en route shortly. She's in-briefing our latest addition."

"Good."

A long silence played out and Hannah waited. She knew Ms. Jones wasn't happy. But Ms. Jones's happiness wasn't something she cared about.

Ms. Jones finally spoke. "I would like to reiterate my stand that the Nightstalkers should be allowed to pursue Burns. He's an unknown entity. This might not be a simple Sanction."

"No Sanction is ever simple," Hannah said. "You've made your position known. Thank you."

And then she hung up.

CHAPTER 5

Scout rode Comanche along the riverbank as far as she could, which wasn't far, since waterfront property was prime real estate. She reached the fence on the far side of the pasture and halted. She stood in the stirrups and looked downriver. The rhythmic thump of the pile driver started up behind her as they went to work on another pole.

The river was smooth and calm. Scout could see the reflection of the few scattered clouds overhead in the surface of the water. It might be a river, but it was a slow-moving river, the flow determined by how much the TVA opened the sluices at Fort Loudoun Dam. There were times when it did indeed seem more like a lake than a river, the water still, logs and branches floating in it seemingly suspended in place for hours on end.

Slow would be good, Scout thought. Whatever had been in her toothbrush had seemed to move with the water. The boat whose engine had died had restarted and was gone downriver. There had been no other traffic since then. Scout was about to turn Comanche around and give him a workout when the hairs on her arm tingled.

Hoping the anal neighbors beyond the farm weren't home, Scout looped Comanche around and then straight at the fence.

He jumped and they cleared the top board easily. Scout pushed Comanche along the riverbank, through someone's backyard, past their dock. Then she came to another fence, which Comanche bounded over.

She wasn't in anyone's backyard now, but rather a stretch of land underneath the power lines. The tower on this side had vines growing up the metal legs. The power lines, all eight of them, crossed the river high enough that they had large red balls attached to them as warnings for low-flying aircraft.

Scout slowly turned the horse, looking for whatever it was that was making her skin tingle. Comanche stirred nervously and started to back up. Since the horse had firsthand experience with a Firefly, and Comanche was smarter than most people she knew, Scout gave her horse free rein.

Then she saw it. A thin line of black through the high grass, as if a line of flame had come out of the river and moved inland about six feet. There was no fire visible, just the grass curling and turning black. Whatever was causing this was moving very, very slowly. Scout watched it for a few minutes. The line was headed directly toward one of the legs of the tower. She guesstimated at the rate it was moving, it would reach it this evening. Of course, she knew her guess was about something no one had probably ever seen before, so who knew?

Then Comanche stirred and began pawing at the dirt.

"I don't blame you," Scout said, patting the horse's neck.

And then Comanche galloped forward, right to the black line being etched into the ground.

"Whoa!" Scout yelled, but the horse ignored her. He reached the line and then raced along it to the riverbank, where he came to an abrupt halt, almost sending Scout flying.

"What is wrong with you?" Scout demanded.

The horse looked over his shoulder and rolled his eyes as if trying to tell her something.

"I know. Bad, bad, bad," Scout said, pulling on the reins and turning Comanche around.

Scout looked up at the tower.

She didn't know what was going to happen when the line reached the tower, but she was willing to lay off every dime in her piggy bank it wasn't going to be good

Then she remembered the Nightstalkers had broken her piggy bank when they took out the Firefly in her curling iron back in North Carolina.

When they showed, and she had complete faith Nada and the rest would show, she vowed to get another piggy bank out of them.

———————

Burns was driving the Prius on I-24, just past Paducah, Kentucky, when the engine died. He steered the car to the side of a bridge on the interstate and sat still for a moment, examining the dashboard. A yellow light was blinking, indicating he was out of fuel. The battery was dead.

Looking around, he saw a dam to his left. The GPS indicated it was Kentucky Dam, the last one on the Tennessee River before it joined the Ohio, which he'd crossed just a few miles back.

"Interesting," Burns murmured to himself.

He got out of the car and opened the hood. He stared at the engine for several moments. Behind him, a pickup truck pulled over. Burns glanced over his shoulder as the driver got out. He was a young, tattooed man in coveralls, sporting the obligatory John Deere cap every male in the flyover states had in their possession.

"Even them fancy electric cars run out of gas, don't they?" the guy said as he walked up.

Burns turned to face the man, who stopped in his tracks when he saw Burns's face. "Fuck, dude. What the devil happened to you?"

"An old wound," Burns said. The suppressed pistol was heavy in his coat pocket.

"Awfully sorry, dude, awfully sorry." The man jerked a thumb back at his truck. "I can ride you to the next exit and we can get you a gas can."

"No need," Burns said as he turned back to the engine. He had a feeling that ride would turn out differently than the man indicated. He reached in, wrapping one hand around a wire. He closed his eyes.

"Hey!" the guy called out. "Be careful!"

Burns's hand glowed gold and power surged into the battery. He held on for ten seconds, then let go. Burns staggered, drained just like the car had been.

"You okay?" The guy came closer. "What did you do? I ain't never seen nothing like that."

Burns could now see the tire iron hidden in the hand the man kept at his side. He put his own hand in the pocket of the coat, fingers curling around the pistol grip. Then he reconsidered. Given all the cars and trucks racing by just a few feet away on the highway, the gun was unnecessary. Burns stepped up to the man, who realized at the last second, his last second, that he'd made a mistake to stop and try to rob this stranger.

Burns swung his arm, sending the man tumbling out onto the highway. A large pickup truck, apropos for the hat, hit him, sending him flying. Both the man's shoes were still on the pavement where he'd been hit. As tires screeched and drivers swerved, Burns got back in the Prius, put on his turn signal, and accelerated around the traffic jam he'd just caused.

Heading southeast.

Following the river.

"We both have flights to catch and things to do today, so you're getting the Cliff's Notes version." Moms jumped into Ivar's in-briefing without a how-do-you-do. Of course, Moms never did a how-do-you-do, so it wasn't a big deal. Doc was with them, because as soon as this was over, he was taking Ivar over to Area 51 and the Can and then the Archives.

Unlike Ms. Jones's office, the CP (command post) that held Moms's and Nada's battered gray desks was secured by a solid steel door.

"Sit," Nada said, pointing at a plush armchair facing the angled desks. As Ivar sank into the chair, Doc perched himself on a table covered with photos and documents.

Moms closed her eyes for a moment, as if remembering all the times she'd given this in-brief. "You don't have a military background," she started with. "So that makes things a bit different. Most of your teammates came out of elite Special Operations units: Delta Force, SEALs, Special Forces, Rangers, CIA, et cetera. So they came with a set of expectations, both good and bad. The good for you is we're not like the normal military or even normal Special Ops. We're a true team and don't do rank or a lot of other military things. I'm the team leader and Nada is the team sergeant. What that means is that you have any problems, any questions, you go to Nada. The reason for that is I answer to Ms. Jones and that's my focus. I'm the liaison between the team and her." She paused. "Well, except for today apparently." She and Nada exchanged another what-the-frak glance.

"Nada takes care of the team. I take care of the mission. Follow?" Ivar nodded.

"But, if you need to, you can come to me. But always go to Nada first. He can solve pretty much any problem you got."

"Pretty much," Nada muttered. He was opening drawers, tossing thick binders on his desk.

"Nada has been a Nightstalker longer than any of us," Moms added. "We're all happy to have you join the team."

"Let's not exaggerate," Nada said. "He hasn't proved his worth yet." He paused in his search and fixed Ivar with his gaze. "Newbies tend to have a high casualty rate."

Moms pressed on. "We don't do rank; we don't do titles; we don't do medals or badges or any of that stuff. Doc there"—Moms indicated him—"has five PhDs, right?"

"Right," Doc said.

"And he'll tell you all about them if you give him the chance," Moms said.

"Lucky you," Nada said.

"You know something about Rifts—" Moms began, but Nada jumped in.

"He even has some theories on them."

"—but we have more missions than just Rifts," Moms continued. "Nuclear, chemical, biological incidents are not uncommon."

"Meaning we get called out on them a lot," Nada said. "Hate the nuke ones," he added. "Especially the nuke ones. Especially the *last* nuke one."

"Doc will tell you about the Acme list," Moms said. "They're our on-call specialists."

"'Always listen to experts,'" Nada quoted. "'They'll tell you what can't be done and why. Then do it.' I wish that was an original Nada Yada, but Heinlein got to it first. You know Heinlein?"

Ivar nodded. "I've read all—"

Nada cut him off at the book. "Great. Eagle will love you for that, but you didn't know who Harvey was, so you're still on the short end of that stick. You're never going to know more than Eagle, so the sooner you accept that, the better for you. Even Doc don't know more than Eagle."

Moms cut in. "Doc will fill you in on what we know about Rifts and the history of them. Stuff you're never going to find on the Internet."

"If you had, we'd have sent Roland to cut your head off," Nada said, "and shove it in a safe." He waited for Moms to continue but she leaned back in her chair, the old springs protesting loudly. She looked tired; hell, Nada thought, they were all tired. Maybe Ms. Jones was right. They needed a reboot. Burns being free bothered Nada and he knew he wouldn't be able to "relax" or really think of much else until they took him down, but orders were orders.

Moms opened a drawer and took out an acetated notebook. She tossed it to Ivar. "That's the team Protocol. You had protocols in your lab at the university, correct? Rules you followed?"

"Yes," Ivar said.

"That's our Bible. You're going to get a lot of information thrown at you in the next few days—"

"Literally," Nada said, hefting a thick binder.

Moms closed her eyes again as she rattled off a few of her favorites. "In the beginning of the Protocol is my philosophy. You can read it, but let me summarize the important stuff right now, so we start off on the right foot. Be honest. Always. Don't hide bad news. I'm the team leader, but there will be times when you'll have to make decisions on your own. If you have to, make the decision and act decisively."

Nada nodded. "In Ranger school, they teach you that doing something, anything, is better than standing around with your finger up your butt in the kill zone. They call it the kill zone for a reason. We tend to enter a lot of places that would be considered kill zones. Don't stand in it and do nothing."

Doc spoke up. "Unless it's best to do nothing at the moment. It depends on the situation."

"Ain't your briefing, Doc," Nada said without any rancor, but that shut Doc up.

Moms reached into the same drawer and tossed Ivar a leather badge case. "For cover, you're a senior field agent for the FBI—"

Nada snorted. "No one's going to buy that cover, Moms. Look at him. They might have toughened him up a bit at Bragg, but he still looks like a geek."

"The badge is real and the ID card is real," Moms said. She looked at Ivar. "Plus, the FBI does have some geeks in it. You act like you're the real deal, they'll believe you. Most everyone you have to deal with is a big believer in the system. That badge puts you way up in the system. Someone thinks they outrank you, you point them in my direction."

"No one outranks her," Nada threw in. "If they think they do, then we might have to kill them."

"Which leads me to this," Moms continued. "Discipline stays on the team. I report to Ms. Jones and she reports to someone, but we'll kill you before we let you go off the reservation. We should have killed Burns."

Even Nada looked surprised at that, but he nodded. "Once a Nightstalker, always a Nightstalker."

"You have to die to get off the team?" Ivar asked, ready to believe just about anything at this point.

Moms shook her head. "No. People move on to other things. Usually when they're no longer capable of fieldwork, they go into Support. Colonel Orlando was once a team member."

"Ended up having a bit of a problem." Nada gestured with his thumb, indicating a drinker. "But he's still a good man. We've got other ex-team members doing important stuff in Support. Just 'cause you're a leg or an eyeball short doesn't mean you can't be useful."

"Be on time," Moms said. She gave a triumphant smile at Nada as she remembered the right order for her ending. "And last, and most important, we are ultimately accountable for the survival of the human race. That trumps the law, national borders, family, everything. Nada?"

"Any op we go on," Nada said, "has three possible classifications: dry, damp, and wet. Dry is something we contain and want to study. Doesn't pose a threat. Doesn't happen often. If it wasn't a threat in the first place, why the hell would we get Zevoned?" Nada asked, his frustration seeping through.

"Don't go all Eagle on me," Moms said.

Nada collected himself. "Okay, then there's damp, which means it's to be contained, and if we can't contain it, we break it. Rare also. Finally, most missions are wet. We contain it until we can completely destroy it. Rifts and Fireflies are always wet."

"'Always'?" Ivar repeated with a questioning inflection, causing both Moms and Nada to look at him hard.

"What do you mean?" Nada asked.

Ivar pointed at himself. "I'm here. Wasn't the mission at UNC a wet one?"

"It was," Nada said.

"Then why am I still alive?"

"Good question," Nada said. "Want me to kill you?"

"We needed you," Moms said. "You reversed the Rift and shut it. You were on our side."

Ivar shrugged. "Okay. Not that I'm complaining or anything."

Nada shook it off and grabbed the stack of binders he'd been piling up. He gave them to Ivar, one at a time. "Nuclear Protocol. Biological. Chemical." He grabbed another binder but paused. "We work under the three Cs—containment, concealment, and control. Containment, first and always. We lose containment, we're fucked and sometimes the world could get fucked."

"So this Burns guy . . . ?" Ivar said.

"Yeah," Nada admitted. "We lost containment. But we maintained concealment. Ms. Jones covered up the Snake going down by saying it was an experimental military aircraft on a training mission. Support got the wreckage out before daylight. We used our badges at the Gateway Arch to take the murder away from the locals and get the body out of there. Concealment is important because panic is a bad thing. Remember *War of the Worlds*? H. G. Wells? Sometimes, next to the armed locals, our biggest problem is the media." Nada nodded toward the door. "They've been all over Area 51's perimeter along with the alien and conspiracy theory wackos for a long time. Which is why we moved out here.

"Last, and most importantly," Nada said, "is control. That's where dry, damp, or wet come in. Pretty much it's always wet."

"I'm picking that up," Ivar said.

"You being a smart-ass?" Nada snapped.

Ivar held his hands up. "No. Just taking it all in."

Nada wasn't placated. He tossed the next binder at Ivar with a little extra energy. "Every mission the Nightstalkers have been on.

Mostly shit caused by scientists." He threw another binder while Ivar was still fumbling with the one he'd just caught and this one banged on his arm, causing him to hiss in pain. "This is the Dumb Shit Scientist Protocol. Maybe you should read it first since you want to take it all in."

"First priority," Moms said in a calm voice, "is the team Protocol. You've got forty-eight hours to get up to speed on it. Doc?"

"Yes?"

"Show him his locker and show him how to rig his gear according to Protocol once you leave here."

"Roger that."

Moms turned to Nada. "Any Nada Yadas you want to lay on him?"

"When I ask," Nada said to Ivar, "just tell me how to kill it. Whatever it is. Got it?"

Ivar nodded.

"He'll have to learn the rest on the job," Nada said. "We need to get moving to make our flights." He got up and walked out of the CP. Moms stood. She went over to Ivar, who hopped to his feet. She stuck out her hand. "Welcome to the team. Don't let Nada get to you. He wants to kill Burns and he's being stopped. He doesn't take well to being stopped from killing those who need killing." She nodded at Doc as she left the room. "Take care of him."

███████████████

Blake had lost both his flip-flops to the fluffer mud and he was beginning to think he'd overdone the "make the cache secure and remote" part of the Protocol. He was halfway between two barrier islands south of Myrtle Beach and the mosquitoes were feasting on him. He'd had to wait on the tide, a necessity of a beach cache, and that had eaten up two hours. It was just a little before noon and a day that had started with such promise was turning to crap.

One key to the Loop was they sacrificed speed of the message being transmitted for security.

He sucked it up, the way he'd sucked up every shitty mission for thirty-four years and the fluffer mud had sucked up his flip-flops. Yes, sir . . . no, sir . . . may I have some more, sir? Even when they dropped the "sir" and "ma'am" shit, it was still shit. Calling someone by their first name when they outranked you didn't mean the order wasn't real.

"'Ours is not to wonder why. Ours is just to do or die,'" he quoted as he pulled his left foot out of the muck with great effort and took another step forward. It took another hour to go fifty yards and make it to the island. He took out his GPS and checked the coordinates. Then he took out his old compass and shot two azimuths to verify.

Protocol.

It had saved his life several times, and he wanted to get back to that pool and the young mother, although he had a feeling she wouldn't be up to chatting with him after he'd dumped her dumb kid in the pool. He'd have to try plan B. He didn't know what that was right now, since he had other important shit on his mind, but he was content knowing there was always a plan B. Just like what he was doing right now was a plan B.

The Loop, which he was part of and was now implementing, was not official Protocol. The Loop was an attempt by operatives and former operatives to have a communication channel outside of official channels. One for all and all for one sort of thing.

It had not been an easy thing to set up. It was rarely used. And it was very slow.

But one had to try, because once in a while, someone needed help outside of official channels.

Blake removed the folding shovel from the sweat-drenched backpack he'd hauled out here. He dug.

At least the sand was soft.

He hit the ammo can at eighteen inches. It took a few more minutes to recover it from the hole. He unlatched the lid. There was a lot jammed into a little space. He peeled open two layers of waterproofing and removed the loaded pistol that was always the last item in and first item out.

He found the cell phone and encryption device. He opened the battery cases and removed the old ones. He replaced them with fresh ones. Then he typed in the message he'd received at the pool. The encryption device hummed for a bit, garbling the message into meaningless groups of five letters that only a device programmed exactly the same way could decrypt.

Blake hit send.

Then he removed the battery from the cell phone. He stood and threw the phone out into the salt water, watching it hit and sink. He replaced the phone with the exact same model. He then zeroed out the encryption device. He took a thumb drive out of his pocket and inserted it into the slot on the side. He loaded a new encryption program, removed the thumb drive, and put it back in the can. Then he put the pistol on top, resealed the two waterproof liners, closed the lid, and put the can back in the hole. He shoveled the sand back in the hole. The incoming tide would take care of concealment.

With bare feet and a bad attitude, but mission accomplished,

Blake began making his way back to the mainland, his car, and eventually the pool and young mother.

He was not optimistic.

Mac had started bitching as soon as the truck carrying them rolled underneath the big sign reading: COLONEL NICK ROWE TRAINING FACILITY. Located at Camp Mackall, west of Fort Bragg, North Carolina, it was the field training facility for aspiring Special Forces soldiers.

Roland was more optimistic, pointing out there were modern buildings at a facility he remembered as having only shacks that were half-assed, leaky, and cold.

"They used to mermite chow from Fort Bragg out here," Eagle observed. "Now they've got a chow hall."

"I don't think we're here for the chow," Kirk said.

Roland looked at his watch. "It's thirteen hundred. We probably missed lunch."

"I don't think we're here for lunch," Kirk said.

A smatter of raindrops on the canvas roof over the cargo bay portended a storm rolling in. They'd flown in to Mackall Army Airfield on one of the blue-liners. Mackall was considered a sub-base to adjacent Fort Bragg and home to Special Forces Selection and Assessment, most of the Qualification Course, the SERE (Survival Evasion Resistance and Escape) compound, and other assorted training schools and scenarios. It was where the Delta raiders on the ill-fated Desert One mission to free the hostages in Iran had trained. The airfield was one almost every Special Operator had flown into or out of or jumped onto the large field the two intersecting runways contained.

The truck had been waiting, the driver shrugging when asked what was going to happen. His job was to drive them out here and that was the extent of his knowledge.

"They better not be putting us through SERE again," Mac groused. They'd all been through the mock POW camp and training and no one was eager to do it again. "I already survived, evaded, resisted, and escaped. What more can they want? Become Houdini?"

"Probably something high speed," Roland said. "Maybe some advanced weapons training?"

"Did you hit your head in St. Louis?" Mac asked.

The truck came to an abrupt halt, which sent them tumbling along the steel floor.

"Get your asses out of there!" An imposing figure wearing a green beret was standing to the rear of the truck, arms bulging under the rolled up sleeves of his camouflage shirt. His uniform was soaked, but he was obviously one of those guys who espoused the theory that the human body was waterproof, which was true, but tended to ignore misery.

The four team members all wore "sterile" cammies. No rank, no badges, no names. Just a number on a Velcro patch on their chest. That had started Mac's complaining as they flew in. When the army took your name and gave you a number, it usually meant something not fun was getting ready to occur.

"Dickhead," Mac muttered, voicing what they all thought as they exited the back of the truck.

"You gentlemen are late," the dickhead said. "My name is Master Sergeant Twackhammer."

"You gotta be shitting me," Mac said in a low voice.

"What was that?" Twackhammer demanded.

"It's on his shirt," Roland observed, immediately bonding with the fellow large human being. "Hey, Master Sergeant Twackhammer. How's it going?"

"Shut up!" Twackhammer shouted. "Your Selection began yesterday. I don't know who pulled strings to get you in, but I'm going to be watching you." To emphasize the point, he put a finger just below his left eye and pulled the skin down. "You gentlemen are late to my course and that makes me very, very upset."

"*Your course*?" Mac said.

Twackhammer started yelling, getting them moving through the supply hut to get field gear; then they were out of there, into what was now a downpour, and over to the Nasty Nick obstacle course, where mud-covered Special Forces Assessment and Selection (SFAS) candidates were being put through the grinder.

"I'm too old for this shit," Eagle said as Twackhammer slid them in line.

So they began the mile-long course, hitting the obstacles every so often, all of which seemed made of a lot of rope (vertical and horizontal), a bunch of mud-smeared tunnels, and lots of wood configured by a mad carpenter making a person jump, leap, shimmy, and climb up and down and sideways.

"Ms. Jones must be really pissed," Kirk said as they completed another obstacle and were forced to wait, as a backlog of students was in front of them, all of them facing a wall that had them stymied.

"Get to the other side!" a staff sergeant was screaming at the candidates.

"I think Moms might have been the one who suggested this," Eagle said, trying to scrape some mud off his fatigue shirt, a futile effort. "I doubt Ms. Jones even knows what the Nasty Nick is."

"Yeah, but how is this supposed to help us?" Mac asked.

"Get to the other side!" the staff sergeant's voice went up an octave as the bewildered candidates clawed, jumped, and fell off the vertical face of the eighteen-foot-high wooden wall. There were no handholds, just a single tantalizing rope that hung down four feet from the top and was knotted on the bottom. Realizing they couldn't reach the rope on their own, the candidates began working together, trying to build human pyramids to get someone to the rope.

No such luck.

Eagle sat down on a fallen tree, watching with a bored expression. Mac, Kirk, and Roland joined him. Across the muddy path, glaring at them through the rain, Twackhammer suddenly appeared.

"What are you girls doing?" he screamed. A major was next to him, his green beret soaked and drooping on his head. Everyone in Special Forces agreed that a beret was the most worthless of headgear. Hell, Girl Scouts wore green berets. The major was quiet, watching, observing, and they knew he was the one who could wash a candidate out with a stroke of his pen. He walked with an odd gait, which meant one of his legs, if not both, were no longer flesh and blood, a common occurrence nowadays with those no longer physically fit for deployment duty and slotted to faculty positions.

"Waiting, Master Sergeant Twackhammer," Roland said. "The wall's a bit crowded at the moment."

"Get your asses off that log!" Twackhammer yelled.

They got to their feet.

"Drop right where you are and give me forty."

The four looked down. They were standing in a couple of inches of mud. If Ms. Jones and Moms had wanted to humble the four, they'd succeeded. Being treated like newbies—when they'd all gone through several training programs like this years ago, served in elite units in combat, and were now Nightstalkers, the best of the best, et cetera, et cetera—was hitting home. It was obvious Twackhammer had no clue who they were. The major, on the other hand, had his head cocked to the side, evaluating.

The major was no fool. He could see the clear difference between these four and the younger men flailing away at the wall, trying to get to the rope, their ticket to the other side of the wall. Besides the obvious scars on Roland and Eagle, all four were older and held themselves differently. Other services and agencies and even foreign governments sent people to go through the Q Course at Bragg, the Special Forces Qualification Course, but even those people were usually younger and more enthusiastic about the opportunity. And most bypassed SFAS, going straight to the Q.

They dropped down and began doing push-ups, but in a way that said "yeah, yeah" rather than the anxious desperation of a candidate. Any Spec-Ops person who had been through a selection and assessment course, and especially if they'd ever been cadre in such a course, understood the reality of what was going on. Certainly it was important to weed out those who didn't belong and to evaluate the candidates, but much of the screaming and the yelling was by rote, a routine that can begin to numb one out.

So they languidly did their push-ups, except Roland, of course, who was done first, knocking them out without even breathing hard. He snapped out five more, just for shits and grins, then hopped to his feet.

Eagle was last, and he was breathing hard.

The major ambled over, obviously not worried about getting his feet wet and muddy since he didn't have feet. He smiled at the four. "Welcome, gentlemen. Someone named Ms. Jones says hi. And gung ho."

Then he moved away.

"What the frak was that about?" Mac asked, wiping a hand across his forehead, which only served to move mud around. "We know Ms. Jones sent us here. She's rubbing it in."

"Gung ho," Eagle repeated. "That's it." He nodded at the other three. "It's an American version of two Chinese words that were appropriated during World War Two. *Gong*, which means 'work,' and *he*, which means 'together.' In China it was actually the name of a corporation, but a marine major named Carlson decided to use it as the motto of the Second Marine Raider Battalion. Now everyone's heard of it."

"You are just full of arcane stuff," Kirk said.

"Huh?" Roland said.

"Great history lesson," Mac said. "Couldn't she have just *told* us to work together?"

Kirk spoke up. "How well do words work on you, Mac?"

Mac bristled for a second, but then his shoulders lumped. "Yeah. I get it."

"I work with everyone," Roland said.

"Maybe that's the problem," Kirk said. "You all did the unauthorized mission to help me in Arkansas. And you"—he indicated Roland—"did an unauthorized mission with Neeley in South America. I think Ms. Jones is trying to get us to stay on the reservation."

"*This* ain't the reservation," Mac said.

The cluster of candidates still hadn't defeated the wall. Some were arguing with each other now, teamwork breaking down in the face of frustration. Lightning flashed in the distance and thunder rolled through the pine trees.

"Still in loner mode," Kirk said, nodding at the ones arguing.

"I think that's the other point," Eagle said.

Kirk laughed as a couple of the candidates jumped as a bolt of lightning struck so close that everyone could feel the static electricity in the air. "City boys."

"Gotta remember," Eagle said, "they're on short sleep, short rations."

"And short brains," Mac said. "Geez, how long do you want to watch this frak-up?"

"Hey." Kirk was pointing. "I think that guy's crying. You can't tell 'cause of the rain, but he's fraking crying. Ranger up, dude. Damn SF weenies."

"He won't make it," Eagle said. "There's no crying in Special Ops, fella."

"The longer these guys take," Mac said, "the longer we're going to be standing here in the rain. How about we gung ho up?"

Roland nodded. "Let's finish this thing and whatever else Ms. Jones wants us to do here so we can get back to the team room and just have Moms and Nada give us shit. This is ridiculous. I set the course record on this thing ten years ago."

"So you know what they're doing wrong, right?" Mac asked with a grin.

"They're not listening," Kirk said. "I never went through the Q Course here, but I went to Ranger school. People think the *N* in *Ranger* stands for 'knowledge,' but we learned to listen to orders. And we had the Darby Queen to negotiate, which wasn't no cake walk."

Some of the candidates were now piling their rucksacks, trying to build a platform, to get them closer to the knotted rope.

"How did you get over the wall, Roland?" Eagle asked. "It wasn't here when I went through."

"I threw a little fellow up there," Roland said. "He got the knot and then held on for his life. I jumped, grabbed his legs, used him as part of the rope." Roland flushed. "Dislocated both his shoulders. But the instructors were impressed."

"I don't think that was or is the correct solution," Kirk said.

"Worked for me," Roland said.

"You aren't in the bell curve," Eagle said.

"No one here is supposed to be in the bell curve," Kirk said.

"The rope is a MacGuffin," Eagle said.

"A what?" Roland asked.

A cluster of candidates had their top man come within a foot of the rope, before the pyramid collapsed into a muddy pile.

"It's a term Hitchcock used for something that seems important and everyone is focused on it, when it really isn't important," Eagle explained.

Kirk was the first to get it, as he usually was. "It's misdirection. What if the rope wasn't there?"

"No way anyone could get over that wall," Roland said. "Even working together with what they got."

"Yeah," Kirk said, "but what was the instruction?" He didn't wait for an answer. "Get to the other side."

Mac laughed. "Well, shoot. Even in Texas we'd figure that out. Eventually." He shouldered his rucksack. "Ready, guys? Watching these newbies is making me wish I was in a different army."

The Nightstalkers shrugged on their weighted backpacks, then simply walked around the wall. Roland was last and he paused, looking at the candidates. "Coming?"

"What the hell do you think you're doing?" Twackhammer screamed.

"We're going to the other side of the wall," Roland said. And then he was gone.

The muddy candidates stood confused, staring at the wall, and then at Twackhammer, and then at the Nightstalkers. It was only when the major started to laugh that they got it. They grabbed their packs and followed the Nightstalkers around the wall.

And they were better soldiers for it.

Gretchen was sipping cheap white wine and getting a wonderful foot massage, which kind of made up for the trimming of her ingrown big toenail. She put the glass down and closed her eyes. Her mind wandered to that boring morass of wondering what she was going to make for dinner, which was inevitably a few hours from now. She did find it odd, perhaps even ironic, that her wife never cooked. Never learned, never wanted to try, and it was not a subject to be discussed. Nope, cooking was Gretchen's, except she'd never really learned either.

You'd think in a marriage of two women that one of them would have learned to cook. What were the odds?

Gretchen, however, could make a mean smoothie and that's about it. She tried to remember what was in the freezer because she might have a couple of chicken fillets to nuke and then half scorch. She opened her eyes and reached into her purse, pulling out her phone. She Googled a recipe for chicken. She'd spent thirty-six years working in IT for the government, although her partner thought she'd worked for the IRS. As if. Gretchen had worked deep in the bowels of the Pentagon for Mrs. Sanchez, but much like the women who worked at Bletchley Circle in England during World War II, once she retired, that was it. One never, ever, discussed that world with outsiders.

There were many reasons for that beyond the secrecy oath they swore. But even that issue outsiders had a problem with; some didn't think oaths were worth that much, but for those in the covert world, their oaths meant everything to them. Also, outsiders didn't understand. They couldn't. One had to live the life, experience it, to understand.

And last but not least, speaking out of house could bring a very unfriendly visit from the Cellar.

As she scrolled through recipes, Gretchen smiled as she remembered watching the movie *RED* with her wife. Her wife had thought it stupid, but Gretchen had just howled and wondered who'd whispered the little truths to the screenwriters. Retired. Extremely. Dangerous.

The covert was over for Gretchen, even though the closest she'd come to the front lines were the bundles of millions of dollars of cash she and Mrs. Sanchez had prepped to be shipped overseas to be used to bribe, acquire, and who knew what else.

The woman rubbing her feet was the best and Gretchen tried to remember her name for the next time.

Then her *other* phone gave its distinctive Warren Zevon ringtone for the first time and Gretchen was reminded for the first time since she retired that her covert life was *almost* over. It was like the mafia: Just when you thought you were out, they pulled you back in, even though the Loop was technically, well, out of the loop.

Gretchen scrambled through her bag and found the second phone at the bottom. She punched the receive button and saw the five letter groupings message on the screen. She nodded, then forwarded it, as she'd been instructed, to the number she'd memorized. Gretchen then sighed and forwarded the message to a second number, not part of the standing operating procedure of the Loop but part of the reality of her continued existence as part of the living. One could only go off the reservation as far as those in power allowed.

She dropped the second phone back in her bag.

The woman doing her feet laughed. "You're naughty!"

Gretchen was confused for a moment.

"Only one reason to have two phones," the woman said with a smile. "You have boyfriend and no want husband to know."

Gretchen smiled back and wished she were indeed naughty.

Maybe she could find someone who could cook.

CHAPTER 6

The term *LoJack* was invented to be the opposite of hijack, which was a little too cute for Neeley.

It was also too easy. Neeley distrusted easy. It wasn't exactly one of Gant's rules that he'd pounded into her during their years together, hiding from the covert world. It was implicit. Gant had taught her a lot, some of it skills that civilians paid a lot of money to learn such as skiing, parachuting, mountain climbing, and so on. However, he'd taught her the hard way. In adverse weather. Carrying heavy loads of gear. At night. And they'd done some of it under the most difficult circumstances of all: when trying to track down and kill someone or, worse, when someone was trying to do the same to them.

But the Support personnel interviewing the driver of the Prius stolen at the Gateway Arch had learned that the car was equipped with a LoJack system. At three in the morning and in a rush, Burns hadn't had the opportunity to be picky. The VIN and unit number had been sent out to police across the country and it had turned up, driving across Illinois and on into Kentucky. Police were warned to note location of the transmitter but to not approach under any circumstances.

Neeley knew this was part of why Hannah had been quick to

take over the mission of bringing down this Burns fellow. They had his location (the transmitter's location, Neeley corrected Hannah, which was not exactly the same as the person) and could continue to track him. The issue was whether to take him down now or see where he was going and what he was planning to do.

While the Nightstalkers might be bitching about having the op taken from them, this really was the Cellar's area of expertise: tracking down rogue agents from the covert world. If Neeley notched her various guns, there would be a lot of notches. Also her knives, her garrote, and her bare hands. Every niche had its artists, those who took the simple job, the craft, to levels others could barely conceptualize but that the artist could embody. Neeley was an artist in death. She had learned early on that the actual, final act, while important, was not the key to success. It was the preparation, the planning, the consideration of every possible contingency that were the keys to making sure the art went one way and not the other.

Thus Neeley was in a hangar at an auxiliary airfield at Fort Campbell, Kentucky. A field that was headquarters for the original Task Force 160, the Nightstalkers, to be confused with the Nightstalkers out of the Ranch outside of Area 51. Neeley thought the cover name using a Special-Ops unit another too-cute idea.

Then again, she thought as she looked at the various displays, she could simply be getting more paranoid, less patient, and just too damn old for this BS. She was seeing ghosts behind every operation lately, although the reality was there were indeed ghosts and shadows and double and triple crosses. She found the Nightstalkers' outrage that the Cellar was taking over this Sanction a bit ironic considering how straightforward most Nightstalker missions were compared to Cellar operations. They might be bizarre and weird, but they were usually clear as to who or what the bad guy/thing was.

The Cellar was the Cellar. Few had ever heard of it. Few needed to hear of it. It was whispered of in the world of covert ops and in the halls of Washington, much like not-so-nice parents might tell their children of a horrible beast hiding in their closet that would come out and torment them if they were bad.

The airfield was near a large fenced compound, where rows and rows of grass-covered concrete bunkers with rusting steel doors had once held a large number of nuclear warheads, a left-over from a supposedly bygone day of the Cold War. Fort Camp-bell was also the home base of the Screaming Eagles of the 101st Airborne Division (Air Assault) and the 5th Special Forces Group (Airborne). It straddled the Tennessee-Kentucky border, about sixty miles northwest of Nashville.

Neeley had landed via Gulfstream just a few minutes ago and she was in a Tactical Operations Center (TOC), set up by TF-160. The signal was on I-24 approaching Nashville. From there, it could go in several directions: southwest toward Memphis (doubtful since it would have turned south earlier), south toward Birming-ham, southeast toward Chattanooga and Atlanta and beyond, or east toward Knoxville. It might even backtrack north toward Indianapolis, but that was doubtful because it could have turned earlier.

Since LoJack worked on FM, it was line of sight. TF-160 had a Quick-Fix helicopter in the air, at high altitude and several miles behind the Prius, tracking it. Neeley looked at the large computer display as the Prius reached where I-24 and I-65 joined together above Nashville. In a few minutes they'd have an idea which gen-eral direction it was moving on to.

No one else in the TOC had any clue why they were following the car. The orders had come in from higher and thus they would obey. It was a mind-set Neeley was used to but sometimes found disturbing, because the people at the top sometimes might have their own agenda. She'd traveled to South America earlier in the year with Roland to deal with two high-ranking CIA agents who'd manipulated data for their own personal advancement.

Neeley trusted Hannah with her life. She had to. Time and again she'd gone on missions, trusting only Hannah's word.

But.

Gant had told her to trust no one.

Ever.

But he'd trusted her. He'd died in her arms.

If it were easy, anyone could do it. The schizophrenic nature of covert operations where the simple operation could actually be a double-cross, which could actually be a cover for a triple-cross, which might simply be some bureaucrat trying to advance their career, not giving a damn how many operatives died because of the lies and manipulations that took their toll.

What was truth?

Neeley's phone buzzed. There was no question who it was, since only one person had her number. Neeley pulled the phone out but paused before activating it. The weight of that thought, that there was only one person who had her cell number, had never pressed down upon her with so much force.

She hit accept. "Yes?"

"Someone is using the Loop," Hannah said without preamble. "Mrs. Sanchez was contacted by one of her former personnel. The message is heading to a third cutout."

"Someone's being very careful."

"The message originated in the Knoxville, Tennessee, area," Hannah said.

"Who do we know there?" Neeley asked as she looked at the map display and spotted Knoxville, to the direct east of Nashville along I-40.

"We're checking the files," Hannah said. "But it seems to be coming from the outside to the inside."

From a civilian? Neeley wondered. She'd been a civilian once herself. A civilian who'd walked into an airport with a bomb packed inside a gaily wrapped package, before the time of 9/11. That was when she met Gant and left the civilian world far behind.

Neeley stepped back into the TOC and looked at the screen. The flashing dot indicating the Prius had just passed downtown Nashville. It then moved onto I-40 east.

"My Sanction is heading in that direction."

"Yes. That is why I called."

Something was off. Neeley had known Hannah too many years. "This is a Sanction, correct?"

"Correct. The Sanction has three confirmed murders."

"Should I allow the Sanction to get to wherever and whatever his objective is?"

A long two seconds. Silence followed. "I'll get back to you on that as quickly as I can."

The phone went dead and Neeley stared at it for a very long time, ten seconds, while her mind went into dark corners.

Which wasn't unusual.

━━━━━━━━━━

Ivar's locker was squared away, his deployment gear was packed according to Protocol, and now they were driving alongside that third-longest airstrip in the world at Groom Lake, aka the heart of Area 51. Doc was at the wheel of a jeep, only slightly more modern than Colonel Orlando's had been, which meant it was ancient. Ivar had to wonder why the Nightstalkers used such antiquated vehicles here.

Doc had been talking, almost nonstop, all morning and into the afternoon, bombarding Ivar not only with the history of Rifts and Fireflies, but also dipping deep into his own well of knowledge to discuss various theories. *His* theories on Rifts. It wouldn't have taken Frasier, the Nightstalkers' shrink, to point out that Doc was overcompensating, threatened by another scientist's presence on the team.

Ivar, being a physicist, of course, didn't make such a psychological analysis of the situation. He just thought Doc was acting pretty much like every professor he'd ever worked for on his path to get his own PhD. Self-centered, convinced they had all the answers when they didn't even know what most of the questions were, and, most of all, being about one-upmanship.

Aka a dick.

Two massive hangar doors cut into the side of Groom Mountain were partially open, and Doc drove right up to them, guards waving them through after scanning their eyes. Ivar caught glimpses of aircraft he didn't recognize scattered throughout the hangar, but Doc drove straight to the far wall. Two guards scanned their eyes once more and then allowed them access to an elevator.

"They rely a lot on eyes being the true window into our souls here," Ivar said.

"Save it for Eagle," Doc said shortly. "He likes that kind of philosophical stuff."

They got into the elevator.

"It takes a while," Doc said as the doors slid shut after they entered.

"How far down?" Ivar asked as the elevator began to accelerate into the Earth.

"Two miles."

That took ten minutes and it seemed Doc had run out of things to talk about, so the only noise was the whirring of the elevator's engine. Actually, Doc never ran out of things to talk about or ways to spread the wealth of his knowledge. His mind had slipped into a dark rut—more a valley, actually—which it always did whenever he went down to the Can. The left side of his brain, the numbers side, was calculating the tons of pressure accumulating around them as they descended and how small a mass of protoplasm his body would be crushed into if it all collapsed.

Sometimes being smart had its disadvantages.

"The Can is a Super-Kamiokande," Doc said as he gave up, knowing he'd be crushed into a tiny, tiny object if everything imploded.

"Like the one in Japan?"

"Yes. Early on when they started digging into Groom Mountain to develop the base, they did soundings and found a large, natural void deep underground. No one thought it was of much use until we realized we needed to build the Can."

"And the Can detects Rifts." Orlando would have been proud, because Ivar made it a statement, not a question.

The elevator came to a halt and Doc opened the metal gate. A corridor carved out of solid rock beckoned. They began the two-hundred-yard walk down it, fluorescent lights flickering overhead.

It ended, opening to a cavern eighty yards in diameter.

"The Japanese have one, we have one, and the Russians have one," Doc said as they walked out onto metal grating suspended over still dark water.

"So you can triangulate." Another statement.

Two people were on duty, staring at computer monitors with the glazed look of someone who spent 99.9 percent of their time doing nothing with nothing happening. Ivar understood that. He'd spent a lot of bench time doing the exact same thing.

Doc and Ivar walked over. "The Can picks up muonic activity, which Rifts give off when they begin to form. Gives us thirty-eight minutes of warning at least. That's the fastest from first indication to activation recorded. We usually get more time."

Ivar looked over the shoulder of an operator. Four large displays were further broken down into data boxes with various electronic readings, graphs, and charts. He began to ask questions of the two operators, much to the irritation of Doc, who finally walked away to a stack of printouts and began going through them.

Even the operators eventually had enough of the questioning and turned back to their screens. Ivar walked out onto the metal grating that extended over the dark pool of water covering the stainless steel tank, which was sixty meters wide and deep. Along the walls of the tank, over 20,000 photomultiplier tubes (PMTs) were patiently waiting for incoming muons. PMTs are extremely sensitive light sensors that can detect a single photon as it travels through and reacts with water. They were all linked together with the output displayed on the computers at the workstations.

The tank was filled with very pure water. The surface was dark black and Ivar found it quite mesmerizing. Pretty much everyone who came down here did. Ivar knelt and glanced quickly over; Doc was flipping through some charts and the two operators weren't visible, hidden behind their large monitors. He pulled a small black orb out of his pocket, pressed the top, was rewarded with a slight buzz, and dropped it into the water. Then he stood, hands on the railing.

After five minutes, Doc had enough, dropping the readouts. "Let's go. All that matters is that we get our Rift alerts."

"Really?" Ivar was surprised. "But if we don't understand the Rifts, how are we going to stop them completely? Moms said—"

"We know enough to shut one when it happens," Doc said.

"Seems a bit shortsighted," Ivar said.

Doc stopped abruptly and faced Ivar. He jabbed a finger in his chest. "When you have more time on the team, then maybe you can question me. For now, I suggest you shut up and learn."

Ivar didn't step back. "Excuse me, Doc, but you didn't know how to shut the Rift in my lab. You didn't even know what the hell that was in my lab. I barely remember what I was doing. This thing seems to be evolving, changing, as Ms. Jones said. Think about what happened in North Carolina in my lab. This guy, Burns, coming through in St. Louis. The scientist who opened the Gateway Rift received a fatal dose of radiation, yet Burns apparently is still moving about. And what he did to the Snake. That's all something new, right?"

"You did not even get your PhD," Doc said. "Do not dare lecture me."

"Oh, fuck off," Ivar said.

Both operators had turned their chairs around to observe the fireworks, which was more interesting than the screens they'd been watching. Which was unfortunate, because in one of the data boxes on one of the screens, there was a slight disturbance—not muonic, and not enough to trigger an alarm, but something, a slight surge.

Something that should have been noticed.

"It's just a piece of paper," Ivar said. "You can wipe your ass with it."

Instead of continuing the fight, Doc headed for the elevator. "You coming?" he added over his shoulder.

The operators turned back to their screens and all was normal.

At least it appeared that way.

Scout was getting antsy. She'd ridden back home, hiding in her room, waiting for her iPhone to come alive with a message from Nada. Her mother was still off doing whatever it was that her mother filled her days with. Probably shopping for a pot or something. And then for something to put in the pot. Then something to put the pot on. Then she'd come home and spend hours trying to figure out the exact right place to put the pot. Decide there was no exact right place. And spend tomorrow returning the pot, along with the thing she'd wanted to put in the pot. And the thing she'd wanted to put the pot on.

The usual crap.

Scout was curled up, arms around her knees, on the window seat in her bedroom staring out at the river.

It was no longer as enchanting as it had been.

A crackling noise caught her attention and she cranked open the window and leaned out. The metal skeleton holding up the power lines had a slight golden glow on the one leg the black line had been heading toward.

Not being an expert on unnatural forces except for her brief stint with the Nightstalkers, Scout figured she ought to be cut some slack for her guesstimate being off as she watched the glow go up the leg, as if steel were turning to gold.

It reached the first arm holding a power line and moved vertical.

Without even realizing she was doing it, Scout's hand went into her pocket and she pulled out a crumpled pack of cigarettes. She'd quit, really, last week, but circumstances were getting a bit weird.

She scratched a wooden match on the roofing tile outside the window just as the glow touched the wire. Her shoulders were hunched, expecting an explosion, a ball of flame, an earthquake, flying monkeys, something.

But nothing. Except the gold didn't spread any more on the tower.

The cigarette dangled from Scout's mouth, unlit as she waited, until she cursed as the match burned down to her fingers. She dropped the match and took the cigarette out of her mouth.

She realized the thump of the pile driver had stopped and spared a glance across the river. The workers were staring at the tower also, gesturing and talking among themselves. Scout felt a sense of fellowship and also relief that she wasn't just imaging all of this.

Everything stayed exactly like it was for almost a minute; then, as if the metal tower digested a big ball of gold, the orb flowed out of the wire, back down the tower, and into the earth.

Scout leaned farther out of the window, in danger of toppling to the ground. She could see what the men on the river couldn't. The golden pulse came out of the leg, into the ground, and along the black line she'd spotted earlier in the day.

Then it was in the water, a very slight golden mist, slowly spreading outward in all directions. It reminded Scout of a nature channel show where a python had imbibed a deer whole and it went down the gullet and the python slithered back into the water in order to digest the large meal.

The men on the barge had already dismissed it and were back at work, pounding away.

"It just ate a lot of power," Scout whispered to herself, not knowing how she knew it, but she knew it.

And there was no doubt that wasn't a good thing.

She pulled herself back in the window and grabbed her iPhone. She texted the same number.

And was rewarded with "NUMBER OUT OF SERVICE."

"Come on, Nada," Scout said.

Captain Griffin was on the roof of the White House, watching the sky with his binoculars. When he scanned south, the Washington Monument crossed his field of vision. As he did every time he saw it, he thought how odd it was that the monument was two tones. The obsessive part of him wanted to run over and paint it all one color, although the two tones came from different shadings of marble used in the construction, not different paint. And the two different types of marble came about because while initial construction of the monument began in 1848, it ground to a halt in 1854 because of the Know Nothing Party.

Really. The Know Nothing Party. Griffin liked that. He could think of a lot of politicians who could be charter members.

Then, of course, there was the Civil War, which put a damper on building as Washington became the most heavily fortified city in the world at the time. Lincoln did insist work continue on the Capitol Dome and managed to see the Statue of Freedom placed on top, although he did not live to see it totally completed in 1866.

And even after the Civil War, for the Washington Monument, there were more politics. So for twenty-three years, like a broken shaft, the one-quarter-completed monument graced Washington's skyline, testament to a broken country.

It depressed Griffin to think that Abraham Lincoln never saw the completed monument. He often wondered how the various presidents felt when they gazed out from the White House. It was a hobby of Griffin's to study the history of Washington, D.C., and the buildings and countryside around the White House. He was a big believer that one's environment affected a person greatly.

They really should have matched the stone, Griffin thought as he completed his sector, then started over, jumping three-quarters right quadrant so that anyone observing him wouldn't see a pattern, because there was no pattern.

Patterns were bad for effective security.

And thinking about security reminded him of the kerfuffle over the holidays when the White House had gone into lockdown and the chairman of the joint chiefs of staff had lost his mind and committed suicide in the command bunker under the East Wing.

So they said.

Griffin had been on leave and was sorry he'd missed the excitement, but the Keep had handled things well and gotten him up to speed on what had really happened. The world was a much more dangerous place than the average person realized.

Or needed to know.

The Monument flashed by in his binoculars again as he circled back. When he redid his kitchen in Virginia, the contractor tried to pawn off two different granites on him. Said it looked cool. Not. The guy was just trying to unload stuff he'd bought for someone else after the other person reneged. Two tones in the same object just didn't work.

He was so lost in thought he almost didn't hear the phone.

Warren Zevon.

He kept the binoculars to his eyes with one hand as he pulled the phone out of his pocket and hit the accept key by feel. Then he glanced down, verified the message, and forwarded it, all automatically.

Then he lowered the binoculars and forwarded the message to the Keep. As it zoomed out of his phone to a tower, then back here to the White House, just one floor below him, where the Keep kept her office, he shook his head. There were those who believed the Loop was secure, a way those in the know could pass messages outside the system.

There was no outside the system. Not in a world where there were people like Hannah in the Cellar and the Keep in the White House and Ms. Jones at Area 51 and Mrs. Sanchez in the Pentagon comptroller and the other powerful denizens who ruled the dark world of covert ops. There was only what they allowed.

The world was a dangerous place and there were people who dealt with those dangers.

And for that, Captain Griffin was very grateful, unlike the many who decried every dollar spent by the government.

He knew the message was encrypted with a one-time program. He shook his head. They should have stuck to nonelectronic encryption. Use the same agreed upon page from *Tale of Two Cities* and a trigraph. Sometimes the old ways were the best.

Captain Griffin put the phone back in his pocket and scanned the grounds. There was a small patch of browning grass amid the sea of green. Some sprinkler head had to be off.

He made a mental note to tell maintenance about it at the end of his shift.

"He's pulling off I-40," the specialist who was sitting at the large display announced.

"Refueling?" someone asked.

Neeley walked over and stood behind the specialist, watching the image. The Nighthawk tracking the Prius was at a high enough altitude and far enough away that it couldn't be heard and was just a distant black speck in the sky from the target vehicle.

The Prius drove past the cluster of gas stations at the exit. It continued along a secondary road, winding its way into the Tennessee countryside.

Neeley's phone buzzed and she stepped outside to take the call. "Yes?"

"It's a Sanction," Hannah announced.

"He's turned off the interstate," Neeley said. "I'm not certain where the target is headed."

"Most likely Knoxville," Hannah said. "A message is being passed on the Loop via five cutouts. It originated in the Knoxville area."

"The terminus?"

"We're past cutout three now," Hannah said. "Two to go to the terminus."

"Shouldn't we wait—"

"I want this shut down now. The Nightstalkers can deal with Rifts and Fireflies and all their other anomalies, but Burns, no matter where he's been or what's been done to him, is rogue. He was rogue before he got sucked through that Rift and he's rogue now. I want this done before it escalates into who knows what. Not even Ms. Jones understands what's going on."

"Roger," Neeley said as she twirled a finger on her free hand at the officer in charge. He sent a crew chief running toward the Nighthawk waiting nearby. Seeing him coming, the crew was already cranking up the engine. "Has anyone been able to at least determine what Burns's real name was before he joined the Nightstalkers?"

"Ms. Jones did remember that," Hannah replied. "Joseph Schmidt. Beyond that, not much. He came out of Delta Force and we're running down all the former members of that team who have 'disappeared.' Unfortunately, there are quite a few and some have been disappeared so well, they never existed as far as we can tell. The Nightstalkers are very efficient about that."

"Okay. Schmidt."

"Be careful," Hannah said. "And make sure you secure the remains. We'll want to ship it to Area 51 for the Archives."

"Roger." Neeley waited, listening to the static from the encryption.

Finally Hannah spoke. "Good luck."

The line went dead.

Neeley closed her eyes. She thought back to Vermont, to burying Gant, to the rest of that winter alone in the bitter cold, barely feeding the fire enough to survive.

You came into this world alone; you leave it alone.

Neeley went back into the TOC.

"He's stopped," the specialist reported. He pointed at the screen. "I ran it. It's a care facility. Elysian Fields."

Neeley considered this misdirection.

"Maybe he's visiting family?" someone suggested.

The problem, Neeley knew, was that there was no way she could check further on Burns's background. Like some other covert units, once someone became a member of the Nightstalkers, their past disappeared. They were gone from the face of the Earth, every record of their existence wiped clean. It was a two-edged sword, because if they went rogue, it was that much more difficult to track down someone who didn't exist. Neeley had run into the problem numerous times in the past.

Hannah had a point and this development backed it. If Burns ditched the Prius, they'd lose the advantage of the LoJack. Neeley shouldered her field pack and ran for the Nighthawk. They were airborne and racing southeast at max speed.

She opened up her laptop and contacted the IT expert for the Cellar, directing him to hack into the database for Elysian Fields. She scanned the list of patients. Fifth one down was a Peter Schmidt. Father? Brother? Neeley checked deeper. Peter Schmidt was seventy-two years old. Diagnosis, advanced Parkinson's. In a coma. So, most likely father.

Sentimentality was a weakness. One Neeley had found useful in the past to track down rogues. She wondered what it would be like to care so much about someone that even though Burns had to know they were after him, he still took the time to break Protocol to visit his father.

Startled by a sudden memory, Neeley's head snapped up. She closed her eyes, trying to remember the conversation so many years ago she'd had with Hannah, about the death of Hannah's parents, a huge force in shaping her into what she was now.

Hannah's parents had died in a car crash. But it wasn't that simple. Hannah had pieced it all together from memory and told Neeley the story while they were on the run, being chased by a rogue Cellar agent, while at the same time being part of Nero's grand plan to find his successor. The manner of her parents' deaths was a large piece of what put Hannah on Nero's radar.

Hannah had been six years old. Her father had been picked up by the local sheriff for public drunkenness, apparently not a rare event. Her mother took her daughter to pick him up from the station, shoving her in the backseat. Neeley smiled grimly, thinking of Dr. Golden and her recurring theme: childhood trauma. She wondered if Hannah had ever told Golden this story of her own trauma.

Doubtful.

On the way home, Hannah made the mistake of speaking, of asking. There were many times when asking any question was not good. Her father had turned around and slapped Hannah so hard he bounced her head off the side window. Then he'd slumped back and passed out.

Hannah had remembered that her mother started talking, but in such a low voice, and her head hurt so much she couldn't remember or tell Neeley what her mother had said. Hannah had fallen asleep in the backseat and woke up only when she heard the train.

She'd remembered few details, just the blinding light of the on-coming train and her mother reaching back to her and grabbing her hand and asking for forgiveness.

Then the train had hit.

The newspaper article about the "miracle" child who survived such a horrific accident must have piqued Nero's interest deep inside his cave underneath the NSA. Such an odd and touching story. What fertile psychological ground. Who knew what could blossom in a person's psyche from such an event?

It was a story Hannah had only told once as an adult: to Neeley. Not even to her husband, who had also betrayed her. Then Neeley realized why she was remembering Hannah's story. What was key about it. It was the final thing Hannah had said to her at the end of that story in the French restaurant in Strasbourg as they got up to leave: *"Because I know betrayal too. But I know something you don't. Sometimes betrayal is the only love left. Remember that."*

Neeley's eyes flickered open as the crew chief tapped her on the shoulder. "Six minutes out!"

Neeley wondered what role Burns's father had had in his life to cause him to deviate from whatever his plan was to visit him.

To make himself vulnerable to visit someone in a coma. What was the point? He wasn't the same man who had raised Burns. He was the husk of a person who couldn't see or hear.

Neeley was split between envying Burns and despising him for his weakness. The chopper was descending and she tapped on her screen, shifting to GPS mode. She'd designated a landing zone out of hearing distance from the home. An unmarked car, keys in, was waiting there for her. Neeley did one last check of her gear, making sure she had a round in the chamber of her pistol and that her various other weapons were accessible.

She was ready.

The chopper touched down next to railroad tracks. Neeley hopped off and the chopper popped back up into the sky and moved away to await her call for extraction. Neeley got in the car and drove, checking the GPS.

It didn't take long to get to Elysian Fields. There were only a dozen cars in the parking lot, the Prius one of them. Neeley walked in the front and flipped open her badge to the person on duty behind the desk and then flipped it shut.

"Schmidt?"

The old black woman in a starched white nurse's uniform behind the desk didn't even blink. "Might I see that badge again? Long enough so I can read it, miss?" Her name tag read Washington.

"Certainly, Nurse Washington." Neeley bit back her frustration. There was always someone who had to do it by the rules. Neeley opened her badge and held it out. What this old woman didn't know was that the people who made the rules also had the power to break them. She remembered Gant's three rules of rule-breaking:

1. Know the rule.
2. Have a good reason for breaking the rule.

3.   Accept the consequences of breaking the rule.

And if this woman didn't let her pass, Neeley was quite pre-pared to break more than just some rules.

Nurse Washington nodded. "Room one-one-six, Special Agent Curtis."

"Thank you," Neeley said. As she walked away, she saw Washington writing something down. More rule-following. Probably calling the local field office to confirm her identity. Which would, of course, confirm it, because Special Agent Curtis, out of Washington Headquarters, was indeed in their database.

As soon as she was around the corner from the busybody, Neeley drew her pistol and screwed on the suppressor.

There was a slender window allowing someone to peer into room 116 and Neeley angled up to it. Burns was standing next to a chair, facing a bed in which an old man lay. The old man was hooked up to various machines and his eyes were closed. Burns had his back to the door.

Another violation of Protocol.

He leaned forward and ran a hand tenderly over the old man's brow, avoiding the breathing tube. Even in the hallway, Neeley could hear the rhythmic thump of the ventilator. Burns sat back down and reached into his long coat. Neeley brought the pistol up, estimating how much firing through the glass would affect the trajectory of the bullet.

But Burns had a book in his hand. A well-worn book that he opened. He began reading from it, his voice low, hard to under-stand. Gently, Neeley grasped the lever to open the door. There was no click and she edged the door open. No squeak on hinges.

She could hear the words now. Burns was reading in German and it took her a moment to access that rusty part of her brain that had learned German while living in Berlin. Burns was reading from *Siddhartha* in the original language.

She brought the pistol up, aiming at the base of his skull.

But she didn't pull the trigger, instead listening to the rhythm of the words. She'd forgotten the harsh lyricism of the original language. She took a step closer.

It was jarring when Burns switched to English and abandoned the words of the book. "I knew you would come."

He shut the book but didn't turn.

Neeley pressed the muzzle of the suppressor against the base of his skull. A violation of Protocol as she was negating the gun's standoff capability by getting within arm's reach. A slight shock ran through the gun and tingled her hand. She sensed, more than felt, the shock rush through her body, then there was nothing.

"I was also drawn to this place," Burns said. "Can you feel it?"

"Feel what?" Getting in a discussion with a Sanction: definitely a violation not only of Protocol but also of Gant's rules. And just plain stupid. Neeley felt it all unraveling, every rule, every Protocol, every piece of common sense.

"The regrets," Burns said. He nodded toward the old man. "He regrets he spent more time at work than he needed to, trying to get that position he never got, getting that extra percentage of pension that his wife did not get to enjoy. So he never really knew his children, even his wife. And then it was gone all so soon. It's a deep pool that rests over this entire place. Regret."

"What do you regret?" Neeley said. "Going rogue?"

"Am I rogue now?" Burns asked. "And I can feel your regrets."

The lights in the room flickered and then went out. At the same time, the ventilator stopped.

Down the hallway alerts were going off as other life-sustaining machines ground to a halt. In the distance, Neeley could hear a generator coughing, trying futilely to come to life and restore power. Voices were shouting as nurses responded to the emergencies.

"Is he your father?" Neeley asked, taking a step back, regaining her standoff distance.

"No." Burns stood and turned. His face didn't shock Neeley. She'd seen the images and worse in battle. "I did a search en route for someone like this. Amazing that there are so many Schmidts. Sort of like there are so many Smiths in English. This was convenient." He glanced over this shoulder at the old man who was now struggling to breathe. "I have no clue who he is. He might well be a distant relative. But then we all are related, aren't we? Some say a good percentage of the population is related to Genghis Khan. Apparently he liked to spread his seed as he conquered the world."

Neeley's finger was on the trigger, but she was hesitating.

Violating Protocol.

"My father," Burns said, as if searching for a memory. "He was a weak man. But my grandfather. He was a very special man."

"You didn't follow in his footsteps," Neeley said.

"You think you know what you don't know," Burns said, his eyes beginning to flicker in color. "But I know what you know."

"Why?" she asked.

"Why did I draw you in?" Burns asked.

Neeley's finger began to pull on the trigger but then Burns's face rippled, as if the structure underneath were alive. The skin smoothed out, then shifted, and—

"Gant?" Neeley knew it wasn't Gant. It couldn't be. He was dead. But that's who she was looking at. Her finger left the trigger.

Gant's eyes began to glow, a slight golden tint easily visible in the darkened room. "The same reason you are here with that gun. Trying to do what we believe is the right thing."

The voice wasn't Gant's and her finger went back on the trigger, pulling, but the light leaping from those eyes was faster, hitting her in the chest and knocking her back. The gun fired, but the aim was off, the bullet thudding into the ceiling as Neeley fell backward.

She had a protective vest on, but she hadn't been shot. Whatever it was that had hit her wrapped tight around her heart and squeezed. She felt pain like she'd never experienced before, an elephant sitting on her chest. Someone was leaning over her. Gant's face dissolved, back to Burns's scarred one. Then everything went black.

━━━━━━

Burns didn't even look back at the old man, whose chest was no longer rising and falling. He tucked the book into his coat, knelt next to Neeley, and removed the car keys and the radio and the cell phone from her pocket. He stood, stepped over Neeley, and walked out of the room.

As he did so, the power came back on.

He went into the parking lot. Her car was easy to find. Burns keyed the radio and spoke in an excited voice: "Hello? Hello? This woman has been hurt! She needs help."

As he waited, he walked around the car, head cocked as if listening, and then reached under the right front wheel panel and grabbed the tracker. He removed it and stomped on it. He heard a helicopter inbound.

The Nighthawk came racing in just above the tree line when the golden light flashed from Burns's eyes and hit it, shutting everything on board down.

The pilots never had a chance to react; they were too low. The helicopter hit like a rock, tumbling, ripping apart, blades churning, breaking, flying through the air, and then the chopper exploded.

Burns got in the car and drove off.

Back inside the facility, Nurse Washington threw open the door to room 116. She immediately saw that the old man in the bed was dead; she'd seen a lot of dead old people from the doorway of rooms in this place and she knew dead.

The woman, the FBI special agent, confirmed as legitimate by the local field office, wasn't breathing either. But she was fresh dead. Nurse Washington had seen that enough also.

Washington yelled, a voice that carried throughout the entire facility. "Crash cart to one-one-six!" She knelt next to Neeley. "Knew that man was a servant of the devil the minute he came through the door. And knew you were trouble, too, the moment you walked in. And I still don't believe you are what you say you are."

Then she began to perform CPR.

CHAPTER 7

Iris Watkins was five feet tall if she really stretched and dripping wet didn't break three figures on the scale. And she had twenty pounds of baby in a halter on her chest and two kids under five fighting her for control of the grocery cart. She tried to grab some 2 percent milk without banging the baby's head into the cooler door when one of those grandmother types stopped her and started going on about how cute the kids were. And then, of course: "My! What a big baby for such a teeny little thing like you."

Why don't you hand me some milk or hold the door for me? Iris thought. As if she didn't hear that all the time. Of course, they'd never seen the father, and he hadn't been a tiny little thing. He hadn't even been a normal thing. He'd been huge, thus the large baby, but that also probably contributed to him being such a large target and getting hit fourteen times covering his team's withdrawal in Afghanistan last year.

But he'd kept firing, up until the last bullet hit him just under the left eye.

Watkins had asked for every single detail from the SEAL teammates who'd accompanied the body back to the States. She had to know and it gave her comfort to understand he'd died fighting, doing what he was trained to, and he died on the battlefield, not in a medevac or in surgery.

It was the way a warrior should die and her husband had been a warrior. He'd died like the Viking he was, weapon in hand, fighting until he gave his last breath.

One of the girls had wandered off and grabbed a box of no-you-can't-have-that cereal loaded with sugar, as if she wasn't hyper enough, and the other was now clinging to Watkins's leg complaining about something, voice working its way up to a squall.

Iris forced a smile to her lips for the old woman, who was doing nothing but getting in the way. She thought how pleasant menopause must be and imagined herself one day shopping all alone without the usual quiz questions: How old, how much does he weigh, he doesn't have your eyes so it must be the father, what does his dad do? The innocent questions, some of which could cause a stab of pain so hard in her chest she thought she'd just collapse into the empty void that was there.

What she held on to was mirroring his courage, in the more subtle, but sometimes even more challenging field of negotiating everyday life, being a war widow in a country that barely remembered it was at war and taking care of their three children.

Then she heard, buried deep in her purse, the ringtone that she could never ignore. She grabbed for the phone, swinging the baby accidently into the cart handle, which brought a shriek. Watkins ignored even that in the call of duty and pulled the phone out as the old woman huffed and puffed away, talking about these young mothers these days.

Watkins typed in the new destination for the encrypted message and sent it.

Then she dumped the phone back into the bag and held her baby tight, murmuring an apology. She was grateful for the check the Loop sent every month, because the death benefits just weren't enough to cover three kids.

And it made her feel a part of . . .

What exactly, she wasn't sure.

She looked in her baby's eyes and she saw his eyes and she felt that searing clash of joy over the life she held and agony over the life she'd lost.

Then she couraged up and got the milk.

———

The Archives elicited more excitement from Ivar than the Can had, perhaps because the Can reminded him of "bench time," which some physicists loved but others avoided.

"Somebody saw this and thought of the ending for *Raiders of the Lost Ark*," Ivar said as they walked in the yawning steel doors in the front of the Area 51 Archive. As far as one could see were rows and rows of crates, vehicles, planes, boats, and weird-shaped objects covered in tarps, until it all faded into a haze. There was a far end; one could barely make it out in the distance. Ivar estimated it was over a half mile away.

"It's bigger than the Boeing Everett Factory," Doc said proudly, as if he'd put in most of the rivets himself. He was beginning to really get on Ivar's nerves, with his "I've been here longer than you and know more than you and am smarter than you and have more PhDs than you" attitude.

Doc blithely continued. "People think the Boeing factory is the biggest building in the world. *And*," he added, quite unnecessarily—Doc was well known among the Nightstalkers for adding the unnecessary, which on occasion had turned out to be necessary—"the Archives are underground, enclosed in this cavern inside Groom Mountain."

Ivar bit back his sarcastic reply that he hadn't known they'd been inside the mountain for over an hour now. He'd worked under a lot of professors like Doc and sarcasm rarely worked. Most scientists took things quite literally. *The Big Bang Theory* was funny; Doc wasn't.

They stepped across the metal rail on which the huge doors rolled shut and entered the Archives, only after having their retinas scanned for the umpteenth time by a pair of guards who looked so bored, they might shoot someone just to watch them die, aka Johnny Cash style.

"*Warehouse 13*," Ivar said, choosing another approach. "Someone definitely took the last scene of *Raiders* as the idea for that."

"This is real," Doc said, obviously not a TV or movie person. He pointed down. "The entire Archives is on large springs to absorb the impact if a nuke hit the mountain above us. They built this long before they built NORAD. The first building was just a World War Two prefab hut, but as you can see, it's expanded considerably since then."

"Why?" Ivar asked.

"During the Cold War—" Doc began, but Ivar cut him off when he was heading for the wrong pass.

"I mean, why did Area 51 need an archive?"

Doc sighed as they strolled down the main aisle. A golf cart came whizzing by, two men in white coats on it, one of them staring at a map, giving directions. It sped around a corner and was gone. Somewhere in the distance it sounded like someone was pounding a sledgehammer on a pipe, a distinct sound, occurring every twenty seconds or so.

"World War Two," Doc said. He, too, had a map, an actual paper map, in his hand and he consulted it. He pointed left. "The earliest stuff gathered is in that corner. From Operation Paperclip."

"Sounds innocent enough," Ivar said, more interested to learn whether they had the Ark of the Covenant in here or at least some crystal skulls.

"You have no idea what Operation Paperclip was." Doc stopped, carefully folded the map, and placed it in his breast pocket. He adjusted his spectacles and looked Ivar up and down, as if he were a specimen that had crawled out from under some rock. "Very few things we deal with here are innocent. Innocence is something one leaves behind when coming to Area 51. Let me tell you about innocence and this great country we call our own. Do you know what the OSS was?"

Ivar shook his head, surprised at Doc's intensity. It wasn't like they were talking about particle physics or quantum mechanics.

"As the Second World War was coming to a close," Doc said, "there were those in the OSS, the Office of Strategic Services, the forerunner of the CIA and Special Forces, who were looking ahead. In a way, they were also *our* predecessors here in the Nightstalkers. They were already looking past the war to the next war. There's always a next war," Doc added.

That struck a chord with Ivar because war had struck close to him just four years ago. "As Plato said a long, long time ago, 'only the dead have seen the end of war.'"

"You didn't get the full in-brief from Moms and Nada," Doc said. "But you get Moms talking, she'll tell you the Nightstalkers were founded the day guys like you and me, scientists, split the atom and then learned how to turn that into a weapon."

"'I am become—'"

Doc's tolerance for Ivar's deep well of quotes was on a tight leash. "Yes, yes. I know what Oppenheimer said. Moms quotes it all the time. But World War Two changed warfare. We not only saw our own country invent, and use, the atomic bomb, but we also saw other weapons of mass destruction developed to even more lethal levels by scientists. All these weapon races got, and continue to be, despite proclamations otherwise, out of control." Doc pulled the map out of his pocket and unfolded it. He nodded. "Follow me. Let me show you something."

They walked down a side aisle, high rows of heavy metal shelving towering over them on each side, as if they were in a super-super-Costco. Doc halted in front of a house-sized white square. Power lines looped down to the top of it and machinery was humming. Doc went up to a window and wiped away frost on a piece of thick glass.

"Take a look," Doc said.

Ivar, who had spent a lot of time in labs, had a hard time figuring out what the contraption was inside the container.

"It's a nuclear weapon," Doc said. "Once the Russians showed they had their bomb, President Truman, who I'll get back to, demanded we build bigger bombs. Of course, he meant larger yield, but back in the late forties, larger yield literally meant a larger bomb. They used liquid deuterium as the fusion fuel—"

"Thus the requirement for it to be kept refrigerated." Ivar couldn't help resorting to playing a physics card.

"Of course," Doc said. "This one was called Ivy Mike. Pretty much impractical as a weapon, as you can obviously see. But it had a big yield. Ten-point-four megatons." He moved on to what was stored next to it. A large, cylindrical bomb, twenty-four feet long and six feet in diameter, rested in a metal cradle.

"They worked on making the bomb smaller," Doc said, "and this was the first deployable, large-yield one they came up with. A Mark-17 thermonuclear bomb. It remains to this date the most powerful nuclear weapon ever built by the United States. Estimated yield around twenty-five to thirty megatons."

"And we're keeping one here in the Archives for . . . ?" Ivar asked. "Isn't that as stupid as the labs that keep the smallpox virus around?"

"And we keep this around for the same reason," Doc said. "To study and understand. We keep a lot of deadly things in the Archives. Which answers your earlier question of why we need an Archive. Which brings me back to Operation Paperclip. While we led the way in developing, and using, nuclear weapons, the Germans and the Japanese led the way in other scientific fields associated with killing, particularly chemical and biological weapons."

Doc tapped his chest as he led Ivar farther into the Archives. "We've faced down not only Rifts, but also nuclear weapons and some pretty serious biological and chemical mishaps over the years, including one or two cases of the smallpox virus you mentioned being played with in ways that weren't smart or secure. You worked in a lab and look what happened there because your professor had visions of a Nobel Prize dancing in his head. He threw all caution to the wind and opened a Rift.

"You need to know the history of all of this. And you can come in here and study a lot of the things we, and our predecessors, have run into over the decades. I know Nada gave you a binder, but that has just an overview. The details, and they are important, are in here. In the original documents."

Doc stopped in front of a missile pointing toward the roof. "A V-2 rocket. Mint condition. The Germans were the leaders in rocket development and if they'd had another year or so, the East

Coast might have seen an advanced version of the V-2 rocket raining down from the skies. If the Nazi scientists had another two or three years, some of those rockets could have had nuclear warheads on them. Think about that. I like to think that every soldier who died storming those beaches in Normandy gave his life so we could stop that from happening.

"Of course, that's the noble side of warfare. There's another side." Doc plinked one of the metal fins. "So at the end of World War Two, OSS operatives, along with intelligence officers from the Joint Intelligence Objectives Agency, a mouthful like many military organizations are, were sent into Japan and Germany. Sometimes they were actually snatching scientists away from army war crimes units. Sometimes they got in firefights with similar units from the Russian Army. The Brits also were in on it, although their efforts came nothing close to us and the Soviets."

Doc glanced at Ivar. "The Russians have had their own version of the Nightstalkers for a while and we've done some joint missions together, but things were tense for a long time during the Cold War. There were times we suspected the other side of doing things that looked a hell of a lot like developing new weapons of mass destruction." Doc shrugged. "And to be honest, I think it was true on both sides. We cleaned up our own messes and theirs sometimes. And they probably cleaned up some of ours in different places."

"World War Two?" Ivar said, trying to keep Doc on track.

"The worst of the Nazi and Japanese scientists everyone was looking for were the ones who worked on biological and chemical weapons. While the United States was still stockpiling World War One mustard gas as its primary chemical weapon should the need arise, the Germans had perfected tabun, soman, and sarin and proven their effectiveness with ruthless use in the camps. The

Japanese had also developed some nasty bugs at Unit 731 in Manchuria and used them on prisoners of all nationalities, sometimes vivisecting the subjects to study the stages of the diseases."

"You're shitting me," Ivar said. "Vivisection of humans?"

Doc snorted. "I'll give the Russians this: They at least tried a bunch of the people from 731 they captured. Sentenced most to labor camps in Siberia, which was, in effect, a death sentence. We gave the Japanese scientists we got a free pass in order to get the knowledge they had. The Japanese even have a memorial to Unit 731 in Tokyo."

Doc moved on, deeper into the Archives.

"At the end of World War Two, President Truman signed an executive order banning the immigration of Nazis into the United States. He also signed the executive order forming Majestic-12. Sometimes orders can conflict."

"No shit," Ivar said.

Doc ignored him. "NASA got the rocket engineers. But the nuke, bio, chem guys came here to Area 51. Both the Nazis and the Japanese. Also, not even known by most of the Paperclip operatives, we were grabbing the leading physicists from Germany and Japan. It was a plan with a double edge—not only gain the expertise of these people, but also deny their own devastated countries their abilities. It's taken over a generation for those countries to begin to redevelop their brain trust. And, of course, we wanted to keep them from the Russians."

"And those physicists opened the first Rift," Ivar said. "Here."

"Correct," Doc said. "That is why we are here and why you must know the history. The men who opened the first Rift were not good men. They were evil men."

"And the ones who built Little Boy and Fat Man?" Ivar observed.

Doc stiffened in anger and then gave a sad smile. "The victor writes history."

"What happened to the ones who opened the first Rift?" Ivar asked.

Doc stared at Ivar. "You're the only person who has opened a Rift and didn't die or disappear through it."

"So did they die?"

"No. They disappeared. And a lot of soldiers and scientists died and disappeared trying to close the Rift. Those were the first Nightstalkers."

"You're giving me the eye like you want to vivisect me," Ivar said.

Doc ignored him and moved on, then halted in an aisle bounded on both sides by modern filing cabinets. "Ms. Jones, in fact most of the Black Ops world, doesn't trust computers. They don't even trust paper records, as evidenced by the destruction of your own file. But they do accept that we need to keep some sort of historical record of what we do. And our research." He waved a hand. "This is Section Twenty-Two-Charlie. The section on Rifts and Fireflies."

Ivar was overwhelmed and excited at the same time. There were at least sixty drawer cabinets.

"Where should I start?" Ivar asked

"At the beginning," Doc said, pointing to the left.

"You were dead for under a minute," Nurse Washington said. The resuscitation cart was behind her, wires for the defibrillator dangling. "Only took one jolt to bring you back."

Only took one jolt to kill me, Neeley thought. She was still on the floor, her chest throbbing with pain. She tried to lift a hand. "My phone."

"Gone. Along with the man who came here to visit Mr. Schmidt, who I assume wasn't his son. Mr. Schmidt is no longer among the living and was past bringing back. And I assume you're not just an FBI agent. There's a lot of people outside. Lots of police. Lots of people with black sunglasses. And"—Washington looked down at Neeley as if to judge how much more bad news she could handle—"an army helicopter crashed just down the road. Four dead. I figure that has some connection to you and the man who was here."

Neeley closed her eyes. More dead and she'd failed. The number of ways in which she'd failed was as overwhelming as the pain in her chest.

"How long since the helicopter crashed?" Neeley asked.

"'Bout fifteen minutes," the nurse replied.

"It won't be long now," Neeley whispered.

"Who loved you?" Hannah asked Moms.

Moms sat in the seat facing Hannah's desk deep underneath the puzzle palace of the NSA, feeling very different than when she faced Ms. Jones at the Ranch. Jones was a known, after working together for so many years. Hannah, while Moms had heard rumors, was a wild card. Her youth and attractiveness disconcerted Moms. Hannah was everything that Moms wasn't, physically, at least.

The one certainty was that the Cellar ruled all: the Nightstalkers and the cluster of other organizations, many of which Moms assumed she had no clue about or what they did.

The person and the setting were unsettling enough, but the question was bizarre.

"Why don't you ask me who I loved?" Moms countered. "Can one really know if someone loves them?"

"You can save the question-answering-the-question for Dr. Golden," Hannah said. "That's shrink play." She leaned back in her chair, steepling her fingers, regarding the woman across from her. "You receive a stipend every month. You went to see Mrs. Sanchez about it."

They were not questions, so Moms followed a Nada Yada and said nothing.

Hannah continued. "She couldn't help you. It's a survivor's benefit. Someone thought enough of you to put your name in that particular box on that particular form. It seems such a simple thing, filling out a form. But it isn't for *that* form. The survivor benefits form is asking a person to rank-order those in their lives in case of their own death. But the ordering can have different meanings. For example, the man you call Kirk on your team, he rank-ordered his family. His siblings that he has to take care of. So much so, he took part of your team off the reservation on an unsanctioned operation."

"That's being dealt with," Moms said.

"Yes, yes," Hannah said. "Sending them like wayward school-children to Fort Bragg. Do you know that what your Mr. Roland did with my agent Neeley in South America was the first time in years she's ever brought someone on a Sanction with her?"

"So it *was* a Sanction?" This time it was a question.

"Of course. Neeley would never stray. But it crossed the line between Cellar and Nightstalker missions."

"As you're crossing them now going after Burns. And we already crossed when you brought me into the White House last year."

Hannah smiled, revealing even, surprisingly white teeth. "Touché. The world is changing. Our areas of operations are increasingly overlapping. But that isn't why I wanted to speak with you."

Moms folded her legs and put her hands in her lap, like an obedient schoolgirl summoned to the principal's office over the PA system. To be praised or punished, it wasn't clear yet.

Hannah said, "Ms. Jones has a speech she likes to give your team. Why we are here."

"You don't have to repeat it," Moms said.

"I'm not Ms. Jones and my reasoning is different from hers," Hannah said. "People like us, you and me, we're the broken ones. The ones not in the bell curve and not necessarily on the good side of the curve."

"And we protect those inside the curve," Moms said. "The average person who goes through their day not knowing how close they come to extinction. How many dangers are out there."

Hannah smiled. "That there are boogie men in the closet." She tapped her desk. "Do you know why *I'm* here?"

"To police the world of covert ops," Moms said.

"On a base level, yes," Hannah agreed. "But as *you* tend to go deeper with your own why we are here, beyond the Rifts and Fireflies to the Trinity Test as the start point for the Nightstalkers, I like to go back and examine history and determine why an organization like the Cellar was and is needed."

Moms waited, ready to be schooled, because no matter how high up you went, someone was always there above you, and every once in a while you got called in.

She wondered who schooled Hannah.

"As you know, there is evil in the world," Hannah said. "You focus on the abnormal evil. Rifts, Fireflies, and the sort. And other problems. Rogue scientists. Stupid scientists. Nature gone amok. But there is a much more insidious evil. The worst kind. The one that hides inside men's souls. In the dark corners of their hearts. The latent evil, the truly dangerous inside of people, which the psychopaths can tap into. And that evil can spread rapidly among those who are not necessarily evil to begin with. I learned this the hard way as a young woman, being drawn into something terrible because I loved someone. Sometimes love can be turned, twisted."

Hannah smiled at Moms's expression. "Don't look so shocked. We all had lives before we were sucked into this dark world we inhabit. I know that sounds simplistic, but if you look at some of the more dramatic examples in the past hundred years and then factor in the speed with which we can interact with each other now via digital means, the world has become a much more frightening place. Where evil people can spread their message much more effectively and quickly.

"We've had Hitler, Stalin, Mao, Pol Pot, Hussein, bin Laden, and others. When will the next version of those arise? Where? And how much more effective will they be with access to the Internet? I believe legends and dogma exist for a reason. The concept of an anti-Christ has its roots in a base fear we all have."

Hannah tapped her desk once more. "The person who sits here has the power of life and death. Judge, jury, and then send the executioner on a Sanction. How different does that make me from those evil people?"

"Your motivation for what you do," Moms said. "You're protecting people from the evil."

"Perhaps. I sometimes think," Hannah said, "that if the Cellar had existed before World War Two, it might have been able to stop some of the carnage. Most likely not the war itself, but some of the horror perpetuated under the cover of the war."

"Can you separate the two?" Moms asked.

Hannah sighed. "I certainly hope so."

"You think the Cellar would have taken out Hitler?"

Hannah shrugged. "Perhaps. But we didn't take out Hussein. So who knows?"

"War has never been clean," Moms said. "I've seen it firsthand. I watched a sniper in Baghdad one time. A simple thing. Most Iraqis can't swim, but they were fleeing us, trying to cross the Tigris. So there was a group. Five. Grabbed on to a large beach ball and were using it as a float to get across the river. A man, two women, and two children.

"And the sniper. He shot the ball, laughing as he did so. A 'good' American boy. From Nebraska or Idaho or one of those wholesome states. He watched those people drown. He put down his rifle and took pictures."

"And what did you do?" Hannah asked.

"I almost shot him."

"But you didn't."

"No."

"Because you are not evil. Was he?" Hannah asked.

"He was caught up in it. You do become inured to it. Callous."

Hannah leaned forward. "Does that scab you cover yourself with grow thicker or thinner with time?"

Moms shrugged. "Depends on the person, I guess. Is that why you're asking me about love?" Moms challenged. "I don't want your job, by the way."

"I plan on having my job for quite a while," Hannah said.

"I don't want Ms. Jones's job either."

"No one really cares what you want or don't want," Hannah said. She pulled open a drawer. She reached in and took out an object, which she placed on the desk, in clear view of Moms, whose legs quickly became uncrossed and hands became fists.

"Where did you get that?" Moms demanded.

It was a picture album, the kind you buy at Walgreens or K-Mart or more likely remaindered at the Dollar Store. Which is exactly where Moms's mother had gotten it with her employee discount as a young teenager. It was obviously cheap, covered in fake imitation leather. Gold letters on the front read OUR WEDDING.

It was anything but a wedding album.

"Dr. Golden tracked it down," Hannah said.

Moms absorbed the implications of that, which raised more questions than one sentence should. She tried to prioritize the questions in her mind, but Hannah didn't give her the time.

"Yes, Dr. Golden was researching your background. Digging deeper than the ones who vetted your security clearance. After all, there is a large difference between being trustworthy with secrets and being trustworthy. Don't you think."

It was not a question, but a reminder.

Hannah continued. "Dr. Golden found it in an old storage unit one of your brothers had forgotten about with the rest of the stuff from your now-abandoned childhood home. Covered in dust and neglect. Which raises an interesting point: Do your brothers love you? Did they love you when you took care of them when your mother was incapable of action most of the time due to her intoxication?" She didn't consult any notes. "You have not spoken to any of your siblings for over six years."

"We don't have siblings or family in the Nightstalkers," Moms said. "I don't believe you have them in the Cellar either."

Hannah ignored that. "Who loves you, Moms?" She reached out and placed a hand on the album. "Your mother cut pictures from catalogues and pasted them in here while she was a teenager. A wish list for her life."

Moms remembered the images her mother would stick on the old beat-up refrigerator, using magnets from the local feed lot to hold them in place. The album was the predecessor to the fridge.

It wasn't a step up.

"A wish list," Hannah continued, "that was ironically canceled by the wedding in front of the judge with no flowers or rings or anything in this book. A wedding you were present for, although certainly you can't be expected to remember it. It's why you see weddings, indeed all intimate relationships, as the end, not the beginning."

"Is that shrink-speak? I thought I got that later with Dr. Golden?"

Hannah ignored her. "Then the pictures change. From the perfect wedding to places. Beautiful places all around the world from old *National Geographic* magazines." Hannah flipped it open. "You had this up until eight years ago; then you gave it to your brother."

"That's private," Moms said. There was an edge to her voice and she was leaning forward in the chair.

"Of course," Hannah said. She looked up from the album and rolled her eyes toward the ceiling. "And, of course, you understand that's almost the definition of irony saying that here, three hundred feet below the NSA? I can order you to go out and kill someone but you're upset about a book that's been gathering dust for years?"

"It's personal."

"And your life isn't?" Hannah didn't wait for an answer. "You used to check off these places, if you happened to have traveled to or through them and write notes to your mother about them.

Postcards from the edge, literally, given some of your missions and assignments. Of course, you rarely traveled to the nice, exotic locales your mother dreamed of. Mostly hellholes, but there were some decent stops en route and on the way back."

"She loved me," Moms said, trying to stop Hannah.

"Not enough to stop drinking," Hannah said. "Not enough to be a mother."

Moms pointed at the book. "She gave me hope. She gave me purpose."

"Rearing your brothers? Then traveling around the world killing people? It's amazing what we get used to. For you, your life is sort of normal. Yet for a normal person your life is so far off the grid, they wouldn't be able to comprehend it."

Moms wasn't giving in so easily. "She at least showed me a world beyond what we had growing up. A world she knew she'd never see but I could. Even if it means killing people," she added bitterly.

"A world beyond that gray, flat Kansas horizon?" Hannah flipped the album shut. "Of more interest, and more importance, is who loved *her*? That's where *your* allotment comes from."

Moms sat back, some of the anger draining from her. "You know."

"That's what makes Mrs. Sanchez's job so difficult and so important," Hannah said. "Money leaves a trail. Many a Predator strike has resulted from following a money trail and Mrs. Sanchez is very good at that. She's been responsible for quite a few strikes.

"The allotment is from a man who loved your mother. Before you were born. He wanted to marry her but instead she married your father. Not planned for in the album of her future life. It is a testament to your mother's beliefs that you are here at all. But part of that was marrying that man. The man who put her in a very small world and kept her there.

"So the man who really loved your mother left. He went into the military. He couldn't bear to stay in that town and see your mother still working at the Dollar Store, when she was able to make it to the job. It pained him to see her at all, so he left, and he eventually died in the service of our country. And he left the money to your mother so maybe she could see some of these places, but when he died, she was long since gone also, so it went to you."

Hannah fell silent.

"Who was it?"

"It doesn't matter." Hannah swept the album off her desk and into the drawer and slid it shut.

"That's mine."

Hannah ignored her. She put her hands flat on the desk, and her dark eyes met Mom's. "Who loved you? Loving someone, like you did your brothers and your mother and like you do your team, just gets you by. Most people go through life throwing love around to those they find worthy of it, but the real power is in who loves us. Because those who love us, they own a piece of us. They find us worthy."

Moms was confused. "What do you mean?"

"Love is like electricity," Hannah said. "When we feel it for someone, it's grounded in *our* hopes and dreams. When someone loves us, it's wild and free. Unleashed. It's power without a ground. It can hurt us or help us. We have to decide which. The problem for you is that you didn't have a you."

"I imagine there's a point to all this," Moms said.

"I—" Hannah began, but then her desk phone trilled.

Hannah picked it up. She listened and Moms watched her face, searching for any tell.

There was none.

"Bring her to me once she's been cleared," Hannah said. "Where is the terminus of the Loop message?"

She listened and then issued a last order before hanging up. "Help the last relayer decrypt and send, then secure the Loop."

Hannah hung the phone up. "It appears things are not as we would like. Neeley was not able to Sanction Burns."

Moms stood. "My team—"

Hannah held up a hand. "I believe a message is being forwarded to one of your team members as we speak."

"Where's the demon core?" Ivar asked Doc as he slid shut the second drawer.

Doc looked up from the cabinet he'd been rifling through. "Ah, the dragon's tail. The very first Rift."

"The records are incomplete," Ivar said.

"Of course they are," Doc said. "Everyone who worked on it disappeared."

Ivar shook his head. "No. I mean even the paperwork before they opened the Rift is wrong. Like they were hiding something."

"They were Nazis and—" Doc paused, searching for the right word—"you know, there was never a word for those who followed the emperor of Japan into that war. Who perpetuated crimes as bad as the Nazis. Nanking. The Bataan Death March. Unit 731."

"Japanese," Ivar said.

"Yes, but we make such a distinction between Nazis and Germans sometimes. Was every German a Nazi? Was every Japanese responsible for those crimes?"

"The records," Ivar said, thumping the drawer. "There's very little on what this group, Odessa, was doing. The theoretical physicists."

"Ah, yes," Doc said. "Odessa. Does the name ring a bell?"

Ivar shrugged. "Not particularly."

"Ask Eagle about it sometime," Doc said.

Ivar tapped the drawer, getting back on track. "There's some mention of the demon core."

"From Los Alamos," Doc said. "Majestic-12 appropriated the plutonium core from Los Alamos that killed Daghlian and Slotin. They nicknamed it the *demon core* because of those accidents."

Every physicist knew of Daghlian and Slotin. Cautionary tales told early in their studies. "What was that thing about the dragon's tail?" Ivar asked.

"Enrico Fermi told Slotin that playing with that core was like tickling the dragon's tail and that the dragon was going to consume him. More like it farted when Slotin's screwdriver slipped, but it was a radioactive fart and it killed him."

"Where's the demon core now?" Ivar asked. He looked about the Archives. "In some big lead box?"

"They never found it after the first Rift," Doc said. "It was assumed that the Odessa group used it to open the Rift and it got sucked through with them."

Ivar frowned. "But how come everyone who has opened a Rift since then hasn't needed a plutonium core? Just algorithms?"

"Good question, isn't it?" Doc said.

"But plutonium has a half-life of a little over twenty-four

thousand years," Ivar said. "Wherever it is, that core is still putting out a lot of radioactivity and potential power."

"Let's hope it's frying whoever is on the other side of the Rifts," Doc said, and then pointedly went back to looking at the file he'd just pulled out.

Wallace Cranston was standing at the craps table in the Bellagio losing his stash, his savings, and his shirt. He was thinking about going to the ATM to get the money he swore he wouldn't get.

His wife's money.

Even though doing that would most likely change that status to ex-wife. But he could feel it in his bones that his losing streak was just about up and he was going to hit it good.

Of course, he didn't even know what day it was, never mind what time it was, but he was on vacation and breathing the lovely oxygenated air they pumped in, and he was on the fourth, or fifth, or sixth day of a fantastic bender, and he felt anything was possible.

He noticed the cleavage on the waitress as she handed him another rum and Coke, and he thought, *Maybe even that's possible*, even though she had the dead eyes of one of Stephen King's bad people from *The Stand*. Which reminded him he'd been to Boulder, Colorado, where the supposed good people had made their "stand," and the locals there had been a bunch of liberal, stuck-up pricks, so he'd rather be here with the bad.

"It's Vegas, baby," he whispered to himself, then took a slug of his drink and started to weave his way toward the ATM. He bounced into it, then used one hand to claim it as an anchor as he pulled his wallet out. He fumbled through it for the cash card he'd swiped before leaving home, hoping his wife hadn't canceled it already.

Then the phone that never went on vacation started to vibrate in his shirt pocket and chime with "I'll Sleep When I'm Dead," which was more than appropriate here in Vegas. Cranston had a theory that people went to Vegas to die and to L.A. to suffer. He glanced back at the waitress with the dead eyes and thought, *You'd like me better if you knew who I was.*

Then again, maybe not.

He pulled the phone out and with surprisingly steady hands accepted the incoming text message. He saw the five letter groupings and knew he'd have to go back to his room to decrypt and forward.

He looked at the ATM and sighed. His wife would never know how close it came. Saved by the bell. By the ringtone. He started to giggle as he walked toward the elevator.

He loved his job.

And that was when the Men in Black appeared, seemingly out of the walls, one on either side, lifting him up off the ground, his feet still churning, searching for floor. They hustled him into the elevator. A third one, they all looked alike, took the phone and glanced at the screen.

"Do you have the decryptor?"

Cranston nodded. "In my room. I was gonna do it."

"We'll help. It'll save time. You don't want to get this wrong."

———

Nada and Zoey were looking at the babies.

They weren't supposed to be in the nursery. AUTHORIZED

PERSONNEL ONLY the placard on the outside door read, like that had ever stopped Nada from going anywhere. In fact, it was practically an invitation.

Nada checked his watch. They had three minutes before the nurse came by again. The staff had a rigid schedule, the bane of all security. They even had a little infrared thing they had to scan on a light on the wall to confirm they were doing their checks on time; someone thought the trinket added to the security of the place, when in reality it made the hospital all that much more vulnerable to those in the know. Nada knew he could have snatched every one of these little beasts, thrown them into a duffel bag, and been on the road before anyone noticed.

But that would be wrong. Probably even to think it was wrong.

"Hurry," Nada said in a voice that said do anything but hurry to Zoey. He'd learned that was the best way to couch things with his niece. She still hadn't quite forgiven him for the park incident and being abandoned to the police. She was stopping at each basinet and whispering baby talk and all sorts of gooey-gooey. A part of Nada suspected it was an act, designed to irritate him, so he feigned not being irritated.

Plus, it was the right thing to do, he supposed, not very up on baby talk. In fact, Nada was known for not being up on talking at all.

It was a bunch of babies, for frak's sake, not the gold at Fort Knox. Was there an epidemic of baby stealing? For all he knew, there was, not having studied the matter.

He followed Zoey, peering over her shoulder at each one. There were some damn ugly ones, but he imagined everyone would lie and say "How precious," "How gorgeous," whatever it was people had to say about babies, because the parents had a lot vested in those little suckers. Nobody would look in and scream in dismay at the sheer ugliness of the bugger and predict it having a life full of pain and misery because of its looks. Whoever said beauty was only skin deep had none. It's easy to diss what one does not have, Nada knew. He considered adding that to his Nada Yadas but didn't see the point.

As he looked at each one, he wondered what kind of different people they'd turn into. Some were fretting and crying in their blankets, their tight cocoons of cloth unraveled, and he figured that's sort of the way their life would turn out for them. Others were sound asleep, snug as bugs, their blanket tight around them. They'd live quiet lives, not making a fuss, security—another word for fear in Nada's opinion—being their priority.

A few were staring around, not making a fuss, just observing.

Those were the dangerous ones. Just staring as if they already knew something was up, that they'd been dealt a hand, and they were just trying to figure out the cards. Something was going on and they wanted to know what it was. Several met his eyes, staring back as if challenging him. He foresaw great things and/or terrible endings for those particular babies.

He wondered where and how each would die. It was a morbid thought he'd never shared with anyone, not even Moms, but every time he'd killed someone, he'd later wondered if they would have lived their life differently if they'd known before about whatever shit-hole situation he'd had to kill them in, that that place and time would be their final moment?

He often wondered where he would meet his own end. A Nada Yada he didn't share with others but that ruled his life was: Things will always turn out how you least expect.

Most likely, if he made it to old age, he'd die with Zoey standing nearby giving him grief.

Zoey cooed into another basinet and Nada looked over her shoulder. There was a big boy in it, his head covered with thick black hair and his eyes dark and wide open. They seemed to be staring right through Nada, even though he knew the eyes couldn't focus yet. The baby couldn't see him. So why was he staring at him? Nada wondered.

"Hurry up, Zoey," he said. "The nurse will be here in thirty seconds."

At the sound of his voice, the baby's head moved, as if trying to zero in with his ears as well as the eyes that couldn't focus. Nada put his big, calloused hand out, as if to stroke the thick hair, but he just waved it in front of the baby's face and the eyes tracked it, which he found most fascinating. Movement could be noticed without focus?

Something to remember if he ever had to draw down on a newborn.

Stranger things had happened to him as a Nightstalker.

Zoey grabbed his hand, reversing roles. "Come on, Uncle. We gotta get out of here."

But Nada suddenly wanted to stay. To whisper something to this boy, to leave some mark. There were great things ahead in this kid's life. Nada didn't know how he knew it, but he trusted it as much as he did when his gut told him he was about to walk into an ambush. He was still alive because he trusted that instinct.

There was a little blue bulb syringe at the foot of the baby, something used to clear his nose or put drops in his eyes or whatever hell maintenance on a baby required a bulb syringe. Nada instinctively grabbed it and stuffed it in his shirt. He followed Zoey through the door they weren't supposed to come in. (No signs on this side about stopping intruders, he noted.) They slid through, scant seconds ahead of the nurse doing her rounds, as punctual as security on any firebase.

Nada felt the blue syringe in his chest pocket and it seemed to be extraordinarily heavy. Remembering the impulsive theft caused him to flush, although it would be hard to see against his pitted and dark skin.

He'd done wrong. A small wrong, but an unnecessary one.

And he didn't know why.

But then his brother was there, bouncing up and down like a kid himself. "It's a boy!"

He sounded a bit too excited about it in Nada's opinion, considering Zoey was right there and she wasn't.

A boy, that is.

"Come, come!" his brother said, turning and heading back down the corridor to the room where Nada's sister-in-law had just given birth.

Zoey was excited too. Give her credit for playing along, Nada thought, running after her father. "Can I see? Can I see?"

Nada imagined he should be showing some sort of excitement, but his brother had already walked away, so he was spared the effort. He followed and his brother halted at the door.

"Only one at a time, Zoey," his brother said. "Let your uncle go first. I know you won't have much time," he added, because Nada never had much time, it seemed.

"Is he crying?" Nada asked.

"No," his brother said. "He's just staring at everything. It's really neat."

Then Nada heard the ringtone, low but never silenced: "I'll Sleep When I'm Dead."

He had to go. Answer the call of duty, even the Loop.

Especially the Loop.

His brother made a face.

Nada felt the weight of that blue bulb on his chest.

Nada hit the mute button on the phone that was never muted and walked through the door to meet his new nephew. "Come on," he said to Zoey, taking her hand and leading her into the room. "Rules are made to be broken."

Burns was taking back roads, two-laners that wound through the Tennessee countryside. It wasn't so much he wanted to avoid police or being noticed; it was that the manic atmosphere of the interstate bothered him on a level he couldn't define. Everyone seemed in a rush, particularly the big trucks. As if getting there quicker would change the time spent.

In his life before, Burns had driven on the interstate without a care, in the same rush. That he felt differently bothered him because it meant he was different, but he didn't know how.

He drove the speed limit. He passed what appeared to be a yard sale, except the items were scattered in front of an abandoned building, as if the residents had evacuated in the middle of the sale and just given up on everything. The despair was like a black hole trying to draw one in along the side of the road.

He passed through a small town and slowed down to the posted speed limit. He had the windows down and he heard children's voices to one side. He pulled off the road and stared at the cluster of kids in a schoolyard.

Some were playing; some squabbling; some off by themselves.

Burns's eyes began to shift color, gold spreading out from the pupils. The scene he was watching changed accordingly: Each child took on a color according to their emotions. Those arguing were a cluster of black; those getting along yellow; the ones who were alone were the most interesting because they were a rainbow of colors, reflecting whatever was running through their heads.

Burns was startled by a rap on the car's window.

"What are you watching those kids for, boy?" a distinctly Southern voice demanded.

Burns's head snapped around and the cop standing there took a step back in shock, seeing Burns's eyes.

"What the fuck?" the cop said, his hand scrambling for his gun.

The cop was a towering mass of red and black in Burns's vision. Full of rage and self-importance and the desire to hurt. Reflexively, a bolt of gold shot out of his eyes and hit the policeman in the chest, passing through his Kevlar vest, wrapping around his heart, and stopping it.

The man crumpled to the ground.

Burns started the car and drove way.

He heard the first scream behind him ten seconds later.

███████████

Moms's phone rang and Hannah nodded, indicating she should answer it.

"Yes?"

"I got a message from Scout via the Loop," Nada said, leading with the headline. "She says, and I quote, 'Nada. Scout. In TN. We have a golden problem.'"

"Send the alert," Moms said.

"As soon as I hang up."

Moms looked at Hannah. "Hold on a second." She put her hand over the phone. "Do you know where in Tennessee we need to go?"

"To find your little Scout?" Hannah asked. She shook her head at Moms's expression of surprise. "We got the message the same time as Nada, which actually was about two minutes ago, so there is a curious time lag there. My secretary has been in contact with Ms. Jones, who, of course, being efficient, has been keeping tabs on your asset. She's just outside of Knoxville, Tennessee. Ms. Jones is on top of this."

"I assume this one is *our* mission?"

Hannah nodded. "Yes. It is."

Moms spoke into the phone. "Ms. Jones has the intelligence. I'll meet you at the objective. Out." Moms headed for the door, then paused, looking over her shoulder. "Who loved *you*, Hannah?" she asked. Then she left, not waiting for an answer.

The rain had stopped a little while ago, so now it was just mud. Nice, thick, North Carolina mud.

The Nasty Nick was just a memory and the four Nightstalkers were in the midst of a long snake of camouflaged men, heavy rucks on their backs, marching down what once was a dirt road, now a mud river, through the pine forest that covered most of Camp Mackall.

No one knew how far they had to go, part of the mind games played in SFAS. This forced march could just be a loop back to Camp Rowe and chow, or it could last into the night.

Roland, Kirk, Mac, and Eagle had settled into the rhythm of rucking, which every experienced soldier has developed. They might be a bit older than the candidates around them, but they were more experienced. Some of those in the column, steam rising off of their drying fatigues, were not so fortunate. The obstacle course had taken its toll. Some with sprained ankles were fading through the ranks. Some, in not the best shape, were also fading. What the Nightstalkers knew, and what the others would learn, was that it wasn't so much one's physical conditioning that would make the difference but how badly one wanted it. Did they want to *wear* a green beret or *be* a Green Beret?

It was early enough in the selection process, still the first week, that their fellows sought to help the ones who were hurting. Weapons were taken to be carried by comrades, even some rucksacks. The Nightstalkers watched but didn't contribute.

"They'll figure it out," Mac said, for once keeping his voice down so that only his fellow Stalkers could hear.

Roland laughed. "I carried three dudes' rucks our first march here."

"Figures," Kirk said. "No one carried anyone else's shit in Ranger school. Ever. We knew from the start."

"Weren't carrying anyone else's by the end, were you?" Eagle asked Roland.

"Nope," Roland confirmed. "Everyone's got to pull their own weight."

"They'll figure it out," Mac repeated.

"Company," Kirk said, as always looking ahead.

The major, who had metal instead of feet, was waiting by the side of the road. He had on a freshly starched uniform that he'd pulled out of some magic bag and his boots were spit-shined, as if he walked above the mud, not through it. He held up a hand and Master Sergeant Twackhammer bellowed out, "Halt!"

The long line of camouflaged soldiers compressed unevenly to a stop. Several men leaned over, hands on knees, to catch their breath.

Twackhammer was walking along the line, making a mental note of those who showed weakness.

They'd be gone before the week was over.

The major came stalking over toward the Nightstalkers. He had a waterproof bag in his hand.

"Your phones are ringing, gentlemen." He held it up and everyone could hear a cacophony of four phones blaring "Lawyers, Guns and Money" in sync.

"Thank you, thank you!" Eagle exclaimed as the four pushed their way out of the column.

Because even a Rift was better than North Carolina mud.

The major opened the bag and passed the phones out. "Learn anything?" he asked.

"One for all and all for one," Mac said as he slipped the phone into his fatigue shirt. "Or something like that."

"Didn't that get you sent here?" the major asked.

Eagle nodded. "We learned what we needed to. There's rules and there are rules."

The major nodded. "There are indeed. A time and a place for everything. Good luck, gentlemen, and thanks for showing these"—he indicated the candidates—"that old men can keep it up."

"I ain't that old," Mac muttered.

"And," the major continued, "that brains count more than brawn."

"I ain't that brawny," Eagle said. "But I got brains."

"I'm brawny," Roland threw in. He glanced at Eagle. "Right?"

"And"—the major wasn't done yet—"that desire trumps all."

When Doc left to go to one of the Porta Potties stationed throughout the Archives (no one ever had to go to the bathroom in the movies, Ivar reflected, and whoever designed the Archives hadn't factored in that essential human element), Ivar ran over and opened his real target, a drawer labeled THE FUN OUTSIDE TUCSON. Ivar grabbed the hard drive that was sealed inside a plastic envelope. Someone had written CRAEGAN on it. He slipped it into his pocket and scurried back to where he was supposed to be. Deeper into the rabbit hole. Crossing the streams. His line of sayings was interrupted by a ringtone.

Ivar looked to the right. Doc was striding down the aisle, pulling out his cell phone, which was blaring "Lawyers, Guns and Money." A second later, the phone Ivar had been issued began playing the same tune.

"New guys always seem to be alerted a second or two later on their first mission," Doc said, slamming shut one open drawer and spinning the combination lock on it. "Let's go."

Scout was crouched next to the seawall, sneaking a smoke and watching the river. The guys working on the barge across the way were done for the day and cast off their little boat and puttered away, leaving the barge and pile driver anchored to the far shore.

Now all was calm.

Or at least appeared that way.

Like in those horror movies where everything seemed just fine, right before all the really, really bad stuff happened, Scout thought as she finished the cigarette and then field stripped it. She ground what remained into the ground, then looked up at the sky, as if expecting to see the parachutes of the Nightstalkers floating down toward her.

Nothing.

Plus, she had a feeling they were going to show up in a way she least expected.

Burns stopped the car in the northern parking area designated for viewing. The Fort Loudoun Dam, the first dam along the six hundred fifty-two miles of the Tennessee River, stretched 4,180 feet across the river. It was at the fifty-mile mark from the origin of the river on the eastern side of Knoxville where the Holston and French Broad Rivers joined together.

Formed behind the dam was Fort Loudoun Lake, covering over 14,600 acres. Which was the purpose. All that water, massed seventy feet above the down-dam side, was power. Gravity translated through water, translated through the three hydroelectric generators built into the power station on this end. They produced—Burns closed his eyes for a moment and focused, accessing the Internet via the phone he'd taken off Neeley—slightly over 155 megawatts of power at peak capacity.

The phone was very good, being a Cellar phone. It was untraceable. It had classified access to the government's version of the Internet. And it had more on it.

Burns shivered.

He opened his eyes, the pupils glowing gold, and analyzed the dam. That was peak *safe* capacity.

They were going to need more. And he had to figure out how to accomplish that.

He smiled as he saw that the answer was right in front of him.

He looked to the east. But first he needed to buy some time.

Because *they* were coming.

CHAPTER 8

The Nightstalkers could come in heavy or they could come in light. Heavy was like Stephen King's *The Dome*, coming down with a thud. Seal an area off, no one in and out, follow up with a good cover story (Oak Ridge being just to the north could provide a lot of possibilities), and then take care of business.

Moms decided on Nightstalker Lite to start, with heavy looming.

She made this decision for several reasons. First, the exact threat was unknown. They had Burns, or whatever Burns was, out there. But no Fireflies, as far as they knew. No Rift, although Burns did have the laptop from the Gateway Rift.

And, being honest with herself as she pulled up to Scout's house, there was the Scout factor. Coming in heavy was disruptive, to say the least. And what Moms had planned was going to be rough enough on the kid's family.

Moms parked the government car that had been waiting for her at Knoxville Airport, just five miles away. The airport was going to be their Tactical Operations Center, a hangar of the National Guard already having been commandeered, and that was where some of the heavy would be arriving.

It was late in the day, the sun hanging low in the west, just above the tree line. Lights were on in the windows of the house and Moms had noted the new construction in the housing development.

At least it wasn't a gated community like Senator's Club in North Carolina. That had been a pain in the ass. But this openness of the former farmland turned development didn't thrill her. Lots of fields of fire for the bad guys, if there were any bad guys out there who wanted to shoot at her. Scout's house was on a dead-end street, and Moms felt naked driving along the road, exposed to the entire area and the high ground across the river.

She was wearing a smart business suit for the moment, part of Nightstalker Lite. And something they'd included in their gear after having to improvise in Senators Club. She walked up to the door and pressed the small button. A chime sounded, loud enough she heard it through the door, some classical notes she couldn't place but was sure Eagle could. A bit much for a doorbell, she thought. Then again, living in shotgun shack, the sheriff damn near broke your door in just knocking on it. A doorbell was a luxury that was pretty low on the priority list where Moms grew up. And visitors usually wanted something, like the title to the land.

The door swung open and a man wearing a sweater stood there, reading glasses perched on his nose. "Yes? Can I help you?"

"Hello," Moms said, taking a step forward. Lite didn't have to mean slow.

"What—" the man began, but Moms slapped him on the side of the neck, short needle hidden between two fingers, and then caught him as he collapsed. She laid him out and then switched out the needle for a fresh one.

"Who is it, dear?" a woman's voice echoed from somewhere inside the house.

The acoustics were terrible and Moms wondered why three people needed such a big house. Of course, it was smaller than Scout's house in Senator's Club, which they'd commandeered for their base of operations.

Moms waited and then heard footsteps.

"Dear?" The voice was already tinged with fear and Moms wondered how such a woman gave birth to Scout. She already didn't like her from the little Scout had said about her. Moms immediately felt a rush of guilt for even thinking that and knew there were deeper—

A rail-thin woman came around one of the many corridors branching off the foyer and Moms strode forward.

"Who are—" the woman began; then she ducked as Moms slapped at her with the needle. Give her some points for speed.

Scout's mother darted right, racing down a hallway.

"Frak," Moms muttered as she took chase.

"Greer!" Scout's mother screamed. "Get out! There's a crazy woman here!"

Moms raced after the voice, noting out of the corner of her eye that the alarm had been triggered.

Which meant nothing since Ms. Jones already had this area isolated electronically.

Okay, Moms was beginning to get where parts of Scout came from as she turned another corner into the kitchen and Scout's mother swung a butcher knife at her. Moms sidestepped, avoiding being sliced open.

It was close. Too close.

Then Moms pivoted, sensing someone behind her. Scout was standing there, an ax in her hands, ready to strike; then recognition flooded her face. "Moms?"

Moms jumped back again as Scout's mother jabbed, almost gutting her. But this opened her up to a strike, and Moms slapped the needle on the back of her neck and caught her, lowering her gently to the tile floor.

She wasn't heavy.

"What the hell?" Scout demanded.

"Sorry," Moms said as she pulled out her phone. "We've got two for delivery and seclusion," she called in. She turned the phone off. "We didn't have time to be subtle. They'll be fine. We're just getting them out of the line of fire."

"Same thing you did to me at Senator's Club?"

"Yes."

"That wasn't nice."

"It was necessary."

"Right," Scout said. "You guys couldn't call? Just show up and knock my parents out?"

"Sorry," Moms said. "We just got the message."

"Took you long enough. But call next time. I can get out of the house and meet you. Whatever." She sighed and looked down at her mother. "She was due for a little rehab soon anyway. The move really stressed her out. Her last rehab trip was a while ago. And Dad needs a break. He's been working too hard. As usual. I guess you're doing them a favor."

Moms looked at the laptop on the kitchen counter. A boat was flickering on the display. She glanced at Scout.

"My dad wants a boat," Scout explained. "Actually, he's been wanting one for years, but now we have a dock, so he might actually get one, but I doubt it. I think not allowing himself one seems to make him feel better than having one would. At least that's what Doc would say, right?"

Moms stared at Scout, with her calm acceptance of the situation and her accurate evaluation of her father.

Scout looked past Moms. "Where's Nada? The rest of the team?"

"En route," Moms said. "Anyone else in the house?"

"No."

"Who is this Greer your mother was warning?"

"Me."

"Oh." Moms indicated a chair. "Tell me what's been going on."

Most people don't realize you can get from Knoxville to the Atlantic Ocean by boat. And those who do realize it think in traditional terms: the Tennessee River, traversing all the dam locks, to Paducah where it joins the Ohio River, to Cairo (Illinois, not Egypt), where the Ohio joins the Mississippi and then down to the Gulf of Mexico and onward.

But starting in 1972 and completed in 1984, the Tennessee-Tombigbee (Tenn-Tom) Waterway connects the Tennessee River to the Black Warrior-Tombigbee River system and then on to the Gulf of Mexico. It is still the largest earth-moving project in world history and few have ever heard of it, and fewer even focus on it, including federal law enforcement. This is just fine for a certain Mexican cartel, which began to use the waterway as a route to ship its various products into the center of the United States, avoiding the traditional drug corridors.

The Tenn-Tom is either a success (according to its supporters) or a failure (according to tonnage shipped, one-quarter of what had been estimated), but for the cartel, it was a blessing. Using a small fleet of luxury yachts, specially modified with hidden compartments, powerful engines to outrace ships at sea, and special armor plating secreted on board to battle off boarding on waterways (the cartel feared its competition more than the Feds), the cartel was enjoying two decades of safe travels, spreading its boats up the Tennessee, the Ohio, and the Mississippi along with its product.

The *Splendor* was a Bahamian-flagged fifty-six-foot yacht. Capable of carrying two tons of product and fourteen battle-hardened crewmembers. It had a helicopter on the rear deck underneath a tarp, a last-ditch escape device.

And zero women in bikinis.

It was the latter that was the oversight. *Splendor* had come up the Tenn-Tom, into the Tennessee River, up through the locks to Knoxville and off-loaded its cargo, all on schedule and according to plan. But now, giving in to the needs of the crew, the captain had the armored yacht anchored in a cove on the north side of the river while they took the two skiffs to a local marina, where they took limousines for a night on the town.

A successful mission deserved a reward.

There was one man left on board for guard duty.

Except as Nada would have told them, it ain't over until the fat lady sings, or in this case, the boat is back home.

———

The one thing Ms. Jones had over Hannah was the ability to bring in the thunder and lightning. The Cellar always operated on the down low. The Nightstalkers often tried that approach, aka Moms going to Scout's house, but when in doubt, they brought in the sledgehammer.

Elements of that hammer were now arriving in Knoxville

First in was an AC-130, which could be considered lightning. Based on the venerable C-130 Hercules airframe, the Spectre gunship was designed to rain hell down from the sky. Along the left side of the plane were a 40-mm Gatling gun, a 25-mm Gatling gun, and a 105-mm breech-loading howitzer. Crews boasted they could put a round in every square inch of a football field in five seconds. They'd backed up that boast on battlefields ranging from Vietnam to Grenada, Bosnia, Iraq, Afghanistan, and several other lesser-known conflicts.

It wasn't coincidence that the plane was the first to arrive. Spectre had been alerted earlier in the day out of Hurlburt Field in Florida by Ms. Jones as potential support for Neeley's mission. Just in case. The reality was that Ms. Jones had scrambled the plane and other resources on the chance that Neeley didn't succeed, which was likely, in her opinion.

She hadn't, but in doing so they'd lost track of Burns, so the plane had refueled in the air and then spent time circling around over middle Tennessee, awaiting orders.

A half hour later, as darkness had completely settled over Knoxville and the vicinity, more support came flying in.

First, four Apache helicopters, loaded with live munitions, out of Fort Knox.

Then a C-130 full of Rangers from Hunter Army Airfield outside of Savannah, Georgia, in case the team needed the elite infantry and to provide security at the FOB. And then, as they had done last year in North Carolina, on board a lumbering C-5 cargo plane was a pair of M777, 155-mm howitzers. Packed along with their crews were a couple of pallets of M982 Excalibur GPS-guided munitions. These were laser-guided rounds, allowing for pinpoint accuracy, especially useful when firing around civilian communities. With a range of twenty-five miles, the big guns covered a lot of ground from the airstrip, from the foothills of the Smokies to the south to north of Knoxville and a good stretch of the Tennessee River east and west. As soon as they were unloaded, they were emplaced in a low field behind the hangar, out of sight of the civilian terminal, and readied for fire missions. Rangers were patrolling the perimeter, and the road that ran around the back side of the airfield had been closed off due to a "water main break."

There was Nightstalker Lite and Nightstalker Heavy, and then there was the FPF: Final Protective Fire. It's a military term. For a firebase, this is where supporting artillery fire would be called in almost on top of the friendlies (and sometimes on top of them) in order to prevent it from being overrun. It was something that was only used as a last resort.

For the Nightstalkers, charged with saving humanity from an array of threats, their on-call FPF lumbered into the air from Minot Air Force Base in North Dakota. The venerable B-52 was carrying pods of AGM-129A cruise missiles on each wing, a total of twelve warheads. Ten of the warheads were conventional; two were nuclear.

Every time the Nightstalkers were alerted, a B-52 with this payload was scrambled.

They'd used the conventional cruise missiles in the past.

They had yet to use the nuclear warheads.

After the Pinnacle fiasco of the past year, the crews on this mission had been vetted by the Cellar. They would launch if Moms sent the correct order.

The B-52 rose up and turned to the southeast to go on station, drilling a hole in the sky over the vicinity of the Nightstalkers at a much higher altitude than the Spectre, waiting until needed or the mission was over and they could return home.

Most of the remaining Nightstalkers skipped the airfield and drive over entirely in the name of expediency.

Plus, they were just too damn cool to actually land with an airplane at an airfield. That was for civilians and the lesser Gods of Earth.

And Nada was racing toward the air-field in the backseat of the only F-22B Raptor ever produced. Every other Raptor in the inventory was an F-22A single-seater, coming in at $412 million per jet, which seemed a bit ludicrous to Nada, when some lunk-head pilot could put one into the side of a mountain with the wrong twitch of the controls. But the 22B had been designed as a two-seat training version, the line dropped after only one test model produced, during budget cuts. Nada shuddered to think what this one cost. The U.S. had probably sent men to the moon for less. The craft was stationed at Edwards Air Force, and Ms. Jones had requisitioned it to race into LAX, pick up Nada, and then roar east at over Mach 2.

Closer at hand to the problem, Roland, Kirk, Mac, and Eagle were already dirty and in full gear, so they simply got on the C-130 cargo plane Ms. Jones commandeered for them from Pope Air Force Base, which picked them at the airstrip at Mackall. They rigged in flight, also putting together several pods of gear—since they didn't have the boxes from the Snake—that they might possibly need. Mac, as always, went heavy on the explosives taken from the 18 Charlie (engineer) committee. Kirk made sure he had adequate commo for the entire team from the 18 Echo (communications) committee. Eagle pouted, because he didn't have his beloved Snake and he hated someone else flying him.

Back at Camp Mackall, Sergeant Twackhammer pouted because they were flying off with a lot of the gear he needed to train new Green Berets.

And Roland went with two full pods of assorted weapons appropriated from the 18 Bravo (weapons) committee, including flamethrowers, just in case they did run into Fireflies. As the 130 made its final approach turn for the drop zone, Roland did one last check of the pods to make sure the drogue chutes were rigged correctly, and then he manhandled all the pods into line, hooking their chutes to the static line that ran from the front of the cargo bay into the tail section.

The loadmaster waved his hands and shouted, "Three minutes!"

The rear of the C-130 opened, with the ramp leveling out and the top portion disappearing into the upper tail section. Lights from houses, cars, and streetlights were clearly visible to the rear, bouncing around as the plane twisted and turned.

Roland hooked up behind everyone else and the pods. The other three hooked up in front of the pods, closer to the edge of the ramp.

They were five hundred feet above ground level, and through their night vision goggles, they could see rolling, wooded terrain below. Passing by to the south was a large cluster of lights: Maryville and Alcoa, two adjoining towns south of Knoxville.

They flashed over a section of lake/river as the loadmaster signaled one minute.

It was going to be tight because they (Roland actually) had to push all the bundles and themselves out along a bend in the river. The pilot had promised to bank hard and follow the river as best as possible, but the banking itself could be a problem.

What they didn't want was Roland to land on someone's roof.

As jumpmaster, Mac knelt down and grabbed the hydraulic arm on the right side of the open ramp. He had a main parachute on his back but no reserve. They were jumping so low that if the main didn't deploy, there wasn't time for a reserve. He peered forward through his night vision goggles. He spotted the blinking infrared strobe ahead and to the right, around a bend in the river.

They were on target.

Mac stood and secured his night vision goggles in a waterproof case. He stared up into the tail, at the glowing red light. The moment it turned green he shouted, "Follow me" and stepped off the ramp.

The C-130 was slewing, following the curve in the Tennessee River around Keller Bend on the north side of the river. Eagle and Kirk followed Mac as quickly as they could move, falling off the ramp. Their static lines played out, pulling the deployment bags on their chutes out, and then the chutes themselves snapped open, all within five seconds.

Which was fortunate, because they had another eight seconds before hitting the water even with open chutes.

On the C-130, Roland shoved the bundles, sending them tumbling. He staggered and almost fell as the C-130 abruptly angled to the right as the pilots turned to follow the river around Jackson Bend on the south side of the river. One of the bundles, filled with weapons, got caught up under the hydraulic arm, and Roland was damned if he was going without his toys.

"Go! Go!" the crew chief was shouting, unusually excited for some reason.

Roland grabbed the bundle, pulled it loose, and tossed it out.

Then he was tossed out of the airplane himself as the pilots abruptly pulled back on their yokes, angling the nose of the plane almost straight up.

Roland found out the reason five seconds later as his chute finished deploying and he checked canopy, as per Protocol, and then looked down to get oriented and saw the high power lines directly below him. Lines that the aircraft had just barely cleared. He grabbed toggles and tried to turn, but it was too late.

He expertly passed between two high-tension lines and then his chute got caught in them. Roland came to an abrupt halt, dangling eighty feet above the river with high voltage racing across the lines above his head.

The only thing keeping him from being fried was that he hadn't completed the circuit with either the river or the ground.

That was about the only good news for him.

For the others, they had softer landings than a normal land jump, which was the good part of a water jump.

The bad part of a water jump was the water. Mac, Kirk, and Eagle splashed down, went under, then bobbed to the surface as their chutes came down on top of them, turning the dark night almost completely black.

They had a couple of minutes before the chutes became water-logged and sank—with them inside. So each one did as they'd been trained. Reached up, found a line, and followed it out to the edge of the chute and clear air. Then they unbuckled and pushed the parachute away, slipped on the fins tied off to their sides, and began, well, finning.

The F-22B Raptor touched down with a scorch of black rubber, expensive rubber, since the government bought "special tires" for the "special" plane, and given the price, they were probably leaving at least a few Gs worth of rubber, Nada estimated, on the Knoxville Airport tarmac. Nada was relieved the pilot actually came to a halt next to the Blackhawk helicopter. He'd been envisioning having to do a tuck and roll, jumping from a moving plane, as fast as they'd been flying across the country.

The blue bulb was still in his breast pocket.

Nada managed to climb out of the cockpit, have the blessed relief of the ground beneath his feet for fifteen seconds, and then he was on board the Blackhawk, opening up a kit bag full of the good stuff and trading in his civvies for battle gear as the helicopter took off.

Nothing but good times ahead.

He realized he was looking forward to seeing Scout as he switched the bulb from his civilian shirt into one of the many pouches on his MOLLE vest. It meant he was carrying two less thirty-round magazines but he was beginning to realize he had to live life on the edge in order to experience it more fully.

As if he hadn't been doing so for decades.

Just differently.

Burns had been driving along the river on the north side, getting as close to it as the roads allowed.

He was searching.

He was currently pulled over on the side of Tedford Road, underneath a set of high power lines. The road was just short of ending at Tooles Bend Road, which went under I-140, a spur of Interstate 40 that connected it with Maryville to the south. It was all quite confusing, but GPS helped a lot.

He turned off the engine and rolled the windows down. He leaned his head out and peered up at the power lines. They were a long way up.

But doable.

Then he heard an airplane engine, the roar familiar: C-130.

He nodded. Of course they were here. He had expected the Nightstalkers to be coming. Burns cocked his head to the side as he examined that thought as much he seemed capable of examining anything.

Had he?

Or had he been told they'd come?

He wasn't quite certain of anything, except the mission that had been imprinted on him. That he had to do. There was no choice.

The sound of the 130 faded into the distance and Burns considered the power lines because he needed those to deal with the Nightstalkers.

They'd do, but something was nagging at him, touching on the edge of his consciousness. Something was ahead. Just past the underpass. Something that was drawing him with more subtle urgency than the electricity overhead. More than the mission imprinted on him. He started the car and drove left onto Tooles Bend and through the underpass. The road was narrow and winding and took a sharp left up ahead, but Burns slammed on the brakes as he sensed the strange feeling off to the side.

Not sound. Not sight.

The echoes of the past. Of emotion. Of anguish.

Burns looked to the right. A dirt road ran off into the darkness through the trees. A pair of chain-link gates were padlocked together and a half-dozen NO TRESPASSING signs were hung on the gate and trees.

As if.

Burns turned the wheel and hit the gas. The car burst through the gates, leaving them hanging forlornly on their hinges. He drove along the dirt road.

He didn't need night vision goggles.

Burns tried to figure out what was drawing him. But as he went down the road, it got more powerful. He came out of the trees. An open field was to the left, sloping down to the Tennessee River. Burns peered in the direction as he stopped the car. The ruins of a large ominous-looking building lurked in the darkness. Smashed windows peered out like empty eye sockets, wide double doors in front yawning open, not inviting but threatening.

Do not enter here, for bad things await.

Burns kept his eyes on the ruins as he reached for Neeley's phone. He gripped it and accessed the Internet, trying to ascertain what this place had been.

It took a while, as if someone had been trying to hide the history of the locale, but eventually he uncovered it: This had been the fieldwork outbuilding of the Lakeshore Mental Asylum in Knoxville. Patients had been shuttled out here for "therapy" in the fields and on the river.

It was not therapy they'd received, Burns could sense.

The place was long since shuttered and closed. A minor mystery for investigators of the paranormal who claimed it was haunted by ghosts of patients drowned in the river and murdered in other nefarious ways.

It *was* haunted. Burns could feel the souls of those who'd passed through here. The torments of their twisted minds. He felt a kinship. He got out of the car and walked into the field. The dirt beneath his feet screamed their anguish.

Burns started twirling, slowly at first, then faster and faster. His long coat with the suppressed pistol in the pocket spread out from his side, becoming a cape. His hands went up into the air as if pleading.

Terrible things had been done here. Evil people, both captor and prisoner.

He tumbled to the ground, dizzy.

He lay there for a few moments staring up the sky, his eyes normal.

Then they regained their golden tint.

What had he been doing?

He sat up. Then got to his feet and walked over to the car and got in.

Burns sat for minutes, even with the throb of electricity running through those power lines not far away, a siren's call for his mission.

Finally, he started the car up and headed back for the power.

Moms and Scout snagged the supply pods first, racing up to each one on a Sea-Doo and using a hook to grab them and then using a tow rope to drag them behind.

Scout was better at it than Moms, who was learning how to operate a Sea-Doo for the first time. Scout snagged five of the seven pods and tied them off at the dock. By that time, Mac, Kirk, and Eagle were swimming upriver, in their direction.

Scout skidded up to Eagle with a spray, stopping just scant inches from him in the water. "Hey, Eagle!"

"Impressive driving," Eagle said as he grabbed and pulled himself on board. "Mac and Kirk are coming, but they're younger and can swim longer."

Scout laughed as she roared back to her dock, passing Moms, who'd recovered the last two pods and was heading for the other jumpers. She quickly found both Mac and Kirk.

"Where's Roland?" she asked as they both climbed on board behind her.

Kirk unsealed his night vision goggles and slid them on. "Oh frak." He pointed over Moms's shoulder upriver.

Roland's parachute was clearly visible draped over the power lines. His large body dangling below it was silhouetted against the stars.

"That's about as pretty a picture of Roland we're ever gonna get," Mac said.

"He knows not to complete the circuit?" Kirk asked as Moms gunned them toward the dock.

"I wouldn't bet on it," Mac said.

"He does," Moms said with complete confidence. *Fake it till he makes it*, she thought.

She pulled up to the dock a little too quickly, hitting the Sea-Doo against the rubber bumper.

"Where's Nada?" Scout asked.

"He's coming," Eagle said as Mac and Kirk scrambled up to the dock.

"I'm going for Roland," Moms said, roaring off before anyone could say anything else.

"I'm helping," Scout said, leaving the three alone on the dock. They watched the two Sea-Doos head upriver toward the electric jumper and then began to fish the pods out of the water and onto the dock.

█████████████

"If I'd wanted to swim, I'd have joined the Navy," Nada complained as the helicopter descended to five meters above the Tennessee River.

"We've got power lines around the bend," the pilot said. "So you need to cast in about thirty seconds."

"Yeah, yeah," Nada muttered as he looked between the two pilots, trying to get oriented. "What the hell?" he muttered as he spotted the chute tangled in the power lines and the body below. "Fraking Roland. He better not complete the circuit."

Burns parked underneath the power lines, just off of Tedford Road. Wires looped overhead and the forest had been clear-cut in both directions underneath the power lines. He reached back to the rear seat and retrieved the Gateway laptop.

He exited the government car and was going to head fifty meters to the nearest tower when he paused as something occurred to him. He went to the trunk and opened it. An assortment of automatic rifles, pistols, and grenades were nestled in their slots. Along with body armor and MOLLE gear. Typical Fed field setup.

Burns shrugged on the body armor. Then chose a .45-caliber pistol; an MK-17 CQC SCAR assault rifle, chambering the larger 7.62-mm rounds; a bag full of grenades; and a MOLLE vest into which he stuffed ammunition for the weapons.

He felt much better and grounded. Old habits died hard.

Familiarity bred contentment.

He shook his head in confusion.

Geared up, he headed toward the base of the closest tower.

"Roland!" Moms called out as the Sea-Doo came to a halt, bobbing on its own wake.

"Yo!" Roland answered, dangling in his harness eighty feet overhead.

"Don't drop your lowering line and complete the circuit," Moms said.

"Duh," Roland replied. "Mac asked you that, didn't he?" He was fiddling with something that Moms couldn't make out in the dark.

"What are you doing?"

"Getting out of here," Roland replied.

"It's too high," Moms said. She could hear a helicopter coming in behind them. "Maybe we can do something with the chopper."

"Like what?" Roland asked in a calm voice. He reached up and looped his thumbs through the cutaways for his main.

"Roland, don't!"

Roland pulled the loops and freefell toward the water. As he fell, he pulled his Gore-Tex wet weather jacket over his head, the arms tied into his gear in the back. It was a makeshift parachute that might have helped if Roland was a Ken doll being tossed from a building.

But he was two hundred forty pounds of Roland.

He hit with a solid thud less than ten feet from Moms and Scout. He promptly disappeared into the dark water.

"Roland!" Scout cried out in alarm.

Nada scooted his butt closer to the edge of the cargo bay and watched Roland fall. "Just great," he muttered. Then he shoved himself off, immediately linking his hands behind his neck and tucking his chin in as he'd been trained for a helicast. Feet and knees together, braced for the impact of hitting the water.

He fell from only ten feet and the water was hard when he slammed into the river.

Roland surfaced, sputtering and splashing about. Moms pulled up next to him and put a hand out. Roland grabbed it and almost jerked her off the Sea-Doo and into the river. Then he got hold of the seat and pulled himself aboard.

"Are you all right?" Moms asked.

"I think so," Roland said.

"Oh frak," Moms muttered as she headed for the dock, because a "think so" from Roland meant he was hurt. She turned to Scout. "Nada just jumped from that chopper. Could you—" She hadn't finished before Scout was racing away as the Blackhawk roared by, gaining altitude to clear the lines.

Ivar had his eyes closed, resting. He'd learned in the first month of Special Operations training to rest whenever there was an opportunity. This flight eastward out of Area 51 was one such opportunity.

They were on board a Snake, not *the* Snake, but the original prototype that didn't have the up-to-date electronics that its follow-on production design boasted. It also didn't have the chain gun mounted in the nose. Still, it flew, it could go vertical and horizontal, and it was available.

Ms. Jones was taking what she could get.

Doc and Ivar were in the cargo bay, surrounded by the various equipment cases scavenged off the Snake at the depot in Area 51. They were thirty minutes out from Knoxville.

Ivar stirred as the phone in his chest pocket vibrated. He pulled it out and stared at the screen: #&%!@

It might have been someone trying to express a profanity without directly saying it, but it wasn't. Ivar reached into his thigh pocket and covertly pulled out a twin to the black orb he'd dumped into the water at the Can and held it in the palm of his hand. He kept the phone in the other.

And waited.

━━━━━━━━━

Nada looked up at the Sea-Doo. "You've grown."

"Hey, Nada," Scout said. "Climb on board."

Nada clambered up behind Scout. "I've got a nephew," he said proudly. "Just born."

"Congratulations. Did they name him Nada, after his uncle?" Scout asked as she revved the engine and they headed for the dock.

"Nope. After his father. He's going to be a junior."

"Argh," Scout said. "Ever notice there's no Mary Junior or Nancy Junior? Junior's a guy thing, as if they live on if their kid has their name. Shoulda named him Nada."

"Wouldn't that be Nada Junior?"

"Nah." Scout expertly scooted alongside the dock, touching it without a bump. "You're his uncle, not his dad. Coulda called him Nada Two, the sequel."

Nada laughed as he climbed onto the dock. "One Nada is enough in the world."

"And it isn't even your real name after all," Scout said. She paused before driving the Sea-Doo onto the lift. "You ever going to tell me your real name?"

"Not tonight," Nada said. "You gonna tell me yours?"

"Not tonight." Scout drove over to the lift, positioned the Sea-Doo, and then hit the controls, pulling the machine up out of the water.

As she was doing that, Moms zoomed up, Roland behind her.

"Doc here yet?" Moms asked.

Nada did a quick count. "Nope. Why?"

"Roland's hurt," Moms said.

"I ain't hurt," Roland protested as he climbed off, his body stiff. "Just banged up a little."

"What the fuck?" Mac asked. "Why'd you cut loose?"

Roland shrugged, keeping the wince off his face. "We're on a mission."

"Sometimes," Mac said, "I think you've hit your quotient of dumb, then you do something more." But at the same time, he was checking Roland's ribs, probing.

Nada reached out and Kirk was ready with a comm link. Nada keyed the radio. "Doc? What's your ETA?"

"Twenty minutes to Knoxville Airport. We've got all the gear. And we're on board the prototype of the Snake. Eagle should be happy, although it's missing some bells and whistles, including the gun."

"Roger," Nada said. "We're going to check out the local area, but I'm sending Kirk and Eagle to the airfield to rendezvous with you. We're still not sure what exactly we're dealing with."

"What else is new?"

Part of what they were dealing with was sitting underneath the metal skeleton holding up the power lines. Burns had attached a lead from the USB port to the leg of the tower. His fingers were flying over the keyboard, replaying what he'd picked up from Eden's mind.

There was a crackle of gold running out of the computer, through the wire, up the leg, and into the power line.

Burns nodded, then pulled out his phone and sent his second message.

Ivar didn't even bother to check the message. He just felt the phone vibrate in one hand and with the other he pressed the black orb.

"We've got Rift forming!"

One of the operators of the Can jumped to her feet as the clicking alert sounded and flashing lights made her words redundant.

The other operator turned to his comm station. As he lifted the phone to call Ms. Jones, an electromagnetic pulse rippled out of the orb deep inside the Can.

Everything inside the room went black.

Burns stood up as power came down out of the tower and into the laptop, and then to the small golden dot that was forming six feet beyond it and eight feet above the ground.

It would take time.

But he had time now.

It took the team some minutes to drag the pods up to the house and put them in the spacious four-car garage. They'd moved outside the SUV and Mercedes and four-wheel ATV that had occupied it.

"How many cars do you guys have?" Mac asked as he lugged in the last pod.

"Just the two," Scout said.

"It's like the wristwatches in North Carolina," Eagle said, wanting to stop this one before it got out of hand. "You can have only two wrists, but lots of watches."

"What's the ATV for?" Mac asked.

"Taking the trash can up to the road," Scout said.

"It's that far?" Mac wanted to know.

"Dad has a bad back," Scout said.

"Couldn't you have done it?" Mac pressed.

Scout glared at him. "Dad wouldn't let me. He likes his ATV."

Nada turned to Scout. "How do you get to the airport from here? Doc and Ivar are there with the rest of our gear. And Eagle needs to pick up the Snake."

"I can drive there," Scout said.

"You're too young," Nada said.

"I've got my driver's permit." Scout reached in her pocket and pulled out her wallet. She carefully extracted said document and proudly displayed it.

All the Nightstalkers stopped for a moment and stared at her, realizing she'd grown and changed a bit in the year since they saw her last.

"Your hair is nice," Kirk said, having a younger sister and a bit of a clue. "I like the new color."

"Thank you." Scout beamed.

"What was the old color?" Mac muttered, and Nada nudged him with an elbow hard enough to send him sprawling to the floor.

"Who's Ivar?" Scout asked. "I don't remember an Ivar."

"Mac, you go with Scout," Nada said. "Eagle, you go, too, and figure out the new old Snake. Shouldn't take long—you trained on it. Mac, hook up with Doc and Ivar, leave the boxes on the Snake, and bring the other gear in SUVs we can park in here. Let's play this like we did in North Carolina."

"Except Scout can drive," Moms said.

"Oh goodie!" Scout exclaimed, grabbing a set of car keys off the rack near the door to the house. "Do I get paid?"

The two lab rats down in the Can were just that. They'd found a flashlight and were groping their way toward the elevator, praying power for it wasn't shut down.

They reached the steel doors for the elevator. There was no light behind the buttons, which wasn't an encouraging sign.

The woman pressed the button.

Nothing.

At the Ranch, Ms. Jones listened to the reports that came in from Russia and Japan. Their Kamiokandes had picked up a Rift forming, but her own Can was silent. She turned to Pitr, who was seated at a desk next to her bed, bringing up the data being forwarded from the other two Cans.

"What is wrong at Area 51?"

"Power outage in the Can," Pitr said. "Support is working to restore it."

"At exactly the moment when a Rift starts to form." It was not a question. But Ms. Jones followed the statement with one. "Where is the intersection from Japan and Russia?"

"Eastern Tennessee."

"But we can't pinpoint it," Ms. Jones murmured. "We have a traitor. The question is whether it's Mr. Doc or Mr. Ivar."

"Ivar," Pitr said without hesitation.

"Perhaps," Ms. Jones said. "Perhaps. We must not overlook the obvious. Have the personnel on duty detained and send Mr. Frasier to interview them."

"I will."

"When will power be restored?"

Pitr looked at his screen. "Twenty-five to thirty minutes."

"Just about the time the Rift will open. Alert the Nightstalkers."

CHAPTER 9

Neeley slid off the examining table and put her clothes back on. Her chest ached, but she was functional. All systems normal. She was a go as far as the Cellar's physician was concerned. She had a feeling the bar wasn't too high; breathing seemed to be the standard.

The doctor had left her the usual assortment of pills, carefully sorted into different colored compartments in the compact case she was supposed to slip into her pocket. There was nothing subtle about it: red if she needed a jolt. Blue if she needed to come down off the red without crashing. Green for crashing when she was safe so she could rest and be ready for the next mission that needed a red.

She tried to remember the last time she'd had a green.

She didn't like using the red because it put a ticking clock on the mission, but she also accepted most of her missions had a ticking clock to start with. Once in a while she had to go red in order to beat it.

Neeley knew who was next: the Cellar's psychologist, Dr. Golden, and that interview was going to be a different story. Just breathing wasn't going to clear that hurdle. Neeley slid the double-edged commando knife into her boot. It had been Gant's and years of sharpening had shrunk the blade. Neeley knew the time was coming when she would have to replace it. But it was a connection, one she needed. She was good enough with it that snapping the blade on bone with an awkward thrust or slice hadn't yet been an issue. She always went for the soft tissue over vital spots.

She looped the belt, with the steel wire garrote hidden on the inside, around her waist. She attached the holster to the belt and then drew her pistol, making sure there was a round in the chamber and the safety was off.

"My finger is my safety," she whispered to herself as she looked in the full-length mirror on the back of the door. The woman looking back was pretty ragged.

"You look like shit," she said to herself, and then frowned. Talking to herself twice in a row.

She sensed someone sliding through the door behind her. Out of the corner of her eye she could see Dr. Golden reflected in the mirror. "What do you make of people who speak to themselves, Doctor?" Neeley asked.

"It's not quite as bad when you talk to yourself in the mirror," Golden said. "Those people in the airport with the Bluetooth, who look like they're talking to no one until you see the little device, they freak me out sometimes."

Neeley turned to face her. "I call those people assholes. I don't want to hear their end of the conversation. Sometimes I just want to start an imaginary conversation just as loud and see how they react."

"You seem the same," Golden said.

"Shouldn't I be?"

"How did it feel to die?"

"Cutting to the chase, aren't we?" Neeley didn't wait for an answer. "Did I see a long white corridor? Did I go to the light? It went black. Total black. Nothingness. Then I was back. Sorry to ruin your expectations."

"Why do you think I have expectations of life after death?" Golden asked.

"You seem the type," Neeley said.

"What type is that?"

"Always asking questions," Neeley said with a grin, and Golden smiled.

"Those white corridors or going toward the light," Golden said, "are more likely the random firing of brain cells as they either are deprived of, or overloaded with, power. Our brains work on electricity. So they're most likely a hallucination."

Neeley stared at the psychiatrist, wondering how she could have known about Burns turning into Gant and then realizing she didn't. It was just a coincidence. But Neeley didn't really believe in coincidences.

Golden opened the door and gestured. "We'll meet in the interview room. I'll be down there in a little bit." She disappeared, shutting the door behind her.

Neeley stood still for a moment, taking deep breaths. Had she really seen Gant? Had Burns's eyes actually turned gold? Was she losing her mind?

"Fuck it." Neeley opened the door and stepped out into the dimly lit corridor that was part of the Cellar complex.

━━━━━━

Nada spotted the convoy coming into the community. Scout was in the lead in her father's SUV, followed by four big black SUVs behind her.

This wasn't going to be easy to explain to the neighbors, but that was the least of Nada's worries at the moment. They had the garage doors open and all four black SUVs rolled in as Scout parked outside. One of the SUVs was driven by a Support person, and after unloading the gear in the back, they carefully buckled Scout's unconscious mother and father inside for the trip back to the field.

And their sorely needed rest, according to Scout.

Nada hit the close buttons for the garage as car doors opened and the Nightstalkers were finally intact as a team, except for Eagle.

"Scout," Nada said, making the one introduction, "this is Ivar. Ivar, Scout."

"Pleased to meet you," Ivar said.

"The same," Scout replied.

"Doc, check Roland out," Moms said. "He decided to do a high dive from some high power lines."

"Roland," Doc said in a tone that indicated his displeasure.

"I'm fine," Roland insisted.

"He grimaced," Scout said. "I never saw him grimace before."

"You never saw him hurt before," Moms said. "I have."

"I'm fine," Roland repeated. He lifted up an M240 machine gun with one hand over his head and twirled it. "See? Fine."

"Let me check anyway," Doc said.

"He's got a couple of busted ribs," Mac said. "Not that anyone respects my medical expertise."

Roland sighed and allowed Doc to take a look.

"My mom would not be happy about this at all," Scout said happily, taking in the piles of weapons, demolitions, and assorted gear scattered about. "Lucky you knocked her out."

"It was mission essential," Moms began. "We—"

"It's okay," Scout said. "Really. I can assure you she's had worse nights."

Nada stood on a plastic case full of something deadly. "All right. We're—"

And then their phones all started ringing: "Lawyers, Guns, and Money."

"What the frak?" Kirk said.

"We're getting Zevoned on a Zevon?" Mac wondered out loud.

"Huh?" Roland said.

"This is curious," Kirk said as he silenced his phone.

One by one the phones went quiet and the team turned to Moms. Scout was literally bouncing up and down. "Fireflies? Killer heavy equipment? Possessed pool?"

Nada held up a hand. "Technically, the first Zevon was actually 'I'll Sleep When I'm Dead,' not 'Lawyers.' Didn't you get it?"

"Someone had our phones," Eagle said.

"The Loop?" Mac said. He turned to Scout. "From you?"

"I have no clue what you're talking about," Scout said. "Do I get a gun?"

"Yes, from Scout," Nada said. "No on the gun."

Moms had her finger pressed against her ear, getting an update from Ms. Jones. Even Scout fell silent as they watched her. She nodded and then pulled her finger away. "There's a Rift forming near here, so the 'Sleep' was a good call."

"Coordinates?" Nada asked.

Moms shook her head. "Ms. Jones says the Japanese and the Russians have got it located somewhere in the Knoxville area. Our Can is without power. Going to take them a little while to get it running and get us exact coordinates."

Doc paused, in the midst of wrapping Roland's ribs. "Our Can is down? That is most unusual. And very suspicious timing."

Moms held up her hand, indicating silence, and spoke into her radio. "Eagle, bring the Snake in. We'll load up and recon the area and be ready to shut the Rift as soon as we get a fix."

"Inbound," Eagle said. "ETA ten mikes."

Moms gave a hand signal to Kirk to change freqs to the Ranch. "Ms. Jones, we'll be airborne in ten minutes and monitoring for location. Did you hear back from Cleaner regarding the toothbrush?"

"He did not replace it," Ms. Jones said. "He did scan everything and found nothing unusual."

"Roger. He made a mistake or missed something." Moms turned to the team. "Gear up."

As they proceeded to do just that, Mac, as he was wont to do, asked a question. "If a Rift is just forming now, why were we alerted via the Loop earlier?"

Moms quickly explained the golden glow coming out of Scout's toothbrush, the power outages, and the golden glow in the water.

"So something was still in that toothbrush even after we got the Firefly," Mac said, and it wasn't a question.

"Duh," Roland said, and everyone on the team turned to look at him. Apparently pain had sharpened his wits a bit. Doc had wrapped his ribs tightly, about all that could be done for the three broken ones. He warned Roland not to laugh too much, which didn't appear like it was going to be a major problem.

Doc spoke up. "The question is, if this glow wasn't a Firefly, what was it? So far it's apparently caused no harm other than shorting out the power for short periods of time."

"It hurt my mouth," Scout said.

"If it came through in North Carolina," Doc said, "it's been dormant a long time. Waiting."

"That's not good," Roland said.

"How do we track this thing down?" Mac asked.

"It's in the water," Scout said. "And the water flows that way." She pointed to the left.

"Out of the mouth of babes," Mac muttered.

"Hey!" Scout was offended. "I'm not no baby."

Moms interceded. "But if it doesn't come to land like you say it did at the power line or affect something like the boat, we need a way to locate it. Whatever it is."

"It's power," Ivar said, a split second before Doc said something, apparently the same thing, because he gave Ivar the fish eye. Ivar continued. "So we try to figure out what kind of power, most likely electrical, and we rig a device to track it."

"Get to work on it," Moms ordered Ivar. "You stay here while we take care of this Rift."

Doc looked like he was going to protest and then just shook his head.

They could hear the Snake coming in, landing in the paved circle out front in the cul-de-sac.

"My neighbors aren't going to be happy," Scout said.

"I think we crossed the threshold on that when Roland landed in the power lines," Eagle said. "His chute is still up there. Support will get it eventually."

"Let's move out," Moms ordered.

As they moved out of the house, Nada sidled up next to Moms. "What's with Ivar? Leaving him behind."

"We've got a problem," Moms said. "Someone shut down the Can. Doc and Ivar were just down there before the alert. I put my money on Ivar being the problem."

"I'll keep an eye on Doc, then," Nada said.

The golden glow was now about three feet in diameter.

Burns checked his watch. He stood up. He could hear the muted sound of jet engines echoing across the river. Sound carried really well here, reflecting off the water, and with little to obstruct it. He recognized the sound of the Snake, which was interesting since he'd seen it crash back near St. Louis.

Ms. Jones was nothing if not persistent.

That could be an asset in most situations. But not all.

Scout followed the team up the ramp into the cargo bay, unnoticed among the loading of gear and mission prep. Everyone was checking off their part of the mission Protocol on their team handbooks, slightly out of sync since they were used to loading the Snake in the Barn back at the Ranch.

But not completely. "Oh, no, no, no," Moms said, taking Scout's elbow and leading her back down the ramp. Dust and dirt and mowed grass were swirling about, kicked up by the Snake's engines. The sound was a high-pitched whine and a dog was howling somewhere down the street. Lights were on in several houses and Ms. Jones would have to get Support to work hard to keep video of this off the Internet while spreading a good cover story. A bunch of supposed FEMA personnel were on their way with some cover story.

"You're going to leave me alone with that Ivar guy?" Scout asked. "He's a little bit freaky. *Big Bang* Sheldon, sort of, but not so funny."

"This is a combat mission," Moms said.

"Let's go!" Nada shouted from the cargo bay.

"Please?" Scout begged. "I'll stay on the plane."

"The last plane crashed," Moms said.

"Then I'll stick with Nada."

Who was suddenly standing next to the two of them. "Sorry, Scout."

"I've—" Scout began, but Moms held a hand up, silencing her.

Moms's and Nada's headset crackled with Ms. Jones's voice. "I believe the young lady has earned a place on the team. What is being played out here came through her. Regardless of how we feel about it, she has a role in this."

"This is going to be dangerous," Nada said, knowing his words had no power.

"The stakes are high," Ms. Jones said.

"Roger," Nada said. He pointed toward the cargo bay. "Come on. Rules were made to be broken."

They ran back on board the Snake and it lifted up into the night sky.

Burns knew exactly how they'd come in to try to seal this Rift.

Protocol. The hobgoblin of little minds. Burns began to giggle as the phrase passed through his own mind.

He looked up at the golden sphere, flickering in the air. It was five feet in diameter now. His face was bathed in the glow. He could almost see through. To the other side.

That was the whole point. The other side.

Burns giggled once more.

Then he clapped his hand over his mouth. This was no laughing matter, but he couldn't stop giggling.

Nada grabbed Moms's elbow and leaned close so he could talk to her off the team net. "We do it different."

"Do what different?" Moms was staring at the screen of her iPad, scanning the Google Earth map of the area around them.

"The way we hit the Rift and the Fireflies," Nada said. "If Burns is opening this thing, he knows our Protocols. He'll be waiting. Plus, we're going to be late. Odds are the Fireflies, however many there are, will already be through."

"What do you want to change?"

"No HALO or HAHO parachute jump onto the target. He'll be waiting for that. We come in fast and hard. Everyone fast ropes right onto the target."

"And if it's a trap?" Moms asked.

"Of course it's an ambush," Nada said. "And you know the only way to break an ambush is—"

Moms finished for him: "Assault directly into the ambush with everything you've got." She nodded. "All right. Brief the team."

She switched frequencies, going on the TACNET back to the FOB, getting their Heavy ready.

The lights flickered and then came back on. The two screen watchers ran back through the tunnel to their stations. Computers were rebooting, agonizingly slow.

Then the clicking alarm came back on, along with the strobe light.

"Yeah, yeah," the woman muttered. "We know." She slapped a palm down on the button that cut off the alarm as she adjusted controls with her other hand, zeroing in on the Rift that was forming.

"Got it!" she cried out as she forwarded the data.

████

Eagle had the Snake high, at five thousand feet, circling over Knoxville. They knew Burns was close—how close was the question.

Doc knelt in front of Moms, holding out his iPad. He tapped the screen. "Here. See this?"

"Power lines," Moms said. "The ones Roland jumped into. And? You think Burns is using them?"

Doc shrugged. "He might be. But this whole area is built on power. The TVA." He pointed to the deck of the Snake. "The river is dammed in multiple places, all of which generate power. There's also three nuclear power plants that are run by the TVA along the river."

Nada had leaned over to listen in. "Not another fucking Chernobyl. Ms. Jones would shit."

"How close is the nearest nuke plant?" Moms asked.

"Watts Bar," Doc said. "About sixty miles downriver. And they're getting ready to put their second unit online. The first reactor to be started up in the U.S. in over twenty years. I don't think that's a coincidence. Plus they ship tritium to the Savannah River Site."

"But Burns is around here as far as we know," Nada said. "And—" He paused as Moms cocked her head to the side, indicating a message from Ms. Jones.

"We've got a target," Moms announced. "Lock and load. Eagle, take us in."

The Fireflies flashed through, darting about almost joyfully.

As if they knew what joy was, Burns mused as he watched them go by, lighting up the darkness. Despite the fact that he was no longer a Nightstalker, his training held and he counted them as they came out.

Fourteen.

They went off in different directions on their various missions of mayhem.

"Too late, Nada," Burns whispered. Then he brought the automatic rifle up and scanned the sky overhead for the parachute he was sure would soon appear.

Most likely Roland.

Which meant it would be a big target.

Roland had always been a pain in the ass, Burns thought as he flipped off the safety.

Eagle flew along the river, one hundred feet above the dark water. The plan was to use the river to reach the power lines and then loop underneath them, avoiding the towers and coming in right on top of the Rift and fast roping down. It would require some fancy flying on Eagle's part, but that's why he had the big brain.

Literally.

"Thirty seconds from the lines," Eagle announced. "Opening ramp."

The team was locked and loaded. Scout was all the way forward in the cargo bay, under dire and strict orders from Nada to remain exactly where she was. He'd buckled a harness around her and snapped the leash into a deck bolt, ignoring the dirty look she gave him.

It was just in case.

And to keep her from following the team out.

The back ramp opened wide and the roar of the engines and the air swirling about added to the decibels.

Roland had the M240 in one hand, loaded and ready. He had a flamethrower on his back, the barrel of the weapon resting in an asbestos sheath strapped to one thigh.

Mac had the M203 grenade launcher, a 40-mm grenade ready in the lower barrel.

Moms and Nada had MK-17 CQC SCAR automatic rifles, reluctantly having traded in their venerable 9-mm MP5s over the past year in favor of the heavier cartridge and greater range. They were old dogs but willing to learn new assault rifles when the advantages were obvious.

Doc had his medical kit in one hand and his laptop in the other. This was Protocol when they were approaching a Rift, because it was his job to shut the thing while the rest of the team took care of the Fireflies.

Moms glanced down at her iPad, checking on the status of their support units. She had a lot of firepower on hand and ready.

Nada glanced over his shoulder and gave Scout an encouraging grin, lost in the blackout red lights of the cargo bay. Then he focused at the yawning mouth of the ramp, ready to charge off into whatever new hell awaited them.

What wasn't lost was the fourteen-foot-long wooden pole that abruptly ripped through the floor of the Snake, passing inches in front of Scout and lodging into the roof.

"Fuck!" Eagle shouted over the net as the aircraft rocked sideways and lost altitude, diving toward the river.

It was a sign that he was more than a tad agitated that he used a profanity.

Eagle was flying on instinct, having no idea what had caused the problem, not being able to look over his shoulder into the cargo bay. He just knew they'd been hit by something and he had to keep them airborne.

He slammed throttles forward, drawing every ounce of power he could from the engines, while he fought the dive with both flaps and rotation.

The Snake settled out to a hover less than three feet from the water, stuttering, engines straining.

"What happened?" Eagle demanded as he kept them level.

"We got hit by a telephone pole," Nada said as he got to his feet and observed the cargo bay, his heart racing until he saw that Scout was all right.

"A what?" Eagle asked.

"We got a fraking pole through the cargo bay," Mac clarified unhelpfully. The team was sorting itself out after everyone had become a pile of people, weapons, and gear on one side of the bay. Scout had been dangling in her harness, just above all of them, and she had settled back down on the upright deck with a thump.

"Where—" Eagle began to ask, but then another pole flashed by the cockpit, glanced off the armored side of the Snake with a clang, and disappeared into the darkness. Through his night vision goggles, Eagle could see the barge tied off beneath the cliff ahead. The crane was lifting another pole into place in the pile driver, which was oriented toward them.

"We got Fireflies already through," Eagle announced. "Pile driver on the river has one in it."

"Head for the Rift," Moms ordered. She switched frequency. "Spooky, I've got a target for you."

The gunner was chewing gum, reading her Kindle when the call for fire came in. She lifted her gaze from the latest Bella Andre romance novel and scanned the display. "I've got a barge. No heat signatures."

"That's it," Moms's voice echoed in her ear.

The gunner didn't question the order, the lack of personnel on the target, or the mission. While the Spectre gunship was part of the Air Force Special Operations Wing and had conducted more than its share of hush-hush missions, she'd been able to tell from the attitude of the pilot and copilot just before takeoff that whatever they were doing here over Tennessee was so far in the dark they didn't even dare to start a rumor.

Theirs was but to shoot and scoot.

"Acquired. Request final authorization."

"Authorized," Moms said.

A line of 25-mm bullets shot out of the spinning barrels of the Gatling gun poking out of the side of the aircraft, firing so quickly that the slugs appeared to be a solid line of red even though only every fourth round was a tracer. The 40-mm cannon chugged out rounds, not quite as quickly. And the 105-mm howitzer fired as fast as the crewmen could load it.

━━━━━━━━

As the Snake cleared the shoreline underneath the power line, those in the cargo bay could see the gunship firing downward.

"Minds on the mission," Moms snapped, trying to ignore the pole through the cargo bay and wrapping her arms around the fast rope.

"Ten seconds," Eagle warned.

"Roland, guard Doc once we hit the ground," Moms ordered.

Nada leaned close to Roland and whispered something in his ear, and Roland nodded.

━━━━━━━━

The barge never got a third pole off.

The incoming fire from Spectre chewed it up, ripping the wood decking apart, punching holes in the metal hull. As pieces flew in all different directions, a small golden sparkle lifted out of the sinking hulk and dissipated.

One Firefly down.

The gunner flipped the off switch, and the guns lined up behind her along the left side of the plane stopped firing. The barge slowly settled underneath the dark water of the Tennessee River. The gunner glanced up at the metal plating between two of her screens. As World War II fighter pilots had chalked up kills on the side of their plane, there were little images of various targets taken out by the gunship over the years: technicals (armed pickup trucks), roadside bombers, buildings where terrorists were meeting, and so forth.

She'd have to get the image of a barge.

Burns swung the rifle down as the Snake came roaring in. He fired a sustained burst at the cockpit.

Futile, because the cockpit was armored and he knew that, but Burns let loose more out of irritation that Nada was breaking Protocol and he was missing the chance to shoot Roland.

The Snake came to a hover and thick ropes came tumbling down. Burns aimed at them, but then he was blinded as the halogen searchlight in the nose of the Snake came on.

He fired anyway under the theory that sometimes the big sky little bullet theory worked in favor of the bullet.

Moms was first to touch boots to the ground, Nada a split second behind her. They both let go of the fast rope and began firing toward the Rift as they moved forward, "breaking" the ambush. All they could see was the Rift, its light overloading their night vision goggles. And tracers flashing by from someone firing at them.

Mac and Roland touched down next, followed by Doc.

That's when six deer came charging in from the side. One buck hit Moms, sending her tumbling. Nada avoided getting tagged and fired a burst into the side of the doe that went by him, slowing it slightly.

"Deer!" Nada yelled over the net.

"No shit," Mac said as he fired a 40-mm grenade at a Firefly-possessed deer charging at him. Fortuitously, and unfortunately as it turned out, Roland had modified the grenades so that they armed upon leaving the barrel, rather than the normal safe distance of around fifteen meters. The round hit the deer in the chest about four meters from Mac and exploded on contact.

Pieces of venison flew everywhere and Mac was blown backward by the blast.

Roland was standing in front of Doc, unable to fire in the confusion and the blackout of his night vision goggles.

BOB MAYER

████████████

A cluster fuck.

Burns knew when it was time to make an exit. He tossed a couple of flash-bangs to add to the confusion, averting his eyes and cupping his hands over his ears as they went off. Then he ran to the trees and cut to the right, heading for the car.

████████████

The flash-bangs didn't help the situation for the Nightstalkers.

Moms and Nada were back-to-back, having ripped off their night vision goggles. But the grenades wiped out what little vision they had left with their bright flash, and the thunderous explosion stunned them. Mac was on his back, half conscious.

Doc had been protected somewhat by Roland's bulk. He grabbed Roland's shoulder. "Come on!"

He led Roland forward toward the Rift, but Roland paused, switching out the machine gun for the flamer, and torched the remains of the deer that Mac had blasted. A golden sparkle rose up and dissipated.

Two Fireflies down.

"You okay?" Roland yelled to Mac.

Mac lifted a hand and gave an unenthusiastic thumbs-up.

Roland moved forward to stick with Doc, who was setting up his laptop short of the Rift, next to the laptop Burns had left behind.

"Eagle, what do you have?" Moms asked over the net.

204

"Someone is escaping through the forest to your south. Got lots of heat signatures. Yours, deer, others. It's a mess."

"Doc?" Moms asked, trying to get some vision back.

"The Fireflies are through," Doc said. "I'm going to shut the Rift."

"Spooky, do you have a human moving in the forest to our south?"

On board Spectre, the gunner trained her infrared and thermal sights on Moms's location. "Roger. I've got your team and one more, south of your location, moving toward the road. Also what looks like some deer."

Burns paused and looked up. Of course, with the thick trees all around him, he couldn't see anything, but he felt the electronic fingers from above, coursing over his body, like an enemy's caress, seeking him, finding him, fixing him.

Burns closed his eyes and stood still for a moment. His entire body took on a golden sheen. Then he continued on his way.

"Target gone," the gunner announced. "It just disappeared."

"Fire up the deer," Moms said. "Can you take them out without hitting us?"

"Danger close," the gunner said, "but roger. Smoking the deer."

The young woman leaned forward, hand light on the joystick, and began the delicate surgery of blasting the deer scattered among the team members, selectively using incredibly short bursts of 25 mm, a couple chugs of 40 mm, and an occasional 105-mm shell when there was a sufficient safety margin.

It took her twenty-two seconds to blast the remaining five deer.

When she was done, she was sure she could find a deer image pretty easily online. But whether to put them up was the question. Bambi? Really?

Moms had some vision back. She could make out Doc by the Rift and the laptop that had opened it. Roland was flaming what remained of the deer Spectre had blown to bits, destroying the Fireflies.

A small success in a lost battle.

"Keep a count on Fireflies you've gotten, Roland."

"Always."

She went to the Support net. "All elements, back off, back off. Return to FOB."

The last thing she wanted was for a Firefly to get into Spooky or one of the Apaches or any of the firepower she had on hand. She headed toward Doc to make sure he was doing what he was supposed to be doing.

The Rift snapped out of existence as Doc shut it.

But it was too late.

Burns was loose; the rest of the Fireflies were free.

How many, they had no idea.

Moms switched frequencies once more. "Ms. Jones, we've lost containment."

CHAPTER 10

Neeley walked in the door to the interrogation room, which doubled as Dr. Golden's "counseling" room in the Cellar, expecting to see the good doctor sitting on the other side of the table.

Instead, she was surprised to see Hannah waiting, two cups of coffee on the desk. Hannah stood as Neeley came in, offering one cup across the table.

"No hug?" Neeley asked as she reached out and accepted the coffee.

Hannah grinned. "We're not the hugging type." She sat down and Neeley followed suit.

"We're not, aren't we? Or should that be 'are we'?" Neeley shrugged. "Grammar was never my strength."

"You have plenty of other skills to make up for it," Hannah said.

"Practical ones," Neeley said. "In a certain world."

"You had me worried," Hannah said.

"By dying?"

"Among other things."

"Where's Dr. Golden?" Neeley nodded toward the window. "Observing?"

"Yes."

Neeley sighed. "Charting my childhood trauma?"

Hannah laughed. "We all lived it." She put down her coffee and leaned forward, palms flat on the table. "Are you done? Do you want to stop?"

It was Neeley's turn to laugh. "Blunt, aren't we? I never should have started. Gant wouldn't have wanted me to. But I didn't have much choice, did I?"

"Neither of us did. Nero saw to that."

"Nero's dead," Neeley said. "Is his hand reaching out from the grave?"

"It always has been."

"I didn't think one got to retire from the Cellar," Neeley said.

"Retire from field work at least," Hannah said.

"Do you remember when we were in France?" Neeley asked.

Hannah arched an eyebrow at the abrupt shift in topic. "Of course."

"You told me about your parents."

The eyebrow dropped and Hannah couldn't help but shift her eyes ever so briefly toward the mirror. "I did."

"Do you still believe betrayal is the only love?"

"So you do remember," Hannah said. "But don't misquote me. I said *sometimes* betrayal is the only love left, not the only love."

"I don't understand it," Neeley said. "I thought I did back then. But it makes no sense now."

Hannah sighed. "I should have been more clear. Sometimes betrayal is the only thing some people are capable of. Your young lover who gave you that bomb. My husband keeping his secrets. My mother. By keeping us ignorant of the terrible things they were doing, perhaps they were showing us all they knew of love."

"Bullshit," Neeley said. "They were self-centered assholes using us for their own goals."

"Is that what I am?"

"If you betray me, it is."

A long silence played out in the room, the two women staring at each other.

Hannah broke the silence. "I will not betray you, Neeley."

Neeley nodded. "I didn't think so, but I wanted it on the table."

Hannah got up and walked around the table. Neeley stood also. Awkwardly, Hannah put her arms around her taller operative.

"I love you," she whispered in a voice that couldn't be picked up by the microphones hidden all about the room.

Neeley's mouth opened, as if to say something, but no words came. The two stood like that for a moment, Neeley's arm limp at her side.

Hannah let go and went back to her seat. She sat down and composed herself.

Neeley sat down and picked up her coffee. "Something strange happened in Tennessee."

"Go ahead."

"Burns's eyes changed color," Neeley said.

"I thought you came up behind him," Hannah said. "How did you see his eyes?"

"I violated Protocol," Neeley said.

"That's why we're having this discussion," Hannah said.

Neeley waved off the misdirection. "They turned golden. And . . ." She paused.

"Go ahead."

"His face changed."

Hannah waited.

"I knew about the scars from the mission briefing," Neeley said. "But his face smoothed out and then it became Gant's."

Hannah tapped a finger on the table for a moment, a sign of extreme agitation. "How could that be?"

"I don't know."

"We don't know what Burns is," Hannah said. "So let's assume he's capable of changing his appearance."

"I don't think it's just appearance," Neeley said.

"What do you mean?"

"I think there's Burns and there is something controlling Burns. And they're not the same."

Hannah considered that. "All right. How would he know about Gant?"

"From me. I felt a slight shock when I put the suppressor up against the back his head."

"Another violation of Protocol," Hannah noted, but almost as an afterthought. Both women were off their game, something unprecedented.

The door to the room swung open and Dr. Golden walked in. She nodded at Neeley but went to Hannah's side of the table and slid a piece of paper in front of her. Hannah read it and a frown creased her face.

"Burns opened a Rift," Hannah said. "The Nightstalkers shut it but have lost containment on an unknown number of Fireflies and Burns."

"A cluster fuck," Neeley summarized. She stood. "I'll go and deal with Burns. Sounds like the Nightstalkers will have their hands full tracking down the Fireflies."

Golden finally spoke. "I haven't cleared you for duty."

"You can come with me," Neeley said. "Evaluate me en route and on the job."

Hannah glanced between Golden and Neeley and then nodded at the latter. "Go. We'll finish this later."

Moms had the air force airdrop two F470 Zodiacs into the river. They were layered with Armorflate, an inflatable bulletproof system, and powered by a fifty-five-horsepower, two-stroke pump-jet propulsor.

The team was gathered on the dock, the Snake sitting in the circle at the end of the drive, and a fleet of FEMA personnel were evacuating the inhabitants of Scout's neighborhood with dire warnings of a train derailment nearby. There were chemicals and bad stuff and enough mumbo jumbo that taillights were making an exodus out of the area.

In fact, Ms. Jones had already had a train "derailed" on the line so that overhead imagery would back up their cover story, and it also closed the rail line in the area to further traffic.

So far, Support was having a better mission than the Night-stalkers.

"All right," Moms said, surveying her battered team. "The golden glow was going with the river, so let's assume Burns and the Fireflies are also doing that. I know the clock is ticking, but we've already lost containment. We go racing off in the wrong direction, we're just wasting time. So let's focus here and hash this out before we move. Everyone feel free to put in their dime's worth. What's the target?"

"The Watts Bar nuke plant," Doc said. "It's the most obvious."

"Next most obvious?" Nada asked.

"The dam is closer," Scout said. "Seems like this Burns fellow would have opened the Rift closer to the nuclear plant if that was his target."

"Score one for the girl," Eagle said.

"I am a young woman," Scout corrected him. "Not a girl."

"Correction," Eagle said. "The young woman."

"Perhaps," Doc said. "But this golden glow originated here. From Scout's toothbrush. Originally from the Rift in North Carolina. The question is, how is that connected to Burns, the Rift here, and the Fireflies?"

"And Scout," Kirk said in a low voice, but Nada heard him and so did Moms.

Nada spoke up. "Is Burns trying to complete what they attempted in North Carolina? Expand a Rift into a Portal?"

Doc held up his pack. "I've got the computer Burns used. How is he going to open a Rift, never mind a Portal, now?"

The sound of a chainsaw roared from where the Snake was parked, indicating Support removing the wooden pole from the cargo bay by the most expeditious manner. The pained look on Eagle's face indicated what he thought of that.

"He might have the program in a thumb drive," Doc said. "Ivar was working on a remote site from the computer that opened the Rift in Scout's neighborhood in North Carolina. He shoves a thumb drive in any computer powerful enough, it can generate the algorithm."

"This doesn't feel the same," Scout said in a low voice, which pretty much everyone ignored, especially since it was barely audible above the roar of the chainsaw.

Except Nada. And Moms. And Kirk.

"You know," Ivar said, "there's another potential target in this area. Perhaps an even more likely one, and the entire river thing is a diversion."

"Speak," Moms ordered.

"North of here," Ivar said. "Oak Ridge. When the Manhattan Project was formed in 1939, they picked three main sites. Everyone thinks of Los Alamos, but actually Oak Ridge and Hanford, in Washington, were more important in a way because they produced the fissionable material used in making the bombs."

"Maybe the river isn't a diversion but a route," Eagle said. "Oak Ridge is on the Clinch River, which flows into this river down by Kingston. And part of it borders Watts Bar Lake."

Moms nodded at him. "Thanks. Is Oak Ridge still active?"

"Yes," Ivar said. "And it has a plutonium core that's still active. Going through the Archives, I read that the first Rift ever opened used a plutonium core."

"The demon core," Eagle said.

"That doesn't sound good," Scout muttered.

"Ditto," Nada said.

"It's a core that Area 51 appropriated from Los Alamos," Ivar said. "Killed two researchers."

"Sounds even worse," Scout said.

Ivar turned to Eagle. "What is Odessa?"

Everyone stared at the newest member of the team in surprise.

"What are you talking about?" Moms asked.

"The group that opened the first Rift," Ivar said. "It was called Odessa."

Eagle had instant access to the pile of useless and useful facts in his brain. "I assumed you meant the group at Area 51 and not the Frederick Forsyth book or the movie adapted from it, which was actually based on a real organization, which the group at Area 51 also used. Roughly Odessa stands for Organization of former SS, which the Nazi and Japanese scientists at Area 51 called themselves. They were led by a former SS officer, Colonel"—Eagle paused, having to access deeper thoughts—"Colonel Schmidt. They all disappeared when they opened the Rift using the demon core."

Moms held up her hand as she processed all this. "Okay. So. It could be the Loudoun Dam, the Watts Bar nuclear reactor, or Oak Ridge."

"It ain't that complicated," Nada said. He pointed down at the dock. "The river is the key. We go with the river, we follow the golden glow, and I bet we run into the Fireflies and Burns somewhere along the way. First the dam, then Oak Ridge, then the nuke plant. Meanwhile, you get Support to put additional security down at Watts Bar and at Oak Ridge. Especially any water intake. Also, seal off the dam area. We go downriver to the dam."

Moms turned to Ivar. "You figure out a way to track this golden glow thingie?"

"We don't even know what it is," Ivar hedged. "But," he continued before anyone jumped on his expertise with combat boots, "I've rigged this." He held up a backpack with a long wand attached to it. "It will determine electronic fluctuations, especially in the water. If there's something in there"—he nodded toward the dark river flowing under the dock—"this will find it."

Moms looked over her bedraggled team. "We've got some hours of darkness left. I want to contain and control this before dawn or else it might go viral. We head downriver. Ivar, you're in the lead boat with me and Roland and Kirk. Doc, you're in the second boat with Nada and Mac. Eagle, you fly overhead."

"I don't have the chain gun," Eagle said.

"But you've got eyes and imaging," Moms said. "You're our eye in the sky and our commo link to Support. Also, I want two Apaches on your shoulders. Can you link and slave their weapons to your control system?"

Eagle thought for a second, then nodded. "Yes."

"Good," Moms said. "You control their fire once we make contact."

"Roger," Eagle said.

"What about me?" Scout said.

Moms looked at the young woman/girl.

Before she could say something, Scout volunteered an answer. "I can be on the Sea-Doo. Cover your flank or whatever it is scouts do."

"They scout," Nada said. "Covering the flank is an appropriate mission for a scout."

"She's a civilian," Moms said.

"We're past that," Nada replied. "She was our asset in North Carolina and she's our asset here." He didn't add what only the two of them knew: Ms. Jones had said do it, so do it they would.

"I can drive a Sea-Doo too," Kirk said. "Let's us cover more of the river. I'll take one side, Scout the other."

Moms sighed. "All right."

"Do I get paid?" Scout asked.

"No," Moms said automatically.

"Do I get a gun?"

Moms was about to give the rote answer, but Nada interceded. "Do you know how to use one?"

"Yes," Scout said, all seriousness for once. "I took the daylong course."

"Roland," Nada said. "What do you have for our scout?"

Kirk would have recognized Jimmy DiSalvo for exactly what he was: a meth-head nut job, tweaking so bad he kept loading and unloading the four bullets he had left into the magazine for the 9-mm pistol he'd taken from the store clerk.

The other five bullets that had been in the gun were now in the store clerk at Weigel's back in Farragut. DiSalvo didn't get it: Why get killed over a minimum-wage job?

It never occurred to him to wonder why he'd killed the clerk over one hundred forty-two dollars. And twenty-seven cents. And four bullets.

Three bullets as one escaped DiSalvo's fingers and tumbled down the side of the cliff and disappeared into the water below.

He should have made a wish, although what do you get for a bullet in a lake?

"Stupid, stupid, stupid," DiSalvo kept repeating, hitting himself on the side of his head with the hand holding the three bullets. The contact made him feel better, believing that he was knocking sense into his brain, which needed it; after all, that's what his dad had always told him every time he whacked Jimmy upside the head.

But he didn't want to lose the bullets! That piece of common sense rattled through, so he switched hands.

Except he forgot he had the unloaded gun in that other hand and the next whack was the barrel of the gun rather than his hand. DiSalvo was dazed.

Dazed layered on top of confused while standing on top of a cliff over a lake formed by the brightly lit dam just to his right was not a good combination. DiSalvo staggered, tried to right himself, and then followed the bullet.

He bounced several times off the rocky cliff, hard enough and often enough that by the time he hit the water, he didn't have to worry about drowning.

He should have made a wish.

"Why did you recruit Burns?" Hannah asked.

Dr. Golden was seated across from her, hands folded in her lap, listening in.

There was the slight hiss of reassuring static out of the speakerphone, meaning that the encryption was working. Hannah often wondered if the designer left that static in for the reassurance. Surely technology was advanced enough now that the static could be engineered out?

"His family," Ms. Jones responded, her voice containing its own static.

"More specifically?" Hannah pressed, not used to Ms. Jones being evasive.

"His grandfather was Colonel Johan Schmidt, the leader of the Odessa group at Area 51."

"Ah," Hannah said. "But that still does not explain why you recruited him."

"We don't know what happened with the first Rift," Ms. Jones said. "Schmidt was involved. There is a legacy. I felt that legacy would unfold. So I recruited him for the Nightstalkers."

"That might have been a mistake," Dr. Golden said.

"It might have," Ms. Jones admitted, "but we have yet to see how this current event will play out. Obviously, Burns is central to it. This has been building. Whether by plan or by circumstance, I can't say, although I lean toward the former especially given the events of last year in North Carolina and Scout's involvement now and here."

"I don't like it," Hannah said. "There are too many unknown variables."

"There usually are," Ms. Jones said. "But we have our best people on it."

"Do they know Burns's location or target?"

"Negative on location," Ms. Jones said. "But they have three potential targets in order of priority and proximity: The Loudoun Dam, Oak Ridge, and the Watts Bar nuclear plant."

"Your FPF?"

"On station."

"Very well," Hannah said. "Continue to update me."

She cut the connection and looked across her desk at Dr. Golden. "I hope our best is good enough."

CHAPTER 11

Burns stared at the Tellico Dam while information on it poured into him from Neeley's cell phone.

He shook his head at the human insanity the dam represented: people fighting to keep it from being built to save a tiny fish; sacred Indian land being submerged; land grabs by those in the know.

And it generated no power.

Not directly. Water from the Little Tennessee River was blocked by the dam, which had been built just above where the river had originally joined the Tennessee River. To get to the Tennessee, water flowed through a canal from Tellico Reservoir to Loudoun Lake and then went through the turbines of the Loudoun Dam, adding 23 megawatts of power.

Thus opening the gates of Tellico would reduce the water flow to Loudoun, thus reducing the power outage, which was barely enough at overpeak for what Burns needed.

Not acceptable.

Of course, the gates of Tellico Dam were opened only once a year for maintenance, but it was a loose end.

And one thing Burns had learned as a Nightstalker was to make sure there were no loose ends.

Plus, he still had some time for congruence at the Loudoun Dam to occur.

He looked around and picked up two brick-sized stones. He put them in his backpack. Then he threw the free end of the rope he had tied off down the face of the dam. He clipped the rope through the carabiner tied off to his harness and then launched himself down the dam.

Frasier was humming "I Wear My Sunglasses at Night" as he got off the elevator and walked down the corridor to the Can. His partner ignored him, as he always did when Frasier hummed the song en route to an interview. As he always did. Frasier, being schooled in psychology, knew it was OCD on his part, but he figured it was harmless, other than irritating his partner. Of course, his partner carried a big gun in his shoulder holster, and one day he might get irritated beyond the point of no return, but Frasier figured he had a ways to go before that particular incident occurred.

The man and woman who'd been in the Can when the power went out were seated away from the control consoles, looking decidedly unhappy. And well they should be, Frasier thought as he signaled for the single guard (they were scientists, one guard was all that was needed) to move away.

A new team was at the consoles, while several Support crews were going over every inch of the cavern, searching it. There were even two specially trained dive teams inside the stainless steel tank, working in relays, coming out of the water every five minutes to allow a muonic scan to be done, just in case another Rift occurred.

The two popped to their feet as Frasier and his partner approached.

"Sit," Frasier ordered as he grabbed a folding chair, turned it around, interrogation style, and straddled it. His partner just stood there, looming.

He was a good loomer, which was why Frasier kept him around.

Frasier pulled his sunglasses off, his partner doing it in sync, like a dance team in step.

The two scientists did a double take, staring at Frasier's left eye and then purposely forcing themselves not to stare at his left eye.

It was the usual reaction and the normal one.

Frasier had a solid black left eye. He'd never had the scar tissue around the socket fixed, since he figured that was like polishing the silver around the bullet hole. Or something like that. Of course, most assumed it was just a space filler, but the eye was actually a ridiculously expensive camera and micropro-cessor. Not *Six Million Dollar Man* stuff, where he could actually see, but rather a device that functioned as a sort of lie detector, tracking pulses in a person's neck, perspiration, respiration rate, and so on.

The bottom line was it worked. Coupling the data from the eye with his own experience, his training in micro-expressions, and a natural ability, Frasier was pretty damn confident he could tell when someone was lying.

"It's tough work in the field," Frasier began. He reached across his body with his right hand and tapped his left arm, producing a metallic sound. "I got a deal on the prosthetics. Black was all they had in stock for the discounted eyes in the package deal."

Was that a sigh he heard from the side and behind? Was his partner actually growing tired of his shtick? But he was doing his job, pulling out a notepad to ostensibly take notes, but the real purpose was to reveal the very large pistol resting in his shoulder holster, impressing on these two screen-watchers that this was a no-bullshit visit.

"It's even tougher to work in the field when those we rely on for our data sabotage it."

The woman responded first. "We didn't sabotage the Can! The power went out!"

They didn't exchange glances—one didn't look at the other suspiciously—and his eye told him she wasn't lying.

He shifted his gaze to the man. "And?"

"Hey, dude, I don't know what happened. Some kind of power surge maybe? Talk to engineering. They're the ones who run the power grid. Maybe the reactor burped?"

Unfortunately, he, too, was telling the truth. Frasier wished he wasn't so he could turn him over to his partner; he hated being called dude. Frasier rubbed his scar tissue above the black eye with his artificial hand. He often got migraines, because no matter how good the gear was, his body was not intact and the body yearned for its missing pieces sometimes.

Sometimes Frasier missed them too.

Frasier stood. "All right. You can go."

The two exchanged a glance now, shock and relief fighting for supremacy. They didn't question their good fortune as they scurried toward the tunnel for the elevator.

This time his partner's sigh was audible. "What now?"

"We—" Frasier didn't finish his answer as a diver popped to the surface with a shout, hand held high. A black orb rested in it. "Check that thing for prints. It'll have either Doc's or Ivar's."

Scout had the right bank while Kirk took the left on their Sea-Doos. At Moms's insistence, they stayed parallel to her Zodiac. Ivar was in the bow, the wand for his improvised detection device held over the water. Roland was next to him, M240 at the ready. Moms drove as she peered ahead through her night vision goggles.

Scout was not impressed with Ivar or his machine. She had a feeling whatever was going to happen wasn't going to be subtle or require a special device. The gun Roland had given her seemed rather undersized considering what everyone else, except for Doc and Ivar, was packing. A pistol. With two extra magazines.

She felt totally inadequate, but the look in Moms's eyes had indicated she should be happy to get anything lethal at all. The gun was stuck on a vest Nada had wrapped her in. It was not fashionable, was very heavy, and, according to Nada, helped stop bullets. Then he'd strapped a life vest on top of the bulletproof vest and Scout felt like she was auditioning for the Stay Puft Marshmallow Man. There was also a radio tucked in one of the many pockets on the vest and an earpiece stuffed in her right ear.

She didn't feel as cool as those Secret Service guys with their dark sunglasses. But then again, how cool could they be? If they were so secret, why did everyone know about them? Sort of like why did the Lone Ranger have Tonto? What part of Lone didn't he get? Scout shook these random but irritating thoughts out of her head and focused on the task at hand.

Literally.

Given the bulk surrounding her, she had to work to keep her hands in tight enough to her body to control the Sea-Doo. She scanned the dark shoreline as she drove along. They'd cleared

Keller Bend a little while ago and the river turn left ahead. Scout spared a glance up, but there was no sign of Eagle and the Snake and the attack helicopters with him.

So far this was a lot less exciting than she'd imagined. She juiced the Sea-Doo as she reached the bend, slicing some water.

She knew Moms was glaring at her, wanting her to slow down and fall back into line. She wasn't named Moms for nothing. Mother, Moms . . . what was with older women? Scout wondered. Be careful. Don't do this. Don't do that. As if their warnings could keep her safe from—

Scout blinked and stared ahead in the darkness. She could see white foam ahead, but there were no running lights.

Of course she didn't have any lights on, nor did the two Zodiacs.

Scout slowed down, letting the Zodiacs take the lead because she had a feeling this wasn't going to be subtle.

"I've got two boats and something bigger behind them," Moms said, peering through her night vision goggles. "Eagle, hold until we get a clear picture of what we're up against."

"Roger. Holding at five klicks," Eagle confirmed.

"You gotta be fraking me," Roland muttered as the first target became clear in their night vision goggles. A fourteen-foot bass boat was racing toward the Nightstalker flotilla, no one at the helm.

"No one said Fireflies were brilliant," Mac said over the team net.

"This one is mine," Roland said, resting the bipod of the M240 on the armor plating and tucking the stock into his shoulder.

"Mac will help," Moms said, looking past the bass boat, trying to determine what else was coming their way.

Roland fired, rounds easily punching through the thin aluminum hull of the boat. Mac's first 40-mm grenade landed right in the center with a bright flash.

"Scratch one Firefly," Roland announced, just as Scout screamed, "Watch out!" over the net.

The *Splendor*, racing out of the hidden cove on the north shore, didn't run over Scout. It didn't have to. Its bow wave knocked her off the Sea-Doo and into the river. Its dual engines were revving up to max speed as it roared toward the lead Zodiac.

Moms had a moment to see the blur of the yacht's bow bearing down on her, and then it sliced through the Zodiac, throwing her, Ivar, and Roland into the river. They were tumbled about, nearly chewed up by the twin screws, and spit out into the churning wake.

All their gear that wasn't tied to their bodies disappeared into the dark water, including Ivar's detection wand.

Mac bounced a 40-mm grenade off the bow of the yacht, the steel plating used to protect it from the front anchors as they're pulled up easily deflecting the round as the boat keeled hard toward their

Zodiac. Nada twisted the throttle as he called out over the team net, "Eagle, we need firepower."

"Inbound," Eagle announced.

Nada managed to get enough horsepower, and the Zodiac was maneuverable enough, to escape being plowed under by the yacht.

This time.

Kirk jetted his Sea-Doo to the far shore, into water shallow enough that the yacht couldn't get him, and grabbed the laser designator out of the bag strapped to the side of his craft. He zeroed it in as the yacht turned hard.

Out of the frying pan . . .

Nada was so focused on avoiding the rampaging yacht that the crane on the barge only caught his attention when the cable swung by, missing him by inches, the metal claw on the end of it taking a chunk out of the armor plating and ripping gaping holes into two compartments of the Zodiac.

"Mother-fraker!" Mac exclaimed, staring up at the barge as they raced by, the large tracked crane on board the barge rotating to follow.

"That is interesting," Doc said. "It appears the Firefly is inhabiting both the barge and the crane. I've never seen that kind of continuity before."

"Or it's two fraking Fireflies," Mac said. "Does it really matter?"

"Eagle?" Nada said.

"We're coming in hot," Eagle said. "I've got four in the water, three on your boat, and one on a Sea-Doo near southern shoreline. I assume all are friendlies."

At the Tellico Dam, Burns put a stone into the gears of each of the gate mechanisms.

Mission accomplished, he began the much more difficult task of climbing his way back up the side of the dam, to get ready for the final phase of his mission.

A quarter mile away, in the midst of Loudoun Lake, the golden glow was now coalesced into what was almost a solid ball, twenty meters wide, lying just below the dark surface of the water. It was being drawn toward the intakes for the water turbines.

Neeley dove out of the door of the Learjet, got stable, and then pulled her rip cord.

After making sure she had a good canopy overhead, she scanned the terrain below. It wasn't hard to get oriented on Loudoun Dam.

The straight line cutting across the edge of the lake was easily recognizable from ten thousand feet.

Neeley had never been a fan of jumping out of a perfectly good airplane. Parachuting was something she'd learned because Gant had insisted. A mission-essential skill, according to him. Considering the fact that when they first met he was on the run from the Cellar and every other government organization, Neeley had to wonder in retrospect (as she was wondering about a lot of things) how parachuting was a mission-essential skill in accomplishing that.

Adjusting her toggles, Neeley aimed for the power station.

The helicopter on the back deck of the *Splendor* lifted off and raced upriver.

With no one at the controls.

It flew directly at Eagle in the Snake and the Apaches on his flanks. Eagle had flipped down the display for the Integrated Helmet and Display Sighting System (IHADSS), and the 30-mm guns underneath each Apache were slaved to whatever he targeted.

He was targeting the yacht when a proximity alert went off. Shifting from focusing on the IHADSS to the outside world took a moment, a delay that almost cost Eagle his life as the *Splendor*'s helicopter was on a collision course.

Eagle dove and the chopper passed overhead, barely missing him.

It didn't miss the Apache to Eagle's left.

––––––––––––

A fireball lit up the sky.

"One Apache down," Eagle announced. "And another Firefly."

Nada stood in the front of his Zodiac, two compartments losing air and the boat sluggish to the helm. The yacht was completing its turn, but he estimated he had about a minute and a half before it could bear down on his boat again. The crane on the barge was just out of range, although the tug pushing the barge was in full reverse, trying to correct that.

The Fireflies had managed to gather a lot of power, but none of it was very agile other than the helicopter, which was now in the river along with the Apache it had taken out.

It was a delaying tactic.

Nada began issuing orders:

"Kirk, put a fire mission on that yacht. Eagle, use the second Apache and take out the barge. Moms, you there?"

"Roger. We're in the water but all right. We'll break a chem light once our little problems are dealt with."

"Scout?" Nada asked last, but not least importantly.

"I'm back on my Sea-Doo," Scout reported.

"Stay out of trouble until we deal with this," Nada ordered.

"Oh, right," Scout said. "I'd forgotten about that part."

––––––––––––

"Lion Six," Mac said. "Fire mission! Over."

The crew for one of the M177's replied immediately. "Roger. Over."

"Lion Six. Fire for effect on laser. Danger close. Over."

There was a short pause; then the officer in charge of the M777, 155-mm howitzer responded. "Shot over."

"Shot out," Mac said, keeping the laser steady on the yacht. It was picking up speed, twin turbines planing it out, heading directly for Nada's Zodiac. While the rubber boat might be more agile, it wasn't faster and with two compartments flooding, it was moving slow.

"Splash over," Lion Six warned, indicating the Excalibur round was five seconds from impact.

"Splash out!" Kirk said over the team net.

The round tore through the deck plating and exploded inside the *Splendor*. Curiously, the armor plating layered on the boat contained the explosion to an extent.

Which meant the interior of the boat was shredded, along with the lone man left behind for guard duty, who'd been running around throwing every switch he could trying to regain control.

The explosion did make enough holes in the hull, though, that the yacht quickly began to settle.

Another Firefly down.

Eagle had the crane barge in his IHADSS. The crane was rotating, the steel claw swinging, but once more it was short of Nada's Zodiac.

So far, in Eagle's convoluted media way of thinking, they'd gone through *PT-109* with Moms's Zodiac being plowed under and cut in half and the sinking of the HMS *Hood* with the M177 taking out the yacht. He couldn't come up with a parallel for the barge, so he just said, "Frak it," and relayed the firing command to the surviving Apache.

The 30-mm chain gun fired, but more importantly, one Hellfire missile launched from the pod on the left side of the attack helicopter. Eagle adjusted slightly and a second Hellfire came off the right side.

The first Hellfire hit the crane, blowing it to pieces. The second hit the barge, ripping out the front right portion. Given the weight on board, it did a mini-*Titanic* as the crane slid off and into the water, and the barge went vertical and then down.

Two Fireflies dissipated.

And then there was silence.

Burns stood on the roadway that crossed the Loudoun Dam, above the intakes for the turbines. He could see the golden glow approaching in the water. He checked his watch. He'd heard explosions in the distance and knew the Nightstalkers were coming. They were nothing if not persistent.

Something to count on. As regular as time.

"Armorflate?" Roland said. "Really? False advertising, I say."

"Keep pumping," Nada ordered Roland. "It's for bullets, not cranes." He had Moms, Ivar, and Roland on board, along with his original crew of Mac and Doc. The barge had sliced open two of the air compartments on the Zodiac and damaged two others. Roland was battling the leaks using the foot pump, while Doc worked on bandaging the boat.

Scout and Kirk were on their Sea-Doos, now in tight formation, less than five feet off to each side, their engines almost idling as they kept pace. The flotilla, not even close to being an armada, came around a curve in the river and the waterway widened. A couple of miles ahead, lights glowed in an even line, slicing across the river: the Loudoun Dam.

Moms spoke over the team net. "Eagle?"

"Roger?"

"Get an uplink to FPF."

There was a short silence. "Roger."

The B-52 was lazily circling at forty thousand feet when the alert light flashed on the pilots' control panel and in the lower deck battle station.

Lazy became focused as the crew readied all weapons systems.

Neeley touched down on the road above the dam. Support had already sealed off the road, Route 321, with roadblocks, far enough away from the dam to keep civilians out of eyesight. As she unbuckled her harness, Neeley looked about. It was eerily quiet other than the roar of the water pouring through the spillways, tumbling down to the continuation of the Tennessee River below, to the west.

That roar began to decrease and Neeley readied her MP5 as she walked over and peered down.

Someone was closing the spillways, forcing more water into the intakes for the three generators. She headed for the power-house.

A Firefly was inside the control for the gate mechanisms, closing them off. Burns was inside the power station on the northern end of the dam, watching the power levels begin to spike while the outtakes from the powerhouse gained force.

The entire dam vibrated for a moment as the golden glow reached it, being forced through the intakes and then wrapping itself around the three generators, eating the energy they produced.

Inside the Can, there was no power outage this time as the clicking alert sounded and the lights flashed.

"We have pre-Rift!"

Alarms went off in power stations all over TVA as the power output from Loudoun Dam suddenly ceased. Relays were automatically thrown, power was diverted, but blackouts rippled across the Tennessee countryside.

At the Ranch outside Area 51 and in the Cellar underneath the NSA, both Ms. Jones and Hannah watched the developing situation on their computer displays. The pre-Rift warnings came in from Russia and Japan, but it was no surprise that they pinpointed the location at the power station on Loudoun Dam.

They were helpless at the moment to do anything other than observe. Their forces were in place and this was going to play out on the ground, as combat always had since the first caveman picked up a club.

The lights on the roadway along the top of the dam went out. In fact, the lights all around the lake went out.

"That's not good," Roland said.

"No shit," Mac muttered.

"Someone is stealing the dam's power," Doc said.

The Zodiac was now less than a half-mile from the dam. Nada powered down on the throttle slightly.

"Burns," Moms said.

Everyone's phone began playing "Lawyers, Guns, and Money." Moms answered. "Yes?"

"We have pre-Rift inside the power station," Ms. Jones reported.

"We'll be there shortly."

"Neeley should be there now," Ms. Jones said. "She'll help."

Moms had her own opinion on that, but she kept it to herself.

"This is very different," Ms. Jones said. "Burns, the golden glow. Something is coming together. Something long in the developing."

"Yes," Moms said.

"You need to pay attention," Ms. Jones said. "Be open to possibilities."

"What?" Moms said.

"Good luck." And then the connection was dead.

"The gates are all closed." Mac was peering through a night vision scope.

Moms shook her head and focused on the immediate situation.

"We have to stop Burns from getting all that power," Doc said. "He's going to use it to open a Portal."

"How can he?" Moms asked as they continued toward the side of the dam with the powerhouse.

Roland was ignoring the discussion, checking his M240, making sure it was loaded and that the nozzle for the burner was loose in its sheath.

"Are we sure that a Portal is a bad thing?" Ivar asked.

That earned him a glare from everyone in the boat—except Moms and Nada and Scout.

"Everyone who's ever opened one is dead or gone," Nada said.

"A Rift," Ivar said. "Not a Portal."

Nada looked at Doc. "Just tell me how to stop this."

"I'm not dead or gone," Ivar said, but he was ignored, except by Scout.

"We have to stop him from getting the power he needs from the dam," Doc said.

"I've always wanted to blow up a dam," Mac said. It was the dream of every Special Forces engineer/demo man. Along with a bridge, a skyscraper, and various other engineering feats. The bigger it was built, the more a demo longed to blow it up.

"What are you going to use to blow that?" Moms asked. "Even the Excalibur rounds aren't going to do much damage."

"We need the cruise missiles," Mac said. "Kirk's got the laser designator. I can use it and aim a couple at the weakest points. I've done a target survey on a dam. I know where to hit it to cause maximum damage and structural failure."

Moms nodded. "I'll get them ready for launch."

On board the B-52, the crew listened to Moms's order. On one hand they were happy they weren't prepping one of the nukes for launch. On the other hand, they weren't thrilled with the idea of loosing even conventional warheads over the continental United States.

On the third hand, which was duty, they prepped four cruise missiles for launch.

Burns smiled at Neeley as she came into the powerhouse, steel door slamming shut behind her, his face rippling and then becoming Gant. "You survived. I had hope they might get to you in time at the nursing home."

"Stop with the face," Neeley said, weapon at the ready, laser site flickering on Burns's forehead. "It doesn't work."

"Oh, I think it does," Burns said.

"Why did you have hope that I would live when you were the one who killed me?"

Burns's face flickered, the scars reappearing for a moment and then going back to being Gant's. "I didn't want to hurt you. But you understand. Mission takes priority." He cocked his head. "Your friends are here. My former teammates. The illustrious Nightstalkers. Let's meet them."

"I don't think so," Neeley said, and she fired twice, double-tapping.

The Zodiac bumped up against the dock on the side of the powerhouse. Roland was first ashore, machine gun at the ready, with Nada at his shoulder. Scout and Kirk jumped off their Sea-Doos to join the rest of them.

Mac took the laser designator from Kirk. Ivar and Doc were arguing about the possible dangers of a Portal opening, akin to the band playing while the *Titanic* went down in Scout's opinion, a little speck of calm in the midst of a team in turmoil. That didn't last long as she looked toward the water in the reservoir.

"Uh, people," she said as she watched the blotchy hand reach up out of the water and grab hold of the edge of the dock.

No one, of course, was paying attention to her.

Moms was on the radio, done talking to Ms. Jones and getting permission to blow the dam. The TVA would be pissed, but collateral damage would be minimal outside of the dam and some structures immediately downriver.

"Launch and ride the beam," Moms ordered.

A cruise missile dropped clear from the pods on each wing of the B-52. The two missiles free fell for a few seconds, getting clear of the bomber; then their rockets kicked in and they nosed down, picking up speed.

The first round hit Burns in the chest (go for the largest target first, one of Gant's rules) and the second in the forehead (go where there isn't the possibility of body armor, the footnote to the aforementioned rule).

Burns didn't even flinch.

Both bullets passed into him, not so much hitting as being absorbed. He smiled. "Come, come, Neeley. You're out of your depth here. This isn't a Sanction. This is a Nightstalker mission. I was one of them. Let's go say hello to my old friends."

He turned for the outside steel door of the powerhouse.

Behind him, the golden glow had grown larger, forming a stable pre-Rift.

"Guys," Scout called out in a louder voice.

Nada heard her and turned, but the rest were caught up in their own concerns: Roland wanting to shoot something; Mac searching the dam wall for its weak spot through the laser designator since he had two warheads en route; Kirk facilitating Moms's commo back to Ms. Jones and the launchers of the Tomahawks; Doc and Ivar moving closer to blows about the possibility of even a Rift without the algorithms, never mind a Portal.

"What?" Nada asked.

"Zombie," Scout said, pointing.

At the same moment, the door to the powerhouse swung open and Burns stepped out, his face covered with scars.

Roland fired on instinct, a good, solid, twelve-round burst, every round hitting the former Nightstalker. And being absorbed.

As Roland fired, so did Nada.

In the other direction.

The former Jimmy DiSalvo had climbed out of the water and was staggering down the walkway to the dock in classic zombie style, arms outstretched, body bashed, bloody, and very dead.

Nada's bullets had more impact on him than Roland's did on Burns. DiSalvo's corpse staggered back, chunks of flesh flying off.

But he kept coming.

Until there was a flash of gold from Burns's eyes. DiSalvo's body exploded into vapor and the Firefly that had taken him over fluttered up and dissipated.

CHAPTER 12

"As we always noted," Burns said in the moment of silence that followed that surprising development, "the Fireflies aren't very bright."

"Sixty seconds until impact," Mac called out, ignoring Burns, the exploded zombie, and everything else, his face pressed against the rubber seal of the laser designator.

"Now, now," Burns said, holding his hands up, "let's not be hasty."

Neeley appeared behind Burns, keeping her submachine gun pointed at him and edging around, making sure she didn't get in the line of fire of the team.

Moms's earpiece crackled with information from Frasier. She shifted the aim of her gun from Burns to Ivar. "Why did you sabotage the Can?"

Burns stepped between Moms and Ivar, facing him. "Do you have it?"

Ivar pulled out the hard drive he'd stolen from the Archives and handed it to Burns.

"No way," Moms said. "That dam is toast in forty-five seconds and so is the power for the Portal."

"Abort your missiles," Burns said. "It's not what you think." His face rippled and changed.

"Gant?" Neeley whispered, shaking her head, trying to get rid of the image.

"Whoa!" Scout was pointing. "You see that?"

Once more, the only person who followed her was Nada. She was pointing at a road sign announcing that the roadway on top of the dam was the Greer Bridge.

"My name," Scout said.

"Very good," Burns said, surprising everyone and addressing Scout's apparently inane observation.

"Thirty seconds," Mac said, still focused on the dam.

"That is not by chance," Burns said, his eyes flickering with gold.

"All of this just to get me here?" Scout asked.

"All of us," Burns said. "We need all of us. None of us are here by chance." And then a golden flash from his eyes washed over everyone, and they all had a simultaneous moment of enlightenment, different for each one.

Scout thought of her name and her mother. "What if we've been wrong?"

"Twenty seconds," Mac announced. But he suddenly saw the dam now as a work of progress, of man's achievement, not to be destroyed, and pulled his eye away from the sight.

Electricity can be love, Neeley thought, and she lowered the muzzle of her MP5. "Who loves us?"

"Backwards," Ivar said, remembering the lab. "It's all backwards."

"Who loves you?" Moms said, and she knew the answer: Her team loved her and she loved her team.

Nada reached up and felt the blue bulb in the ammo pouch on the outside of his gear, where there should be two magazines of bullets. Sometimes rules were made to be broken. "Abort, Moms."

"Abort," Moms said into the radio.

CHAPTER 13

Both missiles exploded just above a thousand feet, an expensive fireworks display, lighting up the darkness for a moment, the sound of the explosion rolling across the reservoir.

"FPF, prepare two more missiles," Moms said, shaking her head, not even sure why she'd given the order to abort. "Same target. Fire if you don't hear from me in three mikes, over."

"Roger. Over."

Moms stepped toward Burns. "What's going on? And talk quick or else that dam is gone."

Burns pointed at Scout. "She was the key." His face flickered and went back to its scarred form. "I think you"—he pointed at Moms—"and you"—he pointed at Neeley—"need to bring your bosses in on this. After all, they helped set it all up."

Moms stood stock still for a moment and then pointed at Kirk. He quickly accessed both the Ranch and the Cellar. "We're live with both," he said. "On speaker."

"Report." Ms. Jones's voice was a rasp.

"Good to hear you again, Ms. Jones," Burns said. "It's been a while. And Hannah. I know you're listening. Good to finally make your acquaintance. Your predecessor, Nero, knew my grandfather."

"A Nazi," Hannah said.

"Yes," Burns confirmed. "And a member of Operation Paperclip, which Mr. Nero had a hand in, which means the Cellar had a hand in. Which then Area 51 had a hand in and led to the birth of the Nightstalkers. It's all connected."

Scout spoke up. "Someone want to speak English? Who named the bridge after me?"

Burns laughed. "Out of the mouths of children."

"I ain't no child," Scout protested.

Burns waggled the hard drive that Ivar had given him. "Shall we see the end play?"

He didn't wait for an answer, going through the entry into the power station.

The rest followed, almost a dance, with weapons pointed at Burns and Ivar and people trying not to cross each other's line of fire. They shuffled into the control room for the power station.

Burns walked right up to the golden glow and tossed the hard drive into it. It was caught in the field, suspended. A deep golden iris, less than a foot tall, appeared.

"It will take a minute or two or three," Burns said.

"Two minutes is all you have," Moms said.

Burns turned to face the team. "You've been through this before, haven't you, Ms. Jones?"

"Yes. At Chernobyl."

"But it was stopped." Burns said it as a statement, but Ms. Jones spoke anyway.

"At great cost."

"And, Hannah," Burns said, "Nero didn't leave you many records, did he? He didn't leave you the Cellar report on what happened at Area 51 for the first Rift, did he?"

"He did not."

"Greer," Burns said, and Moms turned to Scout.

"Greer?" Nada repeated. "Really?"

"Really," Scout said. "What's your real name?"

"Fred," Nada said.

"No shit?" Mac exclaimed.

Burns ignored them. "What do you think is going on?" he asked Scout.

"I don't know," Scout said, shrugging. "I was wrong about my name. With my mother. Sometimes we're wrong."

Burns pointed at Doc. "The demon core. Ever wonder about it?"

"It's lost," Doc said.

"It's not lost," Ivar said. "It's the anchor on the other side." He was nodding, finally understanding. "The first Rift needed it. It went through with most of the scientists. But it's right on the other side. It's been what every other Rift has used."

"Very good," Burns said. "And how would you feel if a Rift opened in this world and someone sent through a radioactive core?"

"Piss me off," Roland said.

"Doors work both ways," Nada said.

"Correct," Burns said. "But your people opened one at Area 51 and then have been kicking it shut every time."

"One minute," Moms said.

"Oh frak," Kirk said as the iris elongated, becoming twelve feet high by six wide. They could all see figures on the other side.

"They're only giving you back what you sent to them," Burns said.

And then Professor Winslow from the University of North Carolina stepped through. Followed by Craegan from Arizona State. Followed by a stream of scientists, all of whom had opened Rifts. As the years of the Rifts went back, it was clear that none of them had aged in the slightest during whatever experience they'd had on the other side. Colonel Thorn came through, the man who'd led the very first Nightstalkers, shutting the very first Rift.

And then the members of Odessa came through, the ones who had opened that very first Rift.

EPILOGUE

Blake was sitting by the pool in the Myrtle Beach complex, no grandkids in tow and studying the young mother across the way. She'd flashed him a look earlier, almost a smile, so he was figuring she'd forgiven him for dumping her kid in the pool. She was rubbing sunscreen on her incredibly long legs and her kid was also nowhere in sight.

An interesting development, he thought. Maybe it was time for that flank maneuver after all?

But before he could initiate the maneuver, the mother stood up and walked around the pool, striding with a purpose. So much purpose that Blake looked over his shoulder to see if there was someone behind him she was going toward. But no, he was the target.

"Here," she said, holding out an OD Green plastic case about eight inches long by four wide by one thick.

Blake automatically took it.

She walked away and he was so surprised that he didn't even stare at her ass, instead focusing on the box in his hands. He opened it and there was another encryption device inside, an updated model of the one he'd buried in the cache.

Damn job, Blake thought as he looked at the encryptor.

He looked up, but the woman was gone.

Damn, damn job.

———

Wallace Cranston hated rehab.

———

Iris Watkins swiped her credit card through the device and then signed her name, feeling a piece of her security crumble with the signature. A hundred fifty bucks for the baby's checkup at the pediatrician's office. Taking her receipt, she swung the halter onto her chest and herded the two oldest toward the door.

An older blonde entering held the door for her and Watkins graced her with a smile.

Then the blonde started following and Watkins slid her free hands into her purse, fingers curling around the mace.

"Iris?" the woman asked.

Watkins turned and faced her. "Yes?"

"My name is Gretchen." The woman looked at the baby. "He's got a lot of his father in him."

Watkins blinked. "What?"

"Your son," Gretchen said. She reached into her large purse and pulled out a thick envelope. "This is from Mrs. Sanchez."

"Who?"

"Let's just say someone who knew your husband and valued his service and his sacrifice to our country."

Watkins let go of the mace and took the envelope. It wasn't sealed and she could see a thick wad of bills in it, the end one with Ben Franklin staring out.

"Why?"

"You don't need that special phone anymore," Gretchen said. "There's more money as you need it."

Iris Watkins stuffed the envelope into her purse and pulled out the phone. She handed it to Gretchen. "All right. No more Loop?"

Gretchen smiled. "No more Loop for you. Your family has done enough."

"Thank you," Watkins said, and she turned for her car, but Gretchen's voice stopped her.

"Can you cook?"

"Still looking at the monument?" the Keep asked Captain Griffin.

He didn't move the binoculars from his eyes. "It hasn't changed."

"Other things have," the Keep said. "The Cellar and the Nightstalkers have closed a big chapter in history. I'm still sorting the pieces out with Hannah and Ms. Jones, but I don't think we'll ever know the full story since Burns went back through the Portal the other way and it's shut."

"Permanently, I hope," Griffin said.

"One can hope," the Keep said, but her voice lacked confidence.

Nada sat with Scout on the riverbank. They were smoking electronic cigarettes, one of Nada's conditions for meeting her.

"How are your folks?" he asked.

"Rested," Scout said. She nodded toward the dock where a boat rested in the lift. "My dad finally got his boat. Said life was too short. Support gave him a really good cover story. He thinks he and Mother and I barely survived a train wreck and chemical discharge."

"Support is good at that," Nada said.

"You know something?" Scout asked, and then she took a puff of nicotine. It wasn't as good as a real cigarette, but it would be enough for now. She knew that eventually she wouldn't need this either.

"What?" Nada said.

"It was a very complex plan," Scout said.

Nada remained silent, because he and Moms had been over this several times at forward operating base and they got confused when they got mired in the details of everything that happened.

Scout continued. "Craegan opening that Rift in Arizona, then the drive going to Winslow, while Ivar worked in the lab opening a Portal while you shut the Rift in Senator's Club, and then multiple Ivars coming through, then shutting that Portal. But Ivar was affected. And whatever was in my toothbrush was planted. Then my dad getting assigned to Oak Ridge, so we moved here to the river, near the dam." She shook her head. "Gives you a headache if you believe it was all one long, complex plan by whatever is on the other side just to spit back out all those people."

"It scares me," Nada said. He stood.

Scout stood up. "It scares me too. Because Ms. Jones and Hannah are the best we got and whatever this is outthought them."

"A lot more people than just them."

"What's going to happen to those people?" Scout asked as they walked along the riverbank. "The Odessa people?"

Nada shrugged. "I don't know. But I'm sure the Cellar will handle it."

They paused. The Snake was waiting, engines whining, the ramp open. The team was inside, watching. Nada held out his hand. "Until we meet again?"

Scout shook it. "Until."

Nada turned for the ramp.

"Hey," Scout said.

Nada paused. "Yes?"

"You owe me a piggy bank."

Nada smiled. "I'll bring it."

"So you'll be back?"

"You know it."

On top of the Gateway Arch, a pair of magnets with duct tape partially attached were solidly anchored onto the stainless steel. The Park Service had yet to figure out how to remove them safely.

Even more puzzling was how they got there.

Still caught in the power lines cutting across the Tennessee River, a tattered parachute hung limply. The TVA had removing it on its to-do list, but resources were focused on repairs to the Loudoun Dam, where an accident had caused a power outage.

In the Cellar, Hannah looked at images of both the magnets and the parachute, still there after dawn. Ms. Jones wasn't on top of this.

Hannah reached for the phone, and then she realized what the magnets and the parachute signified. She lowered her head and said a short prayer, not that she was religious, but sometimes it's all you have. Then she got up and headed toward the door. She had an appointment to make.

Ms. Jones stared at the photo. The image of a young man smiled up at her. "Ah," she sighed. He'd died at Chernobyl. Died trying to open a Rift. Perhaps he'd been right. After all these years, she now knew she might have been wrong. Then and every time since, when the Nightstalkers had slammed shut each Rift before a Portal opened.

Who knew? Who knew?

Why were humans always so afraid of the unknown even while some of the brightest minds probed into the unknown?

Ms. Jones closed her eyes, placing her hands over her chest, the photo clutched in her fingers.

Her heart slowed and then stopped. Lights flashed and Pitr

came rushing in, but he halted short of the hospital bed and stared at the old woman.

Her orders had been strict and clear.

A single tear coursed down Pitr's cheek. At least she was finally at peace.

Hannah sighed. "You're not going to ask me to keep a journal or draw pictures or something like that?"

Dr. Golden had her pad out, pen at the ready. "No. You're too smart for that."

"But not too smart to become better," Hannah said.

"Better?"

"At being human."

The prototype Snake landed inside the Barn. The Nightstalkers off-loaded, stowing their gear and then packing into the Humvee. Eagle got behind the wheel while Roland took his place in the gun turret, holding the grips for the .50-caliber machine gun.

As they rolled out of the barn toward the Ranch, they began to sing, as if on cue, Warren Zevon's "Werewolf in London."

The Humvee rolled across the desert, while overhead the running lights of an old aircraft flickered by.

As they reached the chorus, Roland howled from the hatch and the team echoed him.

The Nightstalkers were back home.

⬛

Colonel Thorn's hands were steady on the controls of the C-47 Skytrain as he flew over the Ranch and the team in the Humvee far below. Where they'd dug this relic up, he had no idea, but these folks sure were efficient.

He appreciated that.

He glanced over his shoulder at the German and Japanese scientists sitting on the web seating along both sides of the plane behind him. One of the Germans had somehow wrangled a couple of bottles of schnapps and was passing them down the line. The Japanese were partaking. Nero had told Thorn many years ago that the Japanese had gotten along quite well with their Nazi compatriots in Odessa.

No shit, Thorn thought.

Peering to the right, Thorn could see the long runway at Area 51. The base around here had been built up, to be expected after so much time.

But he didn't bank the plane to begin the long guide to the runway. Instead, he aimed due west.

It took a few minutes before those in the back became aware they weren't going back "home" where they could perform more experiments in secret and under the protection of the U.S. government.

Thorn took it as a positive sign that some lessons had been learned and that this mistake, at least, wasn't going to be repeated.

He flew directly over Papoose Mountain and then Papoose Lake. He heard some argument behind him as the scientists were looking out the windows, wondering why they weren't turning.

Thorn saw the first blast craters of the Nevada Test Site as he cleared the next ridgeline. There were dozens and dozens of them. Hundreds as he looked to the left and right.

Even the scientists behind him grew silent as they saw the shattered landscape wrought by the hand of man.

"Hail Mary, full of grace, the Lord is with thee," Thorn said in a clear voice. "Blessed art thou amongst women . . ." He skipped the next line and went to the end because there wasn't going to be time. "Holy Mary, Mother of God, pray for us sinners, now and at the hour of our death."

He nosed the C-47 over.

The airplane reached terminal velocity, heading directly for one of the large nuclear craters.

Just before it hit, Thorn whispered, "Amen."

AUTHOR'S NOTE

I write factual fiction. I gather real events and add in a fictional premise and characters.

Area 51, aka Groom Lake, does have the third-longest runway in the world, and it was an alternative landing site for the space shuttle.

On August 21, 1945, Harry K. Daghlian did receive a fatal dose of radiation at Los Alamos and died twenty-five days later.

On May 21, 1946, Louis Slotin did receive a fatal dose from what Enrico Fermi did call the demon core.

There have been sixty criticality accidents involving nuclear material. So far. That have been reported.

Operation Paperclip did exist.

Unit 731 did exist.

ABOUT THE AUTHOR

Photograph © Bob Mayer, 2004

New York Times bestselling author, West Point graduate, and former Green Beret Bob Mayer weaves military, historical, and scientific fact through his gripping works of fiction. His books span numerous genres—suspense, science fiction, military, historical, and more— and Mayer holds the distinction of being the only male author listed on the Romance Writers of America Honor Roll. As one of today's top-performing independent authors, Mayer has drawn on his digital publishing expertise and military exploits to craft more than fifty novels that have sold more than 5 million copies worldwide. These include his bestselling Atlantis, Area 51, and The Green Berets series. Alongside his writing, Mayer is an international keynote speaker, teacher, and CEO of Cool Gus. He lives in Knoxville, Tennessee.

ALSO BY BOB MAYER

The Cellar Series
Bodyguard of Lies
Lost Girls

The Presidential Series
The Jefferson Allegiance
The Kennedy Endeavor (Fall 2013)

Stand-Alone Titles
The Rock
Duty, Honor, Country: A Novel of West Point & The Civil War
I, Judas: The Fifth Gospel

Books on Writing/Publishing
The Novel Writer's Toolkit
Write It Forward: From Writer To Successful Author
How We Made Our First Million On Kindle: The Shelfless Book
The Guide to Writers Conferences
102 Solutions To Common Writing Mistakes